Operation
One Night Stand

Operation One Night Stand

CHRISTINE HUGHES

FOREVER
YOURS

New York Boston

Copyright © 2015 by Christine Hughes
Excerpt from *Operation Foreplay* copyright © 2015 by Christine Hughes
Cover design by Christine Foltzer
Cover copyright © 2015 by Hachette Book Group, Inc.

Forever Yours
Hachette Book Group
1290 Avenue of the Americas
New York, NY 10104
www.hachettebookgroup.com
www.twitter.com/foreverromance

First published as an ebook and as a print on demand edition: June 2015

Forever Yours is an imprint of Grand Central Publishing.
The Forever Yours name and logo are trademarks of Hachette Book Group, Inc.

The publisher is not responsible for websites (or their content) that are not owned by the publisher.

The Hachette Speakers Bureau provides a wide range of authors for speaking events. To find out more, go to www.hachettespeakersbureau.com or call (866) 376-6591.

ISBN: 978-1-4555-8999-9 (ebook edition)
ISBN: 978-1-4555-9094-0 (print on demand edition)

To my sister, Holly.
May you always find lipstick when the sexy man
comes around.

Acknowledgments

I've been incredibly lucky and have had so many wonderful days over the course of my career and I've been surrounded by some of the most amazing people. Honestly, a writer's journey is never easy, but I'll take a bad day as a writer over a good day doing anything else—especially when my corner is filled with so much support and love.

I never could have had the courage to start writing had it not been for the unwavering support of my other half. He is my sounding board, my shoulder, my rock. I love you with all my heart, even if you think all the stories in my head are about you. As for my two amazing little people—one day I'll let you read these books. Until then, we'll keep looking for your stories.

To my family, I love you all so much. Thank you for everything. I would not be where I am without you. Mom—I'm sorry you had to find out your daughter had such a bad mouth. Who knew? Dad—thank you for always asking how the writing's going and what I'm working on. Your interest is so appreciated. Nana—ahh, Super G.

You are the best grandma anyone could ever ask for. Now if you'd only make me some arancinis...

Michelle Johnson would be anyone's dream agent. I knew I fell into a pool of awesome when she took me on as a client. And the fact that she encourages snarky, NSFW storyline ideas? She is the Pinot to my Grigio. And I am ever grateful to her.

I have to thank Megha Parekh for her enthusiasm for OPERATION ONE NIGHT STAND. She scooped up this story so fast it made my head spin. I am so happy OONS found a home at Forever Romance. I'd also like to thank Dana Hamilton for her notes and suggestions during the editorial process. Next time I'm in the city, I owe both of you some cocktails.

Kitty Kat has always been the first to finish reading anything I've written. I hope one day to be the first to finish a book you write.

I need to thank Leslie Write, my original writing boo. I feel like you and I have traveled this road together over the past few years. I couldn't ask for a better travel mate.

Many thanks to my writing journal, Sarah Carr. Your notes and comments helped me write a better story. I love trading story ideas and swapping chapters even if we do disagree on who makes the best coffee. Thank you so much. H@JJ!

Thank you to my bitches, Tina and Jodi. I love that you two have come into my life. Who knew I'd ever be part of a trio of cocktail mixers, rimmers, and gigglers? Don't ever stop reminding me to take notes. Even if they don't make sense the next day.

Miss Autumn Wrought. I'm sorry I wore the arsehole hat for so long; I figured you needed some snark. Looks like I was right. Thank you for agreeing to be my beta—still not sure if I am sharing you. And don't worry, I'll break your heart again.

To my friends and fans who've stuck with me through this journey, thank you so much. Your support has not gone unnoticed. I appreciate every single one of you and only hope that I continue to produce work that you enjoy. And if you ever see me out and about—amaretto and ginger is my drink.

Operation
One Night Stand

Chapter One

I had commandeered the sofa. The beautiful, butter-yellow sofa Sarah had purchased when she first moved to her amazingly spacious two-bedroom apartment almost three years ago now probably had a permanent imprint of my ass. The cushions had become a wasteland overflowing with wads of snotty tissues, and creamy brown stains from my new, aptly named addiction—Pint of Tears—smeared the arm. My trusty sidekick, Mr. Bibbles, a childhood stuffed thing—I wasn't sure anymore if he ever really was a bear—lay oddly contorted at my side.

For five years, Steven and I dated. Lived together. Worked together. Dreamed together. That was before it all went to shit. That was before I found him in *my* bed with Betsy the Intern. That was before he figured it was okay to forget about the fact that he was my fiancé. That was before I found myself homeless, refusing to ask my parents for help. I showed up with nothing but a suitcase full of crap—and Mr. Bibbles—at Sarah's door. I didn't even have to ask. Within twenty-four hours, my room was decorated, my bed was made, and I was moved in.

For the past six weeks, I'd lived with Sarah. My best friend, my trusty confidant, and, probably, the only person on earth who'd have put up with my shit for as long as she has. Besides the other third of our trio, Mel. My nightly crying fits, my refusal to leave the house for anything other than work, and my newly minted status as Ice Cream Dreams's most valuable customer wore on my friends.

Every day on the way home from work, before I planted my growing ass on the once beautiful sofa and cried, I stopped at a tiny little ice cream shop called Ice Cream Dreams. They pride themselves on making any ice cream concoction to fit any mood. The first day I walked in, the girl behind the counter took one look at me and Pint of Tears was born. Chocolate on chocolate mixed with chocolate, gummy bears, marshmallow, and peanut butter. It became their best-selling ice cream flavor of the fall. Probably because of me.

Me and my ever-growing, ice-cream-eating, tear-shedding, sofa-arm-smearing ass.

I would silently curse Sarah as she invited me out every Friday. Every Saturday. I would inwardly cringe at the ten pounds I'd gained—while simultaneously thanking my speedy metabolism that it wasn't more—as I watched from my perch on her butter-yellow sofa while she left for the gym with yoga mat in hand.

All I needed was a spoon, a pint, and a remote control.

My new life.

Sucked.

I'd taken to sitting on the couch and watching every single depressing break-up movie ever filmed. Multiple times. From black-and-whites, animated, Ryan Gosling, Jack and Rose to addictions, affairs, Ryan Gosling, Jack and Rose. Oh, and by the way, Rose, I call bullshit. Jack would have pulled your ass from the frozen waters of the Atlantic and shared some space on that door or whatever the hell you were floating on. Then again, maybe you knew something we didn't. Maybe he deserved an icy, watery grave. Maybe you were on to something. Men.

Fuck 'em.

Sideways.

One particular Friday night, I was in the middle of another round of "Which Movie Is More Depressing?" (*When a Man Loves a Woman* was winning, by the way) when I heard Sarah's key in the lock. At the time, I wasn't fazed. We'd gotten into a routine. She'd come home from her date or the gym or dinner out with friends, ask me how I was, ask me if I needed anything, and, when I said no, she'd say good night and go to bed. Once in a while she'd sit on the couch with me, eat out of her own pint of Support System (yeah, another flavor), and watch me as I worked on my ugly crying face. I was pretty sure it was the ugliest crying face ever. I was giving that actress from *Homeland* a run for her ugly crying face money. Which is weird, because without the ugly crying face, she's beautiful. She never would have let Jack sink to the icy depths.

Then again, better to sink than live with the daily heartbreak of a roaming dick.

Instead, Sarah walked in with backup. Melody stormed into the room, ripped off my blanket, and threw Mr. Bibbles across the room. Sarah calmly walked over, grabbed my ice cream and spoon, and placed them on the kitchen counter.

"What the hell?" I shrank into the sofa.

"This is an intervention."

"Mel, you threw my bear!"

"Screw your bear, Caroline. Enough is enough. So Steven cheated on you. That doesn't mean you have to become an ice cream swilling hermit! What the hell happened to you?"

"You are a hot mess, doll face," Sarah quipped as she pulled a new pack of baby wipes from her purse and began wiping the chocolate off my face. Maybe I was.

"I'll see your hot mess and raise you a walking disaster. At least that's what she'll be if this shit keeps up."

"Leave me alone. And don't talk about me like I'm not here." I tried to retreat as far into the corner of the sofa as I could. Unfortunately, the more I squished in, the more tissues squished out.

Sarah hung up her coat before sitting on the coffee table across from me. "Sweetie, we know you're hurting. But it's time to move on. You're still working with him, you're reminded every day of what happened. No wonder you're stuck. You need to get up, get out, and find a new job. Move past this."

"How am I supposed to move past anything? I see Steven every single day. It's not like I can magically unsee him." I fingered the engagement ring I wore around my neck as fresh tears spilled over. I couldn't bring myself to get rid of it. Unfortunately, Steven still worked at the law firm, so I couldn't escape him. Who was I kidding? His daddy *was* the law firm.

"I know it's hard. I can't imagine having to see the two of them day after day," Sarah said, reminding me that Betsy and her welcoming vagina worked there, too.

"Every day I walk in and try to keep my head high but I keep running into her stink eye. She won't stop fucking staring at me." Sarah dodged my wild hand gestures. "Like I'm the one who ruined *her* life by walking in on them." Melody held the box of tissues and I yanked a bunch out and wiped my face. "Not to mention that everyone knows Steven and I broke up. Like anyone in the office needed anything else to gossip about."

"Fuck them. They're a bunch of middle-aged leeches who aren't happy unless someone else in unhappy. And fuck her. Punch her in the face," Melody suggested. "She's just mad she can't fuck the boss's son anymore."

"Right. I know they're still boning like they're the last two people on earth." I blew my nose. "Probably still doing it in the bed Steven and I bought when we moved in together." I could no longer breathe through my nose. "I bet they have sex in the office, too."

Fuck them both.

"I am sure they are not having sex in the office." Sarah laughed as Melody pursed her lips and checked out her fingernails.

"You think they're having sex in the office?" I asked her.

"Of course she doesn't. Right Mel?" Mel didn't answer, so Sarah threw a pillow at her. "Right?"

"I don't think it matters if they are still boning."

"Of course it matters! He begs for my forgiveness every single day. 'Oh, Caroline, forgive me.' 'I love you so much.' 'She means nothing.'" It made my skin crawl. "Bahhh. I want him to shut up. Just shut up!"

"Well, that's something," Melody piped up.

"What?" I asked.

"Mad. Mad is better than what you've been doing."

"And what have I been doing, Melody? I mean besides mourning the loss of a five-year relationship with my fiancé who cheated on me? Besides walking into a work every day and having people actually stop talking the second I come within earshot? Turning it over and over in my head, trying to figure out what *I* did wrong when I know Steven made the decision to cheat, not me?" I stood and threw my tissues. "How should I be dealing with it, Mel? Tell me. I'd love to take advice from a bed hopper who wouldn't know a relationship if it kicked her in the twat." Immediately my hands flew to my mouth.

"Nice." Melody smirked and Sarah gasped.

"I'm sorry. So sorry. I don't know what—"

"Stop. It's fine. I kind of like the sass." Mel winked. "Glad to see you fired up over something other than ice cream and Leonardo DiCaprio's icy death."

"Rose should have made room," I mumbled.

"Holy shit. Enough. I will cancel cable if you don't stop." Sarah rolled her eyes.

"Sorry."

"Look, don't be sorry. Be brave. Be strong. Be happy. Be amazing. Don't be sorry." Melody handed me another tissue.

"Exactly. You need to get up, get out, and meet some people."

"People." Melody waved Sarah off. "Pssh. She means men. You need to meet some men. You need to get your lady parts ready"—Mel grabbed her crotch—"and give them some love."

"My lady parts are fine the way they are."

"Shriveled up?"

"They are not shriveled up."

"When's the last time you had sex?"

"What does that matter?"

"The fact that you answered my question with that question tells me 'too long.' You need to get out and meet someone."

I dropped my head between my knees. "What if I can't? What if no one else wants me?"

Sarah dropped onto the couch next to me and rubbed my back while Melody headed toward the back of the apartment. In that moment I knew I had hit rock bottom and there was nowhere for me to go but up. But up to where? What or who would be waiting for me at the top of whatever?

The answers were sitting next to me rubbing my back and walking back into the living room, bathroom garbage can in hand.

"Look," Melody began as she placed the garbage can on the coffee table and sat next to it, "you're beautiful, talented, and smart. Who wouldn't want you? I mean, shit, you're only twenty-eight years old and the world is your oyster! You've had, what? Two, maybe three, boyfriends in your life? How many one night stands? How many nights of just fun? How many nights that were all about you and what you want? Now isn't the time to wonder who will want you, now is the time to take what you want."

"I've never had a one night stand." I crinkled my nose in mock disgust to mask the embarrassing lack of experience in that department. In truth, it had always been something I was too nervous to do, something other people did. I was a "relationship girl." Always with a boyfriend.

"Now is the time for you to live your life. Start over."

"With a one night stand?"

"Sure. Why not?" Sarah asked.

"That's just not what I do." I shook my head.

"You need to do something. Tell Steven to fuck off. Put the damn ring away." I clutched it and Sarah rolled her eyes. "I don't mean get rid of it—"

"I say sell it," Melody added.

"What I mean is take it off, put it away. Kick up your heels. Step out of the shadow Steven kept you in. Christ, Care." Sarah threw her arms up in frustration. "I need wine. Anyone else need wine?"

"You need to ask?" Mel laughed.

"Look, I appreciate what you're trying to do, but I can't just go out and date someone. I can't just go and talk to strange men. That's not me. I've slept with exactly two people and both were boyfriends."

"We are not saying you have to go bang every guy you meet but what's wrong with a one night stand?"

"Steven said—"

"What the fuck?" Melody grabbed her hair. "Who the fuck cares what Steven said, Care? Really? I don't mean to be a bitch here but, seriously, I am pretty sure you need to stop with the Steven references. He's lucky I didn't castrate his cheating ass."

"But—"

"But what?"

"I don't want people to think I'm a slut."

Melody laughed. "I had a one night stand last weekend. Does that make me a slut?" Melody stared at me.

"That's not really a good example, Mel." Sarah handed her a glass of red before handing me mine. "You had a one night stand the weekend before that, too."

"And the weekend before that," I added.

Melody opened her mouth and closed it quickly before shaking her head and taking a large swallow of wine. "Look, my point is that you can." She stood and plucked the wadded-up snot rags from the sofa and tossed them in the trash. "There comes a time when you need a reality check. Realize this truth: you'll never be good enough for some people. Say it over and over again until it sinks into your sad little skull." I ducked away when she rapped her knuckles on my head. "And when you realize that, ask yourself whether it's your problem or theirs."

The harsh bitch of reality coldcocked me across the heart. I wasn't ready to realize anything. Fresh tears spilled down my face. "Mel, I just want to move on. I want all this past me."

"Of course you do. And we'll help you. Come on, get up." Melody put down her glass and grabbed my arm, yanking me out of my seat. I looked back longingly at my spot before turning to face her.

"Drink the wine."

I took a sip.

"No. Drink the whole thing."

I looked to Sarah and she nodded. I brought the overpoured glass to my mouth and drank. I drank and drank until the glass was empty and Sarah took the glass from my hand.

Wiping the tears from my cheeks and brushing the hair out of my eyes, Melody continued, "We have a plan."

"Yes. We've got it all figured out." Sarah smirked as they walked me down the hall.

That plan began with a very invasive cold shower and a loofah, quite a bit of complaining on my part, and fresh pajamas. When I was finally cleansed of tears, snot, and sticky trails of ice cream, the girls sat me on the couch—Mr. Bibbles was nowhere to be found—handed me another glass of wine, and laid out their plan. I sat and listened. And drank. And tried to understand. All I ended up doing was drinking more.

"You want me to what?" I reached forward and tried to pour the empty bottle into my glass. Melody hopped up and ran to the kitchen. I held my finger to my lips until my glass was filled. I needed the silence to process this plan.

"We'll go to a bar—" Sarah began.

"Someplace new," Melody interrupted.

"Yes. And we'll scan the crowd. Look for someone take-home worthy. When you find him, nominate him as the target."

"And do what again?"

"Flirt. Pick him up. Do what you need to do." Sarah was way too into this.

"So what you're saying is, I walk into a bar, point at a hot guy, and declare that I am bringing him home."

"Yes."

"Why can't I just get his number?"

"Because this is Operation One Night Stand, not Operation Get His Number."

"What if I can't find anyone take-home worthy?"

"Then you don't. That's the point. There is no timeline."

"Right. We just go out and watch you troll for the one."

"I'm supposed to marry 'the one.'"

"Not this one." Melody high-fived Sarah.

I rolled my eyes, stood, and paced the room. "Let's leave that alone for a bit. Tell me about the plan. There has to be more to this plan than me getting it on with a hottie stranger guy." I needed the subject to change, even if only for a minute. I wasn't that girl. I didn't sleep around. But, holy hell, I really wanted to be.

"Right. More about the plan." Sarah refilled her glass before handing Mel the bottle. "We need to rip this Band-Aid off. We need to get free and clear of all this"—she waved her arms around, sloshing the red liquid onto the hardwood—"*shit*."

"Shit." I nodded my head and continued to pace. "Remove the shit." I was pretty sure I needed more wine. "Pour me." I held out my glass and Melody poured.

"Are you ready to hear this part?"

"Rip off the Band-Aid." It was my turn to slosh.

"You need to"—Sarah paused—"why don't you sit down for this?"

"Sit down?" I pointed to the couch.

"Yeah. That would be good." Melody agreed. "Drink."

The three of us drank deeply before Sarah continued.

"Youneedtoquityourjob."

"I'm sorry—what? It sounded like you said I need to quit my job." I laughed and took a sip.

When neither one of them corrected me and, instead, averted their eyes and busied themselves with refilling their wineglasses, I nearly choked.

"You can't be serious? I can't quit my job! How would I pay for anything? How the hell would I make rent, Sarah? You gonna foot the bill on your teacher's salary?"

"Wait, wait. Settle your tits, doll," Melody reasoned. "Are you really going to subject yourself to working alongside Steven and his fuck toy? Around all those miserable people? When was the last time you didn't dread going to work? All the Steven business aside, when?"

"That isn't the point."

"It is the point. There is no way you are going to get past this unless you make a clean break," Sarah said.

"How am I going to find a new job?"

"The same way everyone else finds a new job. You look for one. You use your network. Mel and I will help you, and I am sure your parents will help you, until you get on your feet."

"My mom never liked Steven," I mumbled and chewed on a fingernail.

"Neither did I," Melody blurted. "What? I thought we were being honest."

"We are." Sarah pointed between herself and Melody. "We need Caroline to be honest."

"Me? About what?"

"What you want. Do you want to stay in Steven's shadow? Do you want to stare at Betsy the Intern all day long? Do you want to work someplace that chews away everything great about you until you become an empty shell? Or do you want to take life by the balls and live a little?"

"It's a lot to take in so fast."

"So fast? You've become part of the decor, darling. Get your sweet ass off my couch before I remove you from it myself." Sarah smiled.

"And you think I need to have sex with a stranger?"

"I think you're looking too much into it."

"I don't know. I need time to think."

And I did think. And partake in numerous talks about the ins and outs of dating and one night stands—I mean, I had been out of the game for five years. We took a trip the next day to a hair salon and Fred Burke's, a high-end boutique store, and even squeezed in some much needed fat burning with spin class on Sunday. In between all of it, my ice cream was thrown out, Ice Cream Dreams was asked not to sell my ice cream to me anymore, and my résumé and cover letters were revamped. All I needed to do was rip off the Band-Aid. Easier said than done.

Chapter Two

After a short train ride from New Jersey to New York, I walked into work the following Monday completely unsure about what I was going to do.

I managed to avoid both Steven and Betsy for most of the morning. Mostly because I hid from them. I still wasn't sure what I was going to do. Even after a long phone conversation with my dad I didn't feel any better and my dad always made me feel better; the only advice he had for me was to make a list of all the reasons I should stay at my job and a list of the reasons I should leave. It was good advice but I'd been at work for two hours and only succeeded in drawing a line down the middle of a piece of paper. I hadn't even started on the files sitting on my desk nor had I opened one e-mail.

I shook my head and tossed my pen on the desk. Picking up my coffee cup, I made my way to the break room, intending to caffeinate my way through the next hour, when I walked into Betsy. I dropped my mug and she dropped a stack of papers. I stood staring as she knelt down and scrambled to clean up the mess. I wondered how she was able to do so without exposing at least some part of her body. It appeared her idea of business casual differed greatly from mine.

She must've realized I was just standing there because she looked up, annoyance smeared all over her heavily made-up face. "You think you could *help* me since it was your fault?"

"My fault?" She really was not a good person.

"Yeah. Your head's been up your own ass for weeks. And don't think I'm the only one who's noticed."

"Up my own ass." I counted backward from ten.

"What's going on, ladies?" Steven looked entirely too uncomfortable as he approached.

"Nothing, baby." Betsy side-eyed me. "Can you help me pick these up?" She arched her back and looked up at him with big, blinky doe eyes.

"Uh, sure." Steven glanced in my direction before squatting down and quickly shuffling the papers into her hands.

"Up. My. Own. Ass," I repeated.

"What was that?" Steven asked.

"Are you kidding me?" I lowered my voice to a fierce whisper and stepped toward Betsy. She stepped back and into a desk. "My head has been up my own ass for exactly *how* long? It couldn't be six weeks, could it? It could not be since I found you fucking my fiancé in my bed, could it?"

Steven placed his hand on the small of my back. "Care—"

"Don't touch me. Do you have any idea what you did? Do you take any responsibility for what happened?" I felt the gravity of the past six weeks begin to crumble. "For weeks I've been blaming Betsy the Wonderslut—"

"Hey!" She interrupted and I snapped my head in her direction.

"Really? Don't talk." I held my hand up toward her before returning my attention to the real issue. "You asked me to *marry* you. Do you know what that means? That means you only want to be with me. That means you don't go around sticking your dick in the office floozy."

"Betsy didn't mean anything. She was a mistake!"

"Steven!" The tears in Betsy's eyes proved that she was unaware of his lack of feelings toward her.

"I don't believe you. I was supposed to be able to trust you. I mean, what else have you been hiding over the past five years? How many times did you do this?"

Steven leaned in. "Can we talk about this in private?"

I looked around at the small group of people listening in on our conversation. "No. I'm done, Steven. I hope you and Betsy are very happy together. The rest of you"—I waved my arms—"find something else to talk about. I'm done."

"Listen to me, Care. She did not mean anything to me."

Betsy sobbed into her hands, turned, and quickly made for the bathroom. How she managed to stay upright on those heels was amazing.

"Looks like your girl needs some consoling. You might want to go take care of that." I tilted my head, picked up my mug, and headed to the break room to get my coffee.

A few hours later, I was sitting in my office, cold pad Thai sitting on my desk from lunch. I'd just finished running through my backlog of e-mails and putting the finishing touches on a few of the files that needed my attention. Underneath one of the folders was the legal pad that held the beginnings of my list.

I shoved everything else to the side and centered the pad on the desk in front of me. Taking out my favorite pencil from my drawer, I leaned back, observed the teeth marks I'd placed in the never-sharpened pencil, and popped it between my teeth.

It wasn't long before I had both lists filled with reasons. And the more I looked through and thought about it, the more I knew what I needed to do.

At three o'clock I knocked on the office door of the human resources manager, resignation letter in hand. She was kind enough to sit with me while I explained that I was leaving the firm. Band-Aid ripped. I was pleasantly surprised that it didn't hurt as much as I expected it to. Especially since I was about to be out of a job with nothing else lined up.

I hadn't yet locked down a job, hadn't secured an interview, hadn't even had a chance to look, but I knew for certain that I couldn't work there anymore. To my surprise, it was a wonderful conversation and by the end of an hour, she had made a few phone calls, setting me up with interviews.

As I walked back to my office, I found Steven standing at my desk, legal pad full of reasons in hand.

"Excuse me. That's mine." I snatched the pad from his hand.

"You're leaving?"

"Is that what you got out of that?" I smirked.

"You don't have to leave."

"Sweetie, you think I want to leave? You think I want to start over? Of course I don't. But I have to. I can't keep sitting here wondering why you did what you did, wondering what I did to cause it—"

"You didn't do anything wrong."

"I know, Steven. Look. I have to do this for me."

"You hate change."

"Yeah. I do. But right now, Steven, I hate the way I feel when I'm around you even more."

I knew I didn't owe him any explanation but the dejected look on his face was all the fuel I needed to cement the fact that moving on was by far a better choice than subjecting myself to working side by side with such an ass.

I was on cloud nine, contemplating all the newness about to befall me, as I watched Steven stand in my office without speaking. I glanced over his shoulder and was surprised to see Betsy walk slowly to her desk, empty box in hand. I viewed the event with an unusual amount of glee as she packed up her belongings. It truly was a popcorn moment.

I looked away for a few seconds. I felt bad for my obvious schadenfreudean thoughts. The feeling was short lived.

I plopped in my chair and spun as she walked, head down, with a tiny box in her hands, to the elevator. I knew I should be more mature about the situation, but from what I could figure, she left on her own accord. For the same reason I decided to leave.

And of course I thought she deserved a bout of unhappiness. Not as much as Steven, but she knew he was my fiancé and, as much as we should all direct our anger toward the person in our lives committing the indiscretion, she absolutely, one hundred percent, *knew* Steven and I were engaged.

I could not have cared less if she was good at her job, if she was a nice person, or if she was dying a slow death from a severe case of genital warts. It didn't even matter that I had only two weeks left. Two weeks was a slow torturous lifetime in hell if she was within a hundred yards of me. And I wished her nothing but herpes and a bad case of diarrhea. And I sincerely hoped Steven suffered the same.

However, I had to keep myself from squealing with glee as I watched Steven freeze and stare as his piece of ass made her way out the door. He turned to look at me and I painted on the best "who me?" face I could muster. Inside I was doing back flips.

None of it mattered. As soon as I gave notice, the great weight of sadness lifted off my shoulders and my attitude changed. In that moment, I decided that "poor me" was no longer my battle cry. Melody and Sarah were right. I was twenty-eight, with my whole life ahead of me. Who was I to ignore that?

"Did you have to get her fired?" Steven interrupted my silent hear-me-roar mantra.

"*I* didn't do anything. I just quit my job. Looks like she had the same idea. End of story."

"Care—"

"Steven." I glared at him, wishing actual daggers would shoot from my eyes and hit him in the face.

"Hey!" Bobby popped his head in my door and frowned when he saw Steven. "Did you hear? Betsy quit!"

"There you go." I waved my hand toward Bobby to show Steven that I didn't, in fact, have Betsy fired. Not that banging my fiancé is any sort of grounds for termination. "Thanks, Bobby. You can leave my door open."

Dropping his shoulders, Steven looked at me one last time. "It didn't have to be this way."

"There is no other way for it to *be*. You made sure of that when you fucked the intern in our bed while I walked around oblivious with a two-carat engagement ring on my finger. Who does that? A douche bag, that's who. Now, please, close the door on your way out. I have work to do."

"Who are you? My Caroline doesn't talk like that."

"Your Caroline doesn't exist anymore. Read the obituary. It reads: 'Here lies Steven's Caroline. Fucked over by a pretentious douche bag and his plastic intern.'"

I was a bit alarmed at how good it felt to tell Steven what was on my mind. His gaze fell to the floor and his shoulders sagged. He opened his mouth to speak again but must have thought better of it.

It felt even better when I watched him close the door.

As soon as he left, I picked up the phone and dialed Sarah, knowing she was on her way home.

"Did you do it?" Sarah asked in reference to part one of the plan.

"I did. And Betsy the Wonder Slut quit, too."

"A nice extension of the plan. I wasn't expecting that." I heard her chewing.

"Neither was I. And I told off Steven. I am so amped."

"Excellent. Adrenaline is a beautiful thing."

"What are you eating? It's awfully loud."

"Carrots. Not everyone can eat six million gallons of ice cream in a six-week period and still have a great ass."

"True. So listen, I've been giving it a lot of thought and I think part two of the plan would be good for me."

"So you're in?"

"I'm in."

"Excellent."

All weekend, I had been inundated with a three-part plan. Melody and Sarah had done quite a bit of thinking and come up with what they deemed to be a fool-proof method for helping me move on. Part one was complete. I quit my job. I'll find a new one. Especially with help from the very kind human resources manager.

"Just so you know," Sarah continued, "there is an addendum to the plan. Chapter one point five, if you will. You gave two weeks' notice? You don't have to stay longer than that, right?"

"No. I'm done the Friday before Thanksgiving."

"Good, because the three of us are spending Thanksgiving in Jamaica."

"What?"

"We all need to decompress, Care. I need to get away from school, Mel needs to back away from her job for a bit, and you need, well, you need this, too. I'm not taking no for an answer. I'm booking the second I get off the phone with you."

I guess spontaneity was the lesson for chapter one point five of the plan. "Book it."

Part two was a little dicier, a little less old me and a lot more new me. But then again, Operation One Night Stand was a go and I had two weeks to get up the nerve to go through with it. At least I'd be on a plane out of town soon after, so I'd be able to obsess about it in a different country.

I was going to step out into the sun and live my life. And I'd spend a week in Jamaica with my two best friends doing just that.

Chapter Three

Nothing like bar hopping in late November snow. My cute beige heels already had salt scuffing the toes and my brand-new Sevens were wet at the cuff and we'd hit only two bars. Thankfully I knew the second we walked into Murphy's I'd make good on my bet.

Operation One Night Stand was on. Melody and Sarah thought it would be fun to turn the whole thing into an actual bet. Since I had control over the who and the when, the bet was against the fact that I'd find someone on the first night. Sarah and Mel, knowing that I wasn't the most adventurous of our group, bet me fifty bucks that I'd back out and try again another night. Unfortunately for them, I hadn't had sex in two months and I was hurting for a good romp. Of course, I let them think they had me. Two bars down and not a single prospect? Not likely for most. Especially in a college town. Then again, I wasn't a college girl. Four years after I finished grad school and I was still trolling the local scene for the one-nighter I'd never experienced. My life apparently sucked. That, or I was still reeling over my breakup with Steven. Or the fact that I'd just completed my last day at the firm. Whatever. Not the thing to focus on. I was on the prowl, much to the chagrin of my small, tight group of friends. Maybe Melody, who I met the first day of freshman bio, was right: maybe I was going off the deep end.

It was nearing ten o'clock and I had yet to find a suitable bedmate for the night. When it came to guys, I was picky. Not that a one night stand was a necessary thing to cross off my list. The girls found it hard to believe when I said I'd never had one and I guess, at twenty-eight, it was time. But, like I said, the second we hit Murphy's, I spotted my target.

He was tall, with closely cropped blond hair and dark eyes and was surrounded by a group of guys. He looked older than the rest of the guys in his whole group did. Something about the way he stood. Self-confidence radiated across the bar. I had a feeling he was used to getting what he wanted and I figured that worked in my favor. It was more likely he'd see us as kindred spirits, even if it was just sex. And sex was like riding a bicycle right? No way was he going to back down from what I had planned.

We made our way to the opposite side of the bar so I could get a better look at the man I'd be sharing a bed—or a floor, a wall, a stairwell—with later.

Elbowing Sarah, I declared, "Him," and nodded across the bar.

"Blondie?"

"Yep."

"Bet's on. Get 'em, girl. And remember, if at first you don't succeed, destroy all the evidence you tried in the first place." She nudged my ribs and ordered me a drink. Since it was a special night, I avoided my usual beer and sipped on two fingers of cinnamon liqueur on ice.

The bartender was cute and seemed to be in a good mood, so I decided to bring him in on my little plan. If it was going to go my way, I was going to need him. I'd been planning the night for two weeks. So much for one-night-stand spontaneity. Then again, I *was* a planner.

I waited until he came closer before I called him over. Up close, he was more than cute. I could picture him with an open belt and his jeans sitting low on his ass. Holy shit. I could get lost in those eyes.

Damn.

But he wasn't the target.

"I'm Caroline."

"Hi, Caroline. I'm Brian. Nice to meet you."

"Nice to meet you, too. I was wondering if you could help me out."

Eyeing my tumbler, he lifted an eyebrow, pushed his wavy brown hair out of his eyes, and responded, "Sure. What do you need?"

Looking around to make sure Sarah and Mel weren't listening in, I whispered to my new bartender friend, "I have a bet with my girls and I can't lose. It would kill my buzz and I need your help. So, I need to send that guy over there"—I pointed slightly—"a drink. Something fun. Sexy."

"Sexy, huh?"

The way his mouth moved when he said the word "sexy" had me wondering what it would be like to be sprawled across the bar with Brian on top of me, those teeth scraping my skin, that tongue sliding up and down my body. Unfortunately, I had to pull myself out of my own head because I needed to focus. It was just so hard to do so when his baby blues looked at me like that. Like I was the only person in the crowded bar.

"Suggestive." The word came out throatier than I anticipated and Brian's eyes gleamed mischievously.

"Suggestive. Sexy. Kind of like you." He winked and a warm tingle spread between my thighs. Was that all it took to moisten the panties these days? Jesus, I needed to get laid. I was DEFCON 1 horny.

Down, girl.

"Which one again?"

"Blond. Tall. With a bunch of his friends."

Bartender Brian was good. He looked at my target without actually looking at him. I'd have to ask him later how he did that.

"Yeah. Something fun. A shot. Definitely a shot."

"Got it. Be right back."

I watched Brian mix a bunch of stuff into a shaker and pour a shot. When he brought it to the guy, he leaned in and whispered, barely tilting his head in my direction. The target lifted big brown eyes in my direction, nodded thanks as he lifted the shot, and threw it back before turning back to his friends.

Shit. That didn't work. It seemed like a good idea. I'd have to re-think.

Brian poured another drink for some random college girl before returning to me.

"What did you give him?" My hand reached for his and he slid his fingers along the back of my hand.

"Sex Up Against the Wall."

"What?" I could feel my ears redden.

"Like a Sex on the Beach but with a little Harvey Wallbanger."

Again with the wink. Bartender Brian was hot. I needed some air.

"I'll be right back."

"Giving up already?" He stood up and crossed his arms over his chest.

"Hardly." I winked back at him and watched a slow, sexy smile spread across his face.

I made my way across the room. I was going to have to pass tall, blond, and handsome to get to the bathroom. With a newly formed set of balls, I decided to brush past him, walking right through his little group of friends. Feeling slightly badass with my four-inch heels, I knew my ass looked great. It was my best feature. Score one for an hour a day at the gym.

I quickly tugged my shirt, making sure to expose a little more cleavage while keeping my newly purchased bra under wraps. At least for the moment.

Carefully, I kept my eyes on him. It wasn't until I brushed against him that he looked. My hand barely swiped across his crotch. It was a fuller package than I'd imagined.

Eyes locked, I mustered whatever brash sex appeal I could and hoped I was able to convey my desire silently. I was pretty sure it worked since he put his hand on my arm and whispered, "Hi."

I leaned in, prompting him to bend down slightly—he had at least a foot on me—and whispered the greeting back, making sure to keep my whisper breathy while grazing his earlobe with my lips.

I moved on quickly, feeling his eyes watch me walk away. I heard his red-headed friend say something about "hitting that" and I flipped my hair over my shoulder.

Once I finished in the bathroom, I avoided the target. A quick peek over at him, however, stirred the butterflies in my stomach. He was watching me. There is no better feeling than realizing someone you're into is checking you out.

I ran into a few people I knew and quickly exchanged pleasantries before heading back to Bartender Brian.

"Caroline! Nice to see you came back. I saved your seat."

"You did?"

"I saw those shoes. Didn't think it would be right for you to stand on them all night."

"You noticed my shoes?" *Was he gay?*

"Well, yeah. Something was making that ass swing when you walked away."

Not gay.

Why did I care? He was not the target.

"Give a girl the right pair of shoes and she can take over the world."

"Touché."

Bartender Brian slid a drink in front of me.

"What's this?"

"From him." He nodded across the bar. Target lifted his drink and nodded.

"What is it?"

He motioned for me to lean in, meeting me halfway across the bar. Tucking my hair behind my ear he whispered, "Screaming Orgasm."

He lingered a beat longer, long enough for me to feel his breath on my skin. When he pulled away, he smelled like cinnamon. I looked down; my original drink was empty. I ran my finger around the rim of the glass and looked at him.

Shrugging, he said, "I was thirsty. Drink up."

Smiling, I lifted my shot glass and drank. My lips were moist and a drop of the alcohol slid down my chin. Bartender Brian reached over and wiped it away with his finger before putting it in his mouth.

A change of panties would be required if this shit kept up.

"Your turn."

For the life of me I couldn't figure out what he was talking about. I touched my face where his finger was a moment ago. I felt that touch down to my toes.

"Earth to Caroline." He snapped in front of me.

"Huh?"

"Your turn."

"My turn for what?"

"Drinks. Sexy. Suggestive. Mr. Tall Blond and Dumb over there."

"He isn't dumb!"

Brian laughed easily. "If you say so. What'll it be?"

"I don't know. I didn't think that far ahead. Um, Slippery Nipple?"

Bartender Brian pursed his nibblicious full lips before saying, "You got it."

He tucked his towel in the back of his pants before retrieving a cell phone from his front pocket. He turned away from me and began making the drink. He stopped a few times along the way to pull a few beers for some other customers. I watched as some slutty girl lifted herself on the bar, leaned in, and kissed him on the cheek. He dipped his head and smiled, touching her nose with the tip of his finger. The same finger he used to wipe the small bit of my drink that slipped down my chin. *Who is that bitch?*

I shook the thought from my head. Bartender Brian wasn't my target but he did deliver the drink as promised. Once again Tall Blond and Dumb—er, Handsome—locked eyes with me and mouthed the words, "Thank you." He quickly threw it back before leaning into Brian. Brian laughed and high-fived him. *I wonder what they're talking about.*

"Hey!" Melody yelled in my ear. "Get fucked yet?"

She was always a bit of a close talker but when she was drinking, the closeness was magnified. Honestly, all I had to do was lick my lips at that moment and we'd be making out French style. Not that there'd be anything wrong with that. But at the moment, Melody's tongue wasn't on my list of things to do so I took a step back. Unfortunately, there wasn't anywhere to go and I was practically bent backward over the bar.

"Hey, Mel. No, I didn't. What are you up to?"

"I ran into that Jeff guy. Steven's friend."

"Jeff is here?" My stomach lurched. Wherever there was Jeff, Steven wasn't too far behind. A new start. I needed that without him. Operation One Night Stand needed Steven not to be there. I'd just finished my last day of work with him. I was beginning my new life without him. The last thing I needed was him anywhere near me.

"Yeah. Steven's not here. Yet."

The fact that Steven and I had broken up two months ago wasn't lost on me. I'd barely escaped becoming a hermit. And yet, two months later, there I was with more confidence in my pinky than I'd had during any of the five years we'd dated. I was embracing my confidence and refusing to shirk away from my fears. It wasn't easy. I didn't expect it to be.

I wondered, briefly, if Betsy the Intern would make an appearance. Of course, she was probably crying her eyes out on Steven's shoulder. But I'm not angry. Not anymore. I'm not even that sad. As mortified as she was when Steven publicly declared that she didn't matter, I was even more mortified that I would ever date someone who would do something as cliché as fucking an intern. I don't have anything against interns—everyone has to start somewhere—but come on!

"What can I get you?"

Realizing I was still half sprawled on my back on top of the bar, I rolled my eyes upward. Bartender Brian looked down at me and smiled.

"Hi." He really had nice teeth.

"Hi." I started to get up.

"No, no. Don't get up on my account." He gently placed his hand on my shoulder, effectively keeping me where I was. "So, need something to drink?" he asked Melody. I noticed her noticing him. I frowned a bit at the thought of her thoughts infringing upon the perverted scenes that ran through my head but I had to remind myself, yet again, that Brian wasn't the target.

"Sure. What do you recommend?" Melody leaned in and purred the question like she always did. I swear to God that girl was sex in heels.

"Body shots."

"Say what?" I, again, attempted to sit up and once again, Bartender Brian placed his hand on my shoulder and Melody clapped.

"Let me demonstrate."

I felt like my eyes were going to roll into the back of my head as I watched him pour a shot of tequila. With a shot in one hand and a saltshaker in the other, he leaned down and licked my neck. As he did, my eyes fluttered closed and I moaned.

Yes.

Moaned.

I heard him chuckle quietly.

I wanted nothing more than the bar to swallow me.

Before I knew it he shook salt onto my neck and leaned back down. Instead of merely licking the salt off, he added lips and teeth and *oh my God.*

I gasped so hard for air I swear I was drowning. Then he placed a lemon wedge on my lips.

This shit doesn't happen to me. Ever.

I didn't see him take the shot but I heard the shot glass hit the bar top.

I held my breath and waited as he raked his fingers through my hair, then bit around the lemon wedge, scraping his teeth on my lips. He must've bit the lemon because drops of juice and tequila fell onto my mouth. He used his lips and tongue to clean it up.

"That was fucking hot!" Melody clapped her hands.

"Thanks. I not only serve the drinks, I use them as entertainment." With one hand in front of him and one behind, he bowed. Fucking bowed. I was a lick away from orgasm and he's accepting applause.

Fuck.

"A little help here." I was not able to sit upright. Melody grabbed my hands and pulled me up.

I whipped my head around. Bartender Brian was across the way chatting up a group of guys who were with my target, and a fresh drink was sitting in front of me. A few people sitting next to me at the bar clapped as I came to my senses. A loud chorus of cheers had me ducking my head to avoid the attention.

"What the hell was that?" Sarah asked, laughing.

"What?"

"Look at you making out with the bartender! Looks like someone jumped off the celibate carousel."

"I did not! I was not making out with the bartender. He was just, he was just—" I looked at Melody for an answer.

"Don't look at me. Bartender Boy is hot! I say you focus on him!"

I grabbed my purse and hopped off the barstool.

"No. I made a deal and I picked my target. You'll see. I'm going to win this bet!"

"Caroline!"

Turning around, Bartender Brian smiled as he slid another drink my way. "Pink Panty Dropper."

"What!" *How did he know what color my underwear was?*

He laughed, pointed to the drink, and said, "Pink Panty Dropper from Tall Blond and Dumb."

"Oh. Okay. Thanks." I was a little unsteady and I didn't think it had anything to do with the drinks. Determined not to let my focus wane, I downed the shot, slammed the glass on the table, and said, "Pop My Cherry."

Brian reacted just as I thought he would. The look on his face was priceless. Grabbing a hold of my lady balls, I leaned across the bar, took a page from his book, and whispered, "Send him a drink. Pop My Cherry."

Just as he had, I lingered a beat longer than I needed to, making sure to graze my lips against his cheek. *Fuck it*, I thought. *If I am going to embrace my inner slut, I may as well bear hug her till she can't breathe.*

"Yes, ma'am." Brian white-knuckled his towel as he walked to the back of the bar and began mixing the drink. He snuck a glance at me, smirked, and shook his head.

I needed to know my target's name. "Bartender Brian!"

"Yeah?" He yelled over the noisy chatter of the bar.

"Find out his name!"

"I already know his name."

"What is it?"

"Not sure if I should tell you or not." He walked away, drink in hand, down to the other end of the bar.

"How's Operation One Night Stand going?" Sarah placed her empty glass on the bar and sat on the suddenly vacant stool next to me.

"It's going."

"Get his name yet?"

"Brian won't tell me."

"Who the fuck is Brian?"

"The bartender. Bartender Brian."

"Why don't you go ask his name yourself? Maybe Brian doesn't want you to know the guy's name."

"Why would he care whose name I know?" I took a sip of my cinnamon drink, remembering for a moment how Brian smelled when he drank it.

"Um. Hello?" Sarah rapped her knuckles on my head. "For such a pretty girl you are fucking dense. Brian's into you."

"No, he's not. He's a bartender. It's his job to flirt and whatever. He gets more tips that way."

"Tips, huh? I'll give you a tip. Ditch Ken doll over there and get nasty with Bartender Brian. He is quite a bit yummier." She licked her lips hungrily and growled, snapping her teeth together.

"Will you stop it?" I smacked her arm.

"I'm telling you. The bartender is the guy for you."

"You're just saying that so I'll lose the bet."

"Ugh. Caroline. Listen to me. I am your friend. Fuck the bet. I am telling you. Bartender Brian is the way to go."

"You ladies talking about me?"

I nearly choked on my drink. *How much had he heard?*

"Hi. I'm Sarah. Caroline's roommate."

"Nice to meet you, Sarah." Brian wiped his hands on the towel tucked into the back of his pants before offering it to her and shaking her hand. "What can I get you?" He picked up her empty glass, sniffed it, and said, "Amaretto and ginger."

"He's good." Sarah wiggled her eyebrows at me. I kicked her.

"I'm pretty good at most everything I do. Right, Caroline?" His eyes sparkled dangerously. I was beginning to think Sarah was right.

"I wouldn't know. I haven't seen most everything you do."

"We can fix that, you know. Say the word," he said as he over-poured Sarah's amaretto and splashed it with ginger ale.

"Can we now? So you're a handyman, too?" I chuckled.

"That is, of course, unless you're still stuck on Tall Blond and Douchey over there."

"Still weighing my options."

Sarah pinched my knee before she hopped down, drink in hand. I hadn't even noticed I'd finished mine. When I placed the glass on the bar for a refill, a shot glass topped high with fluffy whipped cream was sitting in front of me.

"Blow Job."

"I guess you expect me to swallow?" I asked suggestively.

"Well, that is the recommended ending for such a thing."

Laughing, I was reaching for the shot when Brian's hand covered mine. "Nope. No hands."

"No hands?" *I really should have gone out drinking more in college.*

"Ooh! Blow Job shots!" Melody and Sarah appeared on either side of me, slapping their hands on the bar. "Make it three and make it snappy, barkeep!"

I locked eyes with my target. He was staring at me like this shot was going to be the one that put the nail in the proverbial coffin. I make this work and I win the bet. He made his way through the crowd until he stood behind me. Sarah and Melody exchanged a look I couldn't interpret.

"My name is Ryan." He stuck out his hand over my shoulder and I shook it.

"Caroline," I said as I pointed to myself.

"Having a good time?"

"Yeah. You?"

"Yeah, sure. What do you say we get out of here?"

I looked at Sarah and she shook her head. Melody dropped her forehead to the surface of the bar. Brian stood in front of me with his arms crossed and an unreadable look on his face. Three shots were lined up in front of us.

Fuck it.

"What do I do?"

Melody piped up, "Put your hands behind your back like this." I mimicked her demonstration. "Lean down, wrap your lips around the glass, and lift. Drink the shot."

"Swallow. Don't spit," Brian chimed in, his eyes locked on mine.

Holding his stare I replied, "I never do."

"Let me hold your hair," Ryan offered as he gathered my curls into a manageable mess.

"Ready, girls?" Sarah asked.

Closing my eyes, I leaned down, wrapped my lips around the cool shot glass, and threw my head back. The shot glass was pulled from my mouth before I could think about it and Ryan's mouth crashed down on mine. By the time I came up for air, Bartender Brian had moved to the other end of the bar.

I wasn't quite sure why I was so disappointed to see him go. Not like we were a *thing*. Regardless, a lump formed in my throat. I grabbed Sarah's drink and downed it like it was my last.

"Easy. You okay?" Sarah whispered.

"Yeah, fine. I'll be at our place."

"You're going to our place?"

"Yeah. Safer there than his, considering I don't know him, right?"

"You know, so many people go through life without having experienced a one night stand. You don't have to do this."

"Sarah. I haven't had sex in two months. Two months! Do you have any idea what that does to a woman's vagina?"

"Um, no. But I know what it does for the battery business."

"Ha. Ha. Really funny. I'm at the precipice of becoming an old maid! Look around! All the girls here are young. I am old. Old!"

"Seriously, Caroline. It's not that big a deal. You're just going through a dry spell."

"Dry spell? There are days I have to check and make sure my lady parts are still there. Dry spell my ass. Ladies, I'm getting fucked tonight. My door will be closed. I will be screaming. Don't come in."

Melody spit her drink on the guy standing next to her. Then she yelped. Of all the people in the world, she spit her drink on my ex.

"Steven. Nice to see you." It really wasn't.

"Uh, Care? You drunk or something?"

"Not really, why?" Actually, I kind of was but he didn't need to know that.

He grabbed my arm and pulled me aside. "Care, do you know this guy?" He thumbed toward Ryan.

"I'm sorry. I lost the memo. When the fuck did that become your business?"

"I still care about you."

"Right. That's pretty funny. You really seemed to care when you were fucking Betsy."

"That was a mistake. I am so sorry. I want to make it up to you."

"Ha! It wasn't a mistake until I found out!"

"Look, can we talk somewhere else? I was hoping that, you know, since we don't work together anymore that maybe…"

"Maybe what? That we'd have another go? That we'd ever be something again? Fuck off Steven and take your dictating intern with you."

"Everything okay over here?" Brian's voice made me jump. I realized I had yelled loud enough to cause a scene and a number of people had stopped their chatter to hear the exchange between Steven and myself.

"Yeah, we're good. Why don't you mind your own business?" Steven responded to him with his usual air of snobbery. *God, what did I ever see in this guy?*

"Don't talk to him like that!" I slapped away his grip on my arm.

"What, are you fucking this guy, too?"

"Too? Too? You should talk, Steven! You make me sick, you lying fucking bastard. Fuck you."

"Knock it off, Care. You're making a scene." I saw him scan the bar.

"Get the hell away from me. I wear heels bigger than your dick. Take it somewhere else. No one here cares."

"That's enough! I think it's time for you to leave." Brian miraculously appeared between Steven and me; Ryan stood next to him. I thought I might faint when he reached behind him and placed his hand on my stomach, effectively shielding me from Steven's jerk-face rhetoric.

"Fine." Steven threw his hands up in the air. "This isn't over, Caroline. You can't throw away five years on a pretty boy and a fucking *bartender*." He spat the word like it was beneath him.

"No, but you can throw it away on Betsy the Intern. Just go away. I don't want to see you ever again."

Steven walked out with his entourage of assholes. I felt both defeated and liberated.

"I'm a bit put out that I'm not the pretty boy," said Brian. "You okay?"

"I'm good. Thank you."

"No problem. You're awfully feisty."

"That's just the new me."

"You ready?" Ryan put his hand around my shoulder.

"Huh?" I was a bit disoriented by the previous display and more than slightly embarrassed. "Oh, right. Sure."

I grabbed my coat and handed it to Ryan. He obviously didn't know what to do with it, so I took it back and shrugged on my coat.

"You sure about this?" Sarah looked at me with equal parts "go get 'em" and "what the fuck are you thinking?"

"Yeah. It's just sex, right? Not like I'm looking for a relationship with Tall Blond and Dumb, right?"

"I just don't want you to regret anything in the morning."

"Then I'll sleep till noon." I smiled.

"If you're sure. Call me if you need anything."

"Will do." I leaned onto the bar. "Brian!"

"Yo!" He turned around, delivering a drink to a thirsty patron before making eye contact.

His gaze was so penetrating, it felt like a thousand gymnasts were using my stomach as a trampoline.

"Thanks again for that. Sorry you had to get involved."

"That's what I do." He rapped his knuckles on the bar. "Take care of yourself, Caroline." *What's with the tone?*

Effectively dismissed, I watched as he pulled another beer and took an order from an overly flirtatious girl who looked like she was barely out of high school. *Not my problem.*

"Let's go, Ryan."

Chapter Four

I nearly dragged Ryan out of the bar. Snowflakes fell steadily, sticking to the already slick sidewalk. I realized my shoes, no matter how cute, were not going to make it through the night.

"Hey." Ryan stopped. "I left my coat in the bar."

"Oh, right. Um, I'll wait."

"You sure?"

"No. I want you to freeze to death in the snow." He looked at me and cocked his head. "I'm kidding. Go get it."

He laughed and pulled me in tight. His thumb slid across my cheek and he lifted it up to show me a single drop of water. "A snowflake fell from your eyelash to your cheek. I think it's good luck."

"Do I blow on it?" I kept eye contact as I leaned in. I closed my eyes and blew the tiny drop off his thumb. I raised my head, smiled, and said, "Hurry."

He grabbed my face and kissed me hard and I felt it in my panties. "Be right back." He pulled away and jogged the half block back to the bar.

I found a bare wall between apartment entrances and leaned against it, hoping the overhang would shield me from the weather a little bit. My feet were wet, my toes were cold, and I hadn't thought to bring gloves or a hat. I rolled my eyes at the thought. Sure, I was cold, but *Hello, Caroline! Hopefully you are about the have amazing sex with a superhot guy.* Smiling, I closed my eyes and imagined his lips on mine again. Only when I imagined the lips they weren't Ryan's. They belonged to Bartender Brian. And the thought of Brian's lips on mine soaked my panties as much as the real kiss did with Ryan.

Ryan.

Brian.

Someone was going to have to change his name.

Rifling through my purse, I found my lipstick. My fingers were cold and when I pulled the cap off, it slipped from my grip and fell to the sidewalk.

"Fuck." I squatted down and looked around me; it couldn't have gotten far. I was sure it was hiding by my feet in the slushy snow.

I didn't spend too much time looking. My fingers were bright red from feeling around the cold snow and my toes felt like frostbite was going to take over.

"Lose something?"

I looked up to see Ryan standing in front of me wearing weather appropriate outerwear.

"Yeah. I dropped the top to my lipstick." I held up the tube to show him.

"It's freezing out and you're worried about lipstick?" He stepped closer. "I don't think you need it."

"No?" My back was pressed against the brick wall.

"No. But if you need them warmed up—" He slid his hand under my ear and threaded his fingers through my hair. And then he kissed me.

His lips melted into mine and I moaned softly. Our mouths parted slightly and he gently pulled my bottom lip into his mouth. He sank his teeth in for a moment before pulling away. He rubbed his nose along mine.

"Warm?"

"Fuck." The word tumbled out of my mouth and I slapped my hand against it. "I meant," I mumbled through my hand, "yes."

He chuckled before offering to carry me home on his back.

"Hop on," he said as he squatted down in front of me.

"What?"

He looked at me over his shoulder. "Your shoes are soaked, your lips are blue. There isn't a taxi in sight. You said you lived close, now hop on."

I hiked my purse up on my shoulder, wrapped my arms around his neck, and hopped up as his arms hooked around my legs.

"So, where are we going?"

"Huh?" I was momentarily distracted by his stubbled jawline.

"Where do you live?"

"Oh, right. Next building." I pointed and he headed for the stoop.

I fumbled for my keys and dropped them, like I had the lid to my lipstick. We both knelt down at the same time and bonked heads.

"Ouch." I rubbed my head.

"Sorry." He rubbed his.

Time stopped for a moment as we stared at each other. He held my keys and my hand reached up to his face. He leaned in and kissed me slowly as we stood. He stepped forward and backed me against the door as he fumbled with the keys. When he finally opened the door, he stepped over the threshold and lifted me up at the same time. My legs wrapped around his waist and my arms circled his neck. His hands held me up by my ass, his fingers gripping tight. The kiss was deep, rough, and needy. He stepped forward clumsily, knocking my back into the wall, and my fingernails dug into his coat.

"Stairs," I directed between kisses. Instead of climbing them he sat, with me straddling his lap. One hand splayed wide and pulled me into him while the other snaked under my hair and grabbed a fistful. He gently yanked back and ran his tongue along my exposed throat.

He shifted his leg over so it was between my legs. He continued to pull me in and I rocked back and forth. The seam of my jeans hit me in just the right spot. Our kisses were sloppy and consuming; he wrapped both arms around my waist and I ground down onto his leg.

"Oh my God," I whispered.

"Don't stop, Caroline." He wrapped his arms tighter.

I buried my face in his neck and thrust until I could feel my panties being soaked. I let out a breathy moan.

"Ryan. Holy shit!" An orgasm racked me and I held on to him tight until the wave passed.

After a few minutes he chuckled and asked, "Are you okay?"

"I'm great. Just very, very thankful for the seam of these jeans." I leaned back with his arms still wrapped around me.

"You wear them well." He leaned in and kissed the corner of my mouth.

"Thank you."

"I'd like you to take them off."

I climbed off his lap and kicked off my shoes.

"I didn't mean here." He leaned back on the steps and smiled.

"Oh, so I shouldn't do this?" I unbuttoned my jeans and cocked an eyebrow.

He ran his finger along his lips. "I didn't say that."

I laughed, reached down, grabbed my shoes, and ran past him up the stairs. He jumped up and chased me. I had only half a flight on him. I was glad I was only going up to the third floor.

"I have the keys you know!" he yelled up to me.

"I know!"

He and I hit the third-floor landing at the same time and he followed me to my door.

"Tease."

"I need to open the door."

"The keys are in my pocket."

I reached in and found something other than keys and mentally thanked the one-night-stand gods for gifting me with such a well-endowed target.

"Those aren't keys," he whispered when my hand gripped him through the pocket of his jeans.

"I know."

He produced the keys and handed them to me. I turned to unlock the door and I could feel his excitement press up against me as he kissed my neck. It felt like unlocking the door took forever but when I finally did, he stumbled into the apartment behind me before he slammed the door closed and turned the lock. For a few seconds we stared at each other. The sexual tension was palpable, like tiny sparks of electricity flying through the room. One tiny word slipped from his mouth.

"Fuck."

We collided in a tangle of hands and lips and tongues. Our coats dropped in a heap on the floor. The buttons on my shirt were too much for him and he ripped it open instead as I unbuckled his belt and whipped it out of his pants. I tossed it across the room and it hit a lamp, knocking it over to shatter on the floor.

I.

Did.

Not.

Care.

"Ryan," I mumbled before sinking my teeth into his lip. He responded by sliding his hand down the back of my jeans and squeezing my ass. He picked me up again and started down the hallway.

"Wrong room." My hand shot out to the doorjamb as he tried to enter Sarah's room. "Across the hall."

He turned around and used his foot to shove my bedroom door open. He dropped me on my bed and leaned down to unbutton my pants. He slid them over my hips hard enough to lift me off the bed.

"Panties off." He was already dropping his pants to the floor and stepping out of his boxer briefs.

I froze. In my whole life I'd never seen anything so girthy. Instinctively my hands flew to cover my lady bits.

He reached down, pushed my hands aside, and dipped his fingers inside me. "You okay?"

"Better than." I placed my hand behind his head and pulled him into a kiss. We both crawled back on the bed until he was able to settle between my legs.

I heard a wrapper open, then it was a few seconds before he positioned himself above me. Need took over and I thrust my hips toward him, feeling the tip of him hit me. Ryan pulled my right leg up and grabbed my ass as he pushed deep inside me. I cried out. I'd never felt anything so completely. He filled me, stretched me, and I couldn't get enough.

"More," I demanded and quickened the pace.

"You want more?" He smiled and pulled out before slamming back into me.

"Brian!" I yelled, and he stopped for a minute and his eyes widened. It was a second before I realized I'd said the wrong name. I tried to play it off. "Oh, Ryan! Fuck me harder!"

I am pretty sure he caught the flub but he picked up the pace and banged me until I thought I would pass out. The bed rocked and the headboard hit the wall so hard I thought pictures would fall off the wall.

"God damn Caroline. You feel so fucking good." His voice was gruff and sexy.

I shifted position and we rolled.

I smacked my head on the nightstand. "Ow, fuck!"

We both stopped our frenzied fuck fest to laugh.

"Sex injury?" He chuckled.

"It fucking hurts," I said between tears of laughter and pain.

"Do you need ice?"

Fuck no, I didn't need ice. I needed sex. "I'm good." I rolled my hips.

"You sure?" He thrust into me.

Instead of answering I kissed him and he leaned back so I was sitting in his lap. He kicked out his legs and held me steady. Once I got my rhythm, he reached around and unhooked my bra. I slipped it off and he tossed it.

"Caroline." He grunted my name. "Caroline. Slow down. I'm going to come."

Instead of slowing down, I held on and sped up, thrusting and rolling like a porn star. I was owning this motherfucking one night stand.

"Caroline." His hands grabbed my hips. "Caroline." His fingers dug into my skin. "Oh fuck!" He grabbed me and pulled me in tight as he thrust up. The muscles in his shoulders and arms tightened. I could feel his legs tense under me. "Fuck." He dropped his head to my shoulder and shuddered.

He let go of me and fell back. I climbed off him and slid off the bed.

"Where are you going?" He reached for me.

"To get a drink. Water. You want some?"

"You have anything stronger?"

"Yeah. Be right back."

I padded to the living room and pulled a bottle of whiskey off the shelf. I grabbed two glasses and a bottle of water from the kitchen before heading back to the bedroom. Ryan was still lying on his back, his dick limp, though he had removed the condom. Truth be told, I was a little put out that the only orgasm I had came from a hundred-dollar pair of jeans.

"Here." I handed him a glass before unscrewing the top of the bottle. I poured him two fingers before swigging straight from the bottle. I winced and coughed and chased the drink with half a bottle of water.

"You okay?" he asked.

"You keep asking me that." I reached into my drawer and pulled out an oversize T-shirt.

"What are you doing?"

"Getting dressed."

"Why?"

"Um…" I waved my arm toward his flaccid penis.

"Oh this?" He sat up and downed the whiskey. "This isn't done. This is a break."

"A break?" Holy shit. Steven never took a break. He pumped, dumped, and passed out. "I just thought—"

"Thought what?" He stood and crossed the room, took the bottle of whiskey from my hand, and took a large gulp. Part of me was jealous because he didn't choke on it. "You thought we were done? No. No. No. Did I make you come?"

I shrugged. "It felt good."

"That's not what I asked. Did I make you come?"

"No."

"No. I didn't. I intend to remedy that tonight. I intend to remedy that a few times."

My mouth dropped open and my skin tingled. Goose bumps covered me and I could feel myself grow wet at his words.

"You are going to feel me here." He kissed my mouth. "Here." He reached around and grabbed my ass. "And here." He dropped to his knees and darted his tongue out, barely flicking my clit.

My knees gave out and he caught me before I fell. He handed me the bottle of water and stood.

"Drink that water, Caroline. You're going to need it." Ryan chuckled and walked out of the room toward the bathroom. I tilted my head and watched his bare ass until it left my sight. I shivered and chugged the rest of my water, anticipating what he had in store for me the rest of the night.

Chapter Five

I shifted under the covers, slowly stretching my arms and pointing my toes until I thought they'd detach from my body. The soreness I was feeling lazily brought me back to a night of mind-blowing sex. My shoulders still ached from when Ryan pinned me to the wall. My hamstrings screamed and I remembered spending quite a bit of time with my legs up in the air. My hair was a rat's nest of tangles covering the lump that had formed from banging my head on the nightstand. Falling off the bed during sex was not as graceful as it looked in the movies. My ass felt like it had been stretched in a torture machine. And to top it off? My bedroom smelled like a brothel.

Ahh. The musky smell of sex.

Last night was definitely not for the faint of heart and had it not been for the ridiculous confrontation with Steven at the bar, I may not have actually gone through with it. I was no longer a virgin to stranger sex.

I opened my eyes, thankful I'd had the forethought to turn off the lights and keep the curtains closed. Rolling over, I reached for the glass of water I always kept by the bed.

Looking up, I tilted my head slightly. *What the hell is that?* Attached to my slow-moving ceiling fan was my pink bra.

At least the hanging bra signified something other than the relationship I had with sweatpants, movie channels, and ice cream since Steven and I broke up.

"So, how'd it go?" Sarah startled me out of my reverie as she walked into my room carrying a huge mug of coffee and I pulled my blanket up to cover my boobs.

"Wouldn't you like to know?" I rolled over, picked up my phone, and looked at the time. Five after twelve. "Told you I wouldn't regret anything in the morning."

"That you did." She made herself comfortable on the edge of my bed and handed me a tank top she found on the floor. "So, details?"

I closed my eyes, remembering what there was to remember about Operation One Night Stand. "It was, uh, nice."

"Nice? There's a broken lamp in the living room and the front door was left open. I thought we had been robbed. Until I found your torn shirt on the floor." She held up the tattered blouse with her index finger. "I think there's more to it than 'nice.'"

I smiled. It was more than nice. It was crazy. I leaned over my bed and picked up what was left of the new pink panties I'd bought specifically for the night.

"Holy shit, Care! When you go all in—"

"*He* went all in." I wiggled my eyebrows at her and squealed.

"Nice!"

"I didn't know it could be like that! I had no idea there were so many different ways to bend. Honestly. Thank God for yoga."

"So you feel good?"

"Yeah. Sore but," I smiled before I pulled my knees up and winced. My hand flew to my crotch. "Ouch!" I couldn't tell what hurt worse, my vagina or my ass. It didn't matter. I needed the pain to go away.

"What's the matter?" Sarah jumped up. "Oh, fucking gross Care!"

Sarah leaned down and picked up off the floor what should have been the most embarrassing clue as to what actually went on last night.

"Seriously?" She turned the item over to read the label. "Lots O'Lube?"

My best friend was holding up a white tube of Lots O'Lube, complete with a bright green shamrock next to the name.

"Huh?" Instinctively, my sphincter tried to shrink back to its normal size.

So that's why my asshole feels like someone lit a match to it.

"Ha! You little whore!" Her laugh echoed in the space.

I squeezed my eyes tight in an attempt to control the throbbing. "I think I may have overdone it."

"You think?"

"My vagina hurts." I flopped to the fetal position, my hands cupping my very sore lady parts.

"Just your vagina?" She cocked an eyebrow.

"No. Not just my vagina. That skin between the vagina and the asshole. I feel like it ripped."

"Your taint?"

"Do girls *have* taints?" I shook my head. "Who cares? I feel like I've been stretched to max capacity."

"That big, eh? I'll get you some ice. Be right back."

I placed my coffee mug on the nightstand and flopped back onto my bed. Hugging my pillow to my chest, I closed my eyes. Every touch, tug, pull, kiss, and slap of the ass from the night before flooded my brain. My stomach fluttered at the thought of his mouth on me. Eating, tasting, sucking, licking, kissing. He was a sex god. And that made me a sex goddess. At least I felt like one last night. It was perfect, until…

"Here you go." Sarah tossed an ice pack at me and I not so discreetly wrapped it in the scraps of my tattered shirt and placed it on my crotch.

"Better?" She shoved clothes off my chaise and leaned back.

"Yeah. Thanks."

"So," she began, "now you've gotten that out of your system and you aren't so anxious and all 'Caroline' about it, tell me, was it worth it?"

"Absolutely. It was amazing. And his dick was huge. I mean, like, cucumber big. And his abs, oh my God! His abs! Physically, a perfect specimen."

"But?" Sarah knew me better than anyone.

"But I think I messed up. I don't think I'll be seeing him again."

"Messed up? How? I thought it was a one nighter? Who cares if you don't see him again?"

"Well…"

"Fess up, sister. What happened? Did you bite when you should have sucked?"

"God no! Nothing like that! I sucked like a champ, if I do say so myself. It's just that, well…" I took a breath. "Toward the end of all the crazy, uh—"

"Fucking." Leave it to Sarah to have the right word.

"Yeah, that. I sorta, kinda called him by the wrong name."

"You didn't!" Her eyes popped out of her head, reminiscent of old-school cartoons.

"Oh, honey! Well, you were with Steve a long time. God knows why, but it happens."

"It wasn't Steven's name."

Sarah sat up straight. "Well, then whose name did you use?"

"Brian's."

"Brian who?"

"Brian from last night."

"Bartender Brian, Brian?"

I nodded and took a long swallow of coffee.

"What? How?" For once cool, calm, collected, say-it-like-it-is Sarah was at a loss for words. "Why?"

"I don't know! I mean, Ryan was on top of me, pumping like a machine, mind you, and all of a sudden my brain went to Brian. I mean, for a minute I didn't think he noticed. Brian sounds a lot like Ryan, right?"

"Right," she said, obviously not following my excuse.

"Well, I said it, he looked at me funny, we finished—"

"Wait, you called out a different guy's name and he still finished?"

"Well, yeah. What else was he going to do? No sense in walking away from a sexcapade like *that*, right?"

"Sure, sure. I regularly allow someone to get off after they call me Lucy or some shit. Go ahead."

"It wasn't like that. I was totally in the moment. Totally into it. You owe me fifty bucks by the way." I pointed at her. "I just had one little slip. Ryan whispered in my ear something like 'I want you to have a screaming orgasm' or something and poof! Brian was in my head."

"Wait, hold on. What the fuck does Brian have to do with a screaming orgasm? Other than the fact that he's outrageously hot. And sexy."

"That's the name of the drink he whispered in my ear. I am pretty sure that's when he started flirting with me."

"Not for nothing, he wasn't the only one flirting. Just saying."

"I wasn't flirting! I was focused on the target! On Ryan!"

"Yeah. So focused you called out Brian's name."

"Shut up!" I threw a pillow at her and she ducked.

"Go take a shower. We have to meet Mel for spin class then lunch."

"Spin class?" My body went rigid.

"Yep. No pain no gain." Sarah let out a huge laugh, the kind that calls you an idiot without voicing the words out loud.

My stomach growled and I realized I hadn't eaten anything since lunch yesterday.

"Sarah?"

"Yeah?"

"You think I fucked up my first one night stand?"

"Far be it from me to judge. Seriously. I've had more than my fair share of one time romps. But"—she stood and walked to my door—"I have never gotten anyone's name mixed up."

She laughed as the door closed and I threw another pillow, which bounced off the wall. Pouting, I slumped back onto my bed. Part of me was thrilled to have finally popped my cherry, so to speak, on the one-night-stand thing. But another was disappointed that it hadn't been with Brian. Regardless of my feelings on the subject, I was a girl who'd just been banged to within an inch of her life and had the ice pack on her crotch to prove it.

Chapter Six

An hour later, Sarah and I met up with Mel in the lobby of the gym. I, of course, felt like I'd just spent a week riding stallions when, in fact, it had been only one night. Neither the ice pack nor the cluster of pain pills I took alleviated the strange throbbing sensation between my legs. Every step felt like a cross between round five of a boxing match with my labia, a pool of fire, and the prelude to an insane orgasm. Either way, the sensation was a bit disturbing.

"Good morning, sunshine!" Melody sang a bit too loud for my taste. It may be half past one in the afternoon but I was still in no shape to be in public.

"Take off your sunglasses. You look ridiculous. It's overcast outside and you're indoors." Sarah yanked my sunglasses off my face and I winced.

"What the fuck, Sarah!"

"You are not the only person to ever drink too much. Own it. For one night, you were a drunken slut. No one can take that away from you!"

"Let your freak flag fly, bitch!" Melody waved her arm above her head and swung her hips in a way that made me dizzy.

"Leave me alone," I growled, snatching my sunglasses back from Sarah and shoving them as close to my face as I could. "My vagina hurts."

"Ha! What?" Melody shrieked a little too loudly. "Pounded in the pussy, were we?"

"Not *just* the pussy," Sarah mumbled.

"Yeah, shut it!" I took a long swig of my water. The bottle was already half empty and I wasn't sure how I'd make it through an hour of Warden Suzy, our spin instructor.

"Shut up! That's hysterical!" Melody was finding my pain entirely too funny.

"I am right here! You don't need to mock me. For your information, it was amazing. He was—"

"Hung like a horse."

"Sarah!" I punched her in the arm.

"Oh, sorry. 'Radiated cucumber big.'" She held her hands a foot apart to demonstrate the metaphor.

"Ladies! Get your asses in here! This is spin class, not gossip hour!"

We all rolled our eyes. Sounded like Warden Suzy was in a mood.

"Get the fuck out of here!" Melody whispered. "I need all the deets. You'll spill at lunch!"

"As long as I don't lose my appetite." Sarah laughed as we entered the room.

"Get on your bikes, ladies! We need to work the weekend off your asses! I can see some of you went a little overboard." I swear to God, the warden was looking at me when she said that. "We will remove the aforementioned excess today. Now mount up."

In unison, twenty-two people in the room mounted their stationary bikes while I, the twenty-third, stood and stared at it.

"What's wrong with you?" Sarah whispered, her gaze half focused on me, the other half on Warden Suzy.

"I don't think I can do this."

"You've done this almost every Sunday for the past two years. You're good. Get on before she notices and calls you out."

Whenever Warden Suzy called someone out, they were forced to spin next to her, facing the class. Thankfully, it had never happened to me, but I'd seen enough mortified faces to know I never wanted it to.

"But my crotch hurts."

"Man up."

"Fine," I whined as I settled the too-tiny bike seat between my legs. I honestly felt like I was sitting on jagged rocks. I could barely even bring myself to wear underwear and the bike shorts I was wearing did absolutely nothing to alleviate the pain. I shifted left before leaning right. Sliding forward then nudging back, there really was no comfortable way to sit on a bike seat. Of course, after the night I'd had, the odds at finding any comfort on any seat were stacked against me.

Whether you are a man or a woman, spin class will bruise you in places you had no idea could be bruised. It is crotch torture. But once you see the transformation your body makes after a few classes, you'll put up with the pain. And, to be fair, the pain really does lessen the more you ride.

However, after last night's festivities, I felt like a newbie again. Biting my lip, I focused on the music and Warden Suzy's shouts about slaying the cellulite monster and shrinking our fat asses to drown out the pain.

A bead of sweat formed at the base of my neck and slipped haphazardly down my back, absorbing into the fabric of my sports bra.

With each pump of my legs, my grunting became more and more pronounced. Sarah and Melody, on either side of me, started to giggle. I scowled and continued on.

My sports bra was completely soaked with sweat no longer confined to rogue beads of perspiration and each new drip slid down to my ass crack. I shifted to find some semblance of comfort.

"Holy fucking hell!" I yelled out, much to the astonishment of nearly everyone in the class. Warden Suzy thought, of course, that I was in beast mode.

"That's right, Caroline! Ride through the pain! Ride, bitch, ride!"

Sarah slumped in her seat, her head on the handlebars, her body vibrating from laughter.

Melody joined in the warden's chorus. "That's right, bitch! Ride it like you own it!"

Of course that did absolutely nothing to take the focus off me. Warden Suzy thought I was working the bike whereas Sarah, Melody, and I knew I was about to die from the aftermath of riding a giant cock all night.

"See ladies! Do it like Caroline! Pump! Pump!" Warden Suzy was so into my grunts, she failed to see that I was in actual pain. "Feel it, ladies! Feel it inside you and ride that bitch until you own it!"

It was too much for Melody; she actually fell off her bike. Thankfully, she was on the end and didn't hit another spinner. I don't think it would have mattered much—she was on the floor in the fetal position laughing above the din of the music. Sarah had just stopped spinning completely, lost in the words of our revered and feared instructor.

"Fuck you," I muttered under my breath.

"Ride, Caroline! Pump!" She snorted.

"All right, ladies! Melody get up! Time to take it harder!"

Honestly, when did spin class become so perverted? Then again, like Melody always said, having a dirty mind makes ordinary conversations more interesting. But this wasn't interesting. It was torture.

"We're going to do up downs. On the count of three."

Oh, shit.

"One!"

Oh, shit.

"Two!"

Oh, shit.

"Three! Uuuup!" Warden Suzy screamed until her voice broke. I forced my legs to hold me up and bit my lip.

"Down!"

I dropped to my seat. Oh my God. I'd never felt such pain.

"Up!"

I pushed myself up. My panties were actually crawling up inside me.

"Down!"

That was it. I joined Melody on the floor, holding my crotch like it was going to fall off if I let go.

"Motherfucker!"

A few classmates whipped their heads around to stare.

"I need to get the fuck out of here," I whispered to Melody.

Between fits of laughter she managed to agree. "Me. Too. I swear I am going to pee myself."

On my hands and knees I crawled to my bike, grabbed my towel and water bottle, and hightailed my ass out of the room with Melody and Sarah hot on my heels.

Stumbling through the door I collided with something solid, causing Sarah and Melody to crash into me.

"What the—"

"Hey there."

My knees gave out and the person standing in front of me caught me before I could embarrass myself anymore.

"You okay?" He looked concerned.

"Brian? What are you doing here?" Suddenly I was acutely aware of the fact I hadn't showered and must've smelled like a cross between sweat and sex. The hair that'd managed to slip out of my ponytail was plastered to my face and I was holding my crotch.

He nodded toward the doors behind me. "Warden Suzy too much for you today?" His eyes flicked down to my hands.

I was still reeling from the fact that Brian, the reason my one night stand wasn't perfect, was standing in front of me, his sweaty T-shirt clinging to biceps that hadn't been visible through his shirt last night.

"Ah, well, yeah. You know." I couldn't make a coherent sentence if someone dangled a pair of Louboutins in my face.

"Hi! We met last night. I'm Sarah; this is Melody."

"I remember," he answered, without taking his eyes off me. "You sure you're okay?" He reached out and touched my shoulder.

"Yeah. I'm good." I crossed my arms over my chest in an attempt to appear casual.

"So I hear." That playful smirk danced across his mouth like it had the night before.

"Brian! Yo! You ready, bro?"

Every hair on my body stood on end. I *knew* that voice. Stiff as a board, I turned in the direction of the person I knew to be there.

Ryan. *They know each other?*

"Caroline."

"Ryan."

"Damn," Sarah and Melody whispered in unison behind me, and I elbowed them in an attempt to shut them up.

The words *get out of here* ran in a loop through my head over and over.

"What are you doing here? I mean, this is your gym, too?" Ryan looked as uncomfortable as I felt.

"Yeah, I, uh, spin class." I gestured to the doors behind me.

Sneaking a sideways glance at Brian, I saw that he had yet to take his eyes off me. He was covering his mouth with his hand. *He thought this was funny?*

"Yeah, well, uh. Nice to see you. We have to go. Plans. You know."

"Hi! I don't think we met. I'm Melody." Shoving me out of the way, she stuck her hand out and Ryan took it while staring at me quizzically. "Nice to meet you."

"I'm Sarah. Caroline's roommate." Sarah pushed herself in front of me.

Ryan's face turned an awfully funny shade of red. The tips of his ears looked like he spent too much time in the sun.

"Yeah, um. Sorry about the lamp."

Brian's eyebrows skyrocketed off his face as he stifled a laugh.

"No problem. People bang into things all the time. We can always buy new lamps."

I nearly choked at the way Sarah said *bang*. I tried to silently convey how uncomfortable I was but she continued.

"So, you don't sound like you're from around here. Where'd you *blow* in from?" She couldn't hide her smile no matter how hard she tried.

Like me, Ryan choked at her choice of words. "I'm from Texas. I'm just staying with a friend until I can find my own place."

How did I miss the accent?

Never one to pass up a chance at homing in on a new recruit, Melody stretched her neck. "Is your friend here?"

Brian coughed and held up his hand with a two-finger salute.

"You? You're his friend? He's staying with you?" I pointed back and forth between the two men as if doing so would somehow make the knowledge less embarrassing.

"Yeah. We went to college together."

I needed the floor to open and swallow me whole.

"Well, isn't that great!" I faked a smile so plastic even Barbie would be proud. "We really, really have to go. Nice to meet you, er, uh, see you again—"

"Ryan." Brian pointed to his friend with a look of mock-seriousness on his face.

"Yeah, I know that. Bye, Ryan. Bye, Brian."

Ryan waved halfheartedly. I think he was still trying to figure out what the hell just happened.

"Hey, Caroline!" Brian called out.

"Yeah?" I turned.

"Looks like you don't need those heels to be noticed from behind."

My mouth gaped open until Sarah reached over and closed it for me. My girls on either side of me, I was ushered into the locker room to shower and get ready for lunch.

Chapter Seven

None of us spoke until we were showered, dressed, and out the door. The girls, however, did laugh at me when I stealthily tiptoed my way from the locker room to the front door. I was on the lookout for Brian or Ryan. Just my dumb luck that the two of them knew each other. No, wait. Not just knew each other. Lived together.

I must've been something to look at because Melody started humming the *Pink Panther* theme song.

Once we hit the street, I whirled around. "You two couldn't help me out in there? You"—I pointed at Sarah—"with your *bang* and *blow* remarks! Do you have any idea how mortified I was?"

"I absolutely know how mortified you were. That's why it was so funny."

Melody fell into a fit of giggles. "Ride, Caroline! Ride!"

"You aren't helping."

"Aw, come on. We figured you'd never run into them again. We were wrong. Chalk it up to an awkward encounter. Look, I love you like a back-alley hooker loves crack but if you can't see the funny, you aren't the Caroline I know."

I sighed and plopped down on a bench, wincing in the process. The throbbing subsided but it still hurt to sit. "You're right."

"This shit really would only happen to you, Care," Melody said.

"I know, right? Like I have some idiot badge on my head."

"You don't have an idiot badge. I promise I would have taken a butt load of pictures of it and posted it all over social media if that were the case."

Leave it to my girls to diffuse me. I really was lucky to have them in my corner.

"Let's eat."

"About time. I'm starving."

We walked the block to the café. Ordering was easy. We chose the three greasiest plates on the menu. Nothing like clogging the arteries after a night of drinking and sex followed by a quick spin in the gym.

"So, that was weird, right?" Melody pulled back the curtain to reveal the elephant in the room.

"What was weird?" I tried to act like I had no idea what she was talking about while I shoved a huge bite of medium-rare cheeseburger in my mouth. I couldn't talk if my mouth was full, right?

"You know what." Sarah glanced at me sideways as she picked apart her BLT.

"Ryan. Brian. Texas and the bartender? Friends. *Roommates*." Melody wasn't going to let it go.

"It's fine, right? I mean, so what? I brought Ryan back to my place last night, was fucked sideways—"

"And upside down," Sarah added.

"And upside down, thank you. And I screamed Brian's name."

Sarah got up to pat Melody on the back as she choked on a French fry. "You what?" she finally asked after she'd taken a long sip of her diet soda.

"You didn't tell her?" I glared at Sarah.

"Not my story to tell." She wiggled her eyebrows at me and I dropped my head to the table.

"Yes. Yes, I may have, inadvertently, kind of mentioned Brian's name while I was having sex with Ryan."

"Well, Jesus Christ, doll. No wonder it was so awkward back at the gym. It was like a reverse rodeo."

"I don't know what that is. Like a reverse cowgirl?"

"Yes. No. Look, it's like the joke says, call a girl by the wrong name and hold on tight while she gets mad." She laughed and Sarah and I stared at her. "No? You never heard that one. Must just be me."

"Look, it's no big deal. I'll probably never see them again—"

"Um, I don't know about you but I like the gym and I like Murphy's and unless you plan on never hanging out with us again—"

"Look, Brian flirted because it's his job. He's a bartender. He's a flirt. And Ryan, well, maybe he'll find a place far away and I'll never see him again. It was just one night. One one-night stand. I finally got it out of my system."

Melody reached across the table and pilfered a fry from my plate. "You see, Care, that's where you're wrong. A one night stand is like this French fry here." She popped it in her mouth and grabbed another. "You can't have just one." She giggled, slopped it in a pile of ketchup, and bit it in half.

"No. No, no, no." I shook my head. "There will be no more one night stands. No more picking up random guys at a bar. No more breaking of lamps."

"No more Lots O'Lube?"

"Lots O'Lube?" Melody's eyes were wide.

"Shut up. No. As a matter of fact, maybe I'll just stop having sex altogether until I get my shit straight."

Both girls leaned back in their seats and considered me.

"Really. Thank you ladies for pulling me out of my pity party. I am sure the ice cream makers of the world were despondent over the whole thing. I just really think I need to focus on me. I start a new job when we get back from Jamaica and I don't need to be distracted."

"But that's exactly *why* you need to be distracted. What happened the last time you focused on one area of your life? Steven took it over, that's what. And not for nothing, I'm pretty sure that guy had more dick in his personality than in his pants." Sarah gave me *the look*. The one that said *Go ahead, try to argue my point.*

I couldn't. She wasn't wrong about that. I pursed my lips.

"I agree with you—leave the relationships alone for a while, but you're wrong if you think you can't have your cake and eat it, too. Have a little side of fun with your work. I'm not saying go out and screw every guy in a ten-mile radius—"

"Right. Five miles should do it," Melody piped in.

"Exactly." Sarah continued, "I don't want to see you in the state of mind you were in two months ago—hell, even two weeks ago. Look, you did nothing wrong. You're twenty-eight years old, you're pretty, and you have a great ass."

"Thank you." Suddenly I saw the burger I was eating nestling into my ass. My appetite waned.

"You're welcome. So you slept with a stranger. Who hasn't? Best part? The target has an accent. Southern is so sexy."

"I think Texas is more southwest," I said, lost in thought.

"Do you think he has a cowboy hat?" Melody piped in.

"Do all people from Texas own cowboy hats? Isn't that a bit of a stereotype? I mean, not all of us from Jersey perm our hair to within an inch of its life and shellac it with Aqua Net," I replied.

"I don't know. That's an eighties thing, girl. Doesn't matter, though, Jersey girls just do it better. I wonder what he looks like shirtless with torn-up jeans and a Stetson."

"Isn't Stetson a cologne?"

"It's a hat, too." Melody winked.

"Whatever. Like I said, one night stand, who hasn't?" Sarah reasoned.

"I certainly have. More than once. It's fun to get validation once in a while. I mean, maybe I have a few extra pounds on my hips. I'm not the skinniest bitch on the block, but I give great head and that cancels out the few extra pounds on my ass. Then again, I *am* a size awesome." Melody took another bite of her grilled cheese. "I am all for girl power, woman power, whatever. But any girl who tells you she doesn't like to feel pretty every now and then or need occasional validation from a member of the opposite sex is a liar, doesn't know how to give a good blow job, and probably hasn't ever had an orgasm. Nothing worse than an orgasmless liar."

"What are you saying?" I couldn't follow Melody's train of thought. It wasn't the first time.

"I'm saying we need orgasms and to say you don't is a lie."

"I can see how you were saying that." Sarah nodded.

"I guess so." I contemplated what they had said while keeping myself busy with my soda straw. "You both have valid points. Just do me a favor and don't let me become a slut."

"Aw, sweetie. Who are we to judge?"

"True."

I sat lost in thought for a bit when my phone rang. I reached into my gym bag and dug it out. I didn't recognize the number.

"Who is it?" Sarah asked.

"No idea. Local, though."

"Answer it."

Right.

"Hello?"

"Caroline?"

"Yes?"

"This is, uh, Ryan."

There's the accent. I am quite sure my eyes bugged out of my head.

"Who is it?" Sarah whispered.

Placing my hand over the phone I replied, "Ryan."

Melody made a crude gesture as she bobbed her head up and down, her fist in front of her mouth. I rolled my eyes.

"Caroline, you there?"

"Oh, sorry. Yeah. How are you?" I stared at my friends, who were trying to keep from laughing.

"Good. So, today was weird. Running into you at the gym, I mean."

"Yeah. Weird. So what's up?"

"Don't be rude," Melody whispered.

"I mean, what are you doing?" I made a face at her.

"Nothing. Look, I was wondering, if you're free, I mean, if you wanted to have dinner on Friday."

"We'll be in Jamaica Friday." I have to say, I was disappointed.

"Well, then the following Friday?"

"The following Friday?" I looked at Sarah and Melody again. I wasn't sure what to do.

"Say yes!" Melody squeaked a little too loudly.

"Did I interrupt you?" Ryan sounded concerned.

"No, just a, uh"—I stood and walked away from the table—"dog."

Melody stuck her tongue out at me while Sarah gave me the finger and barked.

"Oh, so Friday after next?"

"Yeah. Sure. Sounds great." I was fidgety, running my hands through my hair, effectively pulling most of it out of my ponytail holder.

"Excellent. So, I'll pick you up at eight?"

"Yeah, sure. Sounds great. You know where I live." I was a queen wordsmith. All the great ones repeat themselves. Good thing I was starting my new assistant editor job in a week.

"That I do," Ryan replied with what I perceived to be a bit of innuendo. I didn't know what to do with that.

"So, okay. I'll see you next week."

"That you will. Have fun in Jamaica. Bye, Caroline."

"Bye."

I hung up and walked back to the table only to find my two best friends whispering with their heads together.

"So I have a date with Ryan. I don't really know what to do with that."

Melody clapped her hands. "From what I hear, you know exactly what to do with that."

I dropped my head to the table, slowly banging it a few times.

"Ryan." Sarah elongated his name.

I popped my head up and looked at her. "That's what I said."

"Maybe it would be a good idea to practice saying his name. You know, in case you forget."

"Nice, Sarah."

"I'm just saying. Everyone needs a smart-ass sarcastic friend in their lives and I'm so very happy to be of service to you in your time of need."

"Yeah, yeah. You're always just saying." I pushed my plate away, silently repeating his name over and over in my head.

"Come on." Sarah stood and dropped money on the table. "We have appointments. Manis and pedis."

"Girls, this time tomorrow we'll be baking on the soft, warm sands of Jamaica."

Chapter Eight

We arrived at the resort in Montego Bay just before noon and were on the beach, drinks in hand, an hour later.

"This"—Melody sipped her rum punch—"is what we needed. Fuck all that snow. Fuck all that dreary weather. We need sun."

"You aren't kidding." Sarah rolled over onto her stomach after she handed me the suntan lotion. "If I had to deal with one more administrator talking to me about leaving no child behind or whatever the fuck, I honestly think I was going to shoot myself. Common Core my asshole."

I half-listened to the two of them go on about the pleasures of a sun-filled winter vacation. My head was stuck processing the events of the past weekend. I'd finally taken the plunge. I'd had sex with a stranger. Good sex. Excellent sex. Mind-blowing, bucket-list sex.

I'd lived through the awkward next day encounter. Ryan was the perfect target. Tall, built, hot as hell. And he'd asked for a date the following week. I wasn't sure what to do with that. Wasn't a one night stand just that? One night? I was sure I was breaking some weird rule about the whole one night procedure.

Who said, of course, that it had to be anything more? Maybe I'd never have sex with him again. Maybe dinner means just dinner. Maybe dinner meant he felt as awkward as I did when we ran into each other at the gym yesterday. Maybe he'll tell me he has crabs.

"Care?"

"What?" Even with sunglasses I needed to shield my eyes. Melody's metallic swimsuit reflected back at me with the strength of an eclipse. I was pretty sure I'd go blind.

"You okay?"

"What if he gave me crabs?" I looked back at the ocean, picturing tiny little crabs marching toward me.

"You're bald as a baby doll down there."

"So?"

"Oh my God, Care. It's like teaching a newbie. Crabs are lice. Lice need hair. You have no hair. As in none. As in zilch. As in—"

"You think too much." Melody finished Sarah's thought.

"I'm just saying. I don't know him. I don't know where he's been!"

"As in," Sarah continued, "there is no hair down there for crabs to hang on to. I was reading online that the popularity of Brazilian waxing has led directly to the decline of pubic lice."

"So, it's not crabs you should be worrying about. If it starts burning when you pee, or—"

"If your vagina begins to shrivel up, then you should be worried."

The two of them were unbelievable. I was having a real and seriously minor panic attack at the possibility of contracting a sexually transmitted disease and all they could do was joke.

"It's not funny. My vagina will not shrivel up." Just in case, I was going to have to check later.

"Well, not now, because you used it. For a while we were wondering if you'd started collecting cobwebs down there. I was actually thinking of purchasing a feather duster for you. I figured you could get off while you cleaned. But, if you're really worried about shriveling or crabs, one of us could check for you. Sarah, did you bring a flashlight?"

"Har, har. Cobwebs? Really, Melody? Real mature." I searched my bag for suntan lotion and remembered it was in my lap. "Whatever. I don't think I'm having sex with him again."

"You know what your problem is?"

"Enlighten me, Sarah."

"You think too fucking much. Christ, the way you talk about it, you'd think he popped your fucking cherry. This isn't forty-year-old virgin crap. You've had sex before."

"True, but it was so…vanilla." I rubbed lotion wherever I could reach.

"So you're used to vanilla." Melody shrugged her shoulders. "I'd be freaked out, too, if all I ever ate was vanilla then all of a sudden someone served up hot fudge, sprinkles, nuts, and cherries. Deal with it, doll. Ryan gave you the perfect sundae."

"He really did, didn't he?" Lying back, I closed my eyes and thought about him. I thought about his hands, his big hands, which had held me pinned against the wall. I thought about his mouth, the mouth that touched every inch of my skin, his tongue that explored me inside and out. Thank God we had that extra room and thank God I brought my vibrator. It looked like I was going to have to make my own luck.

"This is good, right?"

"What is good?" Sarah asked.

"This. This whole me being on my own thing. Never really did this before."

"You are going to be great. Look, you have a wonderful set of parents, a brother who loves you. I think you were so dependent on the tight family unit you had that when you finally had the opportunity to spread your wings, you chose someone you thought would take care of you. Steven was that person. I don't think he's a bad guy, he's just not good for you."

"He is a bad guy," Melody added.

"Mel—"

"No, I'm good. You're right, this will be good."

"There you go!"

I looked at my empty glass. "I don't know about you, but I need a refill. Be right back."

I left my friends basking in the Caribbean sun as I made my way to the bar.

I immediately regretted not slipping on my flip-flops. I hopped through the sand like an idiot, then tripped over a backpack and face-planted. My face full of sand, I rolled over on my back. *Typical Caroline*, I thought. With a belly full of rum punch, the world spun for a moment.

"Are you okay?"

Turning my head to the side, I looked for the source of the voice but the sun glare blocked my view.

"Did you hurt yourself?"

"I don't think so." The owner of the voice helped me to a sitting position. I took off my sunglasses and was face-to-face with dimples.

Green eyes and dimples. And floppy sun-bleached hair. And bronze skin that rippled with athleticism. This wasn't a gym jock. This guy was lean.

"Let me help you up." The face of the voice came into view as it blocked the sun.

He placed his hands under my arms and lifted me to my feet. He must've thought I was insane. I couldn't stop staring at his dimples. I was enthralled by the fact that he didn't even have to smile to make them appear. I blamed the rum punch for what happened next.

I lifted my hand and poked a finger in his face. Right into the left dimple.

"You okay?"

I quickly pulled my hand back and felt the rise of embarrassment heat me from my toes to the top of my head.

"I'm sorry. I don't know what I was thinking." My stammering attempt at an apology left much to be desired. I had defiled his dimple. I'd never prayed for quicksand but in that moment, it felt like a good idea. "Thank you for helping me up. I'll be going now."

Quickly turning away, I nearly tripped over the same backpack.

"Wait!" Dimples called to me. "What's your name?"

"Um, I really should be going. Sorry again!"

Somehow I was able to make my way to the cobblestone pathway without busting my ass again. I speed walked to the nearest bar and hopped up on a barstool. Thank God for all-inclusive.

"What can I getcha?" The bartender had the slightest hint of a Southern accent under his Jamaican accent that immediately led me to believe he wasn't a local.

"Two things. First, Piña Colada, heavy on the booze. Second, the real deal on where you're from."

"You can tell, huh?" Mr. Not From Jamaica busied himself with pouring the drink ingredients into a blender.

"There's a distinct twang underneath all that 'hey mon' you're trying to pass off as real."

"I guess I need to do better. I'm from Texas."

"I knew it!"

"Don't spread that around. I have an image to protect."

That image was over six feet tall and dark skinned. He ran his hands over his bald head and smiled as he handed me my drink, two slices of pineapple and a purple umbrella garnishing it. I wanted to take my straw and drink him up.

"Name's Wes but everyone around here calls me Marley."

"Marley? Isn't that a bit overkill? I mean, you don't even have dreads."

"My last name's Marley."

"Wes Marley?"

"Yes. Wes Marley, no relation. And who are you, or should I just call you Nosey?"

"Caroline. I'm here from New Jersey with my two friends."

"Ahh. Escaping the winter blues?" Wes asked as he cleaned a few glasses and ran a rag over the bar counter.

"Escaping all right. Not the winter blues, though." My straw sucked air as I finished the last of my drink. "That was fast." I stared at my empty glass before pushing it back toward Wes.

"So what are you escaping, Caroline from New Jersey?" He poured me another.

"Life. The old me. An ex fiancé. Reality. You name it. I'm on the run from it."

"Well, I've got nothing to do. Tell me about it."

"I did a bad thing." Yep. Rum punch and Piña Colada and no food since six in the morning? If I wasn't hammered now, it wouldn't take long to get there.

"You? You look like a nice lady."

"I did!" I crooked my pointer finger, signaling him to get closer, and whispered, "I had a one night stand."

The laugh that boomed out of him was sure to garner looks and interest from all the pretty people on the beach.

"Shhh. There is no need to laugh. I never did that before and now, I think I'm having, what do you call it?"

"Buyer's remorse?" Wes replied with a smirk.

"Yes!" I snapped my fingers. "Thank you. Buyer's remorse."

"So what led you to this buyer's remorse?"

Over the next three Piña Coladas I spilled my guts to Wes Marley, the no-relation, not-from-Jamaica bartender.

I'd just finished my story when I heard my name.

"Care! Where've you been?"

Melody and Sarah walked up to the bar.

"Holy crap! Did you two fall asleep?"

"We took a little nap, why?"

"Pretty sure you're sunburned." I poked Sarah's arm, the white fingerprint disappearing in seconds.

"No way. We used lotion. Besides, it doesn't hurt." The two of them hand-printed their stomachs.

"Caroline's right. You two are gonna be hurting in a few hours. I suggest you get some aspirin and go back to your room."

"Who's this guy?" Mel gracefully sidled up to the bar.

"*This* is Wes Marley, no relation. He's being my therapist. Let me get you two back to the room. Seriously."

Sarah took off her sunglasses and Melody squealed.

"What?"

"Your face. You have definite sunglass lines. Do I?" Mel pulled off her ginormous, look-at-me sunglasses and Sarah's eyes bugged out.

"Holy shit, Mel!"

"I don't feel so good." Melody wrapped her arms around her stomach.

"Hopefully you don't have sun poisoning," Wes offered.

"Sun poi—? No, Care. I want to go lie down."

"On it." I hopped off the barstool and turned to Wes. "Thanks for listening. Sorry if I was a downer."

"No problem, mon!" He replied in his best Jamaican accent. "Anytime. Seriously. What's your room number? I'll send them an aloe lotion I made. It really helps out the white girls from the north."

"White girls! Well, I never!" I playfully stomped my foot before leaving him the room number. I gingerly wrapped my arm around Melody, and Sarah followed as we walked back to our room.

Within minutes of arriving, I had them each take cool showers and dress in the loosest sundresses they packed. I knew, from experience, that the pain would take a bit of time but once it hit, they'd be toast.

Each downed a couple of aspirin and just as Wes promised, the lotion he'd concocted arrived at the room via housekeeping.

By the time I'd rubbed them down with the lotion, they were asleep, my buzz had almost worn off, and my stomach was rumbling.

I felt bad about leaving them but I figured there wasn't much I could do for them while they slept, so I placed a bottle of water near each of them, took a shower, and left to get something to eat. I could have ordered in but I really wanted to escape the confines of the room. I didn't travel all the way to Jamaica to coop myself up in a bedroom. I'd done enough of that in the past weeks.

Wearing a long green halter dress and flat strappy sandals, I felt like a million bucks. The salty air did wonders for my already curly hair and I had gotten just enough sun to kiss my skin with a faint tan.

I walked through the small-town-like atmosphere of the resort and watched, with a little pang of jealousy, as couples walked holding hands, kissing, sharing glasses of wine. It was what I'd always wanted. Someone to share the fun with, share romance with. Steven was always too busy for fun, too stuffy for romance. In the five years we were together, we'd been on only one vacation. If that's what one would call it. We went to Vegas for a conference. Never hit the strip once.

I shook off the thoughts that were darkening my mood. No, I was there to relax, to get away, and to have some fun. I decided to sit at the small café that overlooked the beach.

The menu was simple: sandwiches, light pastas, and wines. Perfect. I ordered shrimp over linguine with a white wine sauce and a bottle of Pinot Grigio. The breeze off the water was intoxicating. After dinner, I decided I was going to sit at the water's edge and relax. I wasn't necessarily stressed but my life was turning in a direction it wasn't a few months ago. This was my time to breathe.

I was halfway into my meal, breaking a piece of bread, when someone asked, "Is this seat taken?"

I looked up. Dimples. I was lucky I had another swallow of wine left in my glass because I was pretty sure I was going to choke on the large piece of bread that was stuck in my throat.

Dimples patted me on the back to quell the cough that erupted when he arrived. "We really need to stop meeting like this."

"Hi." I finally choked out.

"Hi." He motioned toward the empty seat and I nodded for him to sit.

"I'm Jim."

"Caroline."

"Where you from, Caroline?" I had to remind myself not to get lost in his dimples.

"New Jersey."

"New Jersey, huh?" And he gave me *that* look. The look everyone who isn't from New Jersey gives those who are.

"And, no, I don't know anyone named Snooki. And I'm not a mob wife or a member of the Soprano clan."

"Hey, don't get testy!" He laughed and held up his hands. "Your accent just sounded like you were from New York. Maybe they sound the same, I don't know."

"I do not have an accent! And if I do, I sure as hell don't sound like I'm from New York." I wanted to be mad, but barely leveled out at annoyed. His dimples were just too damn cute.

"You're funny." Jim took a long sip of his drink. "So what are you doing in Jamaica?"

"Skiing," I replied flippantly. "You?"

"My brother's getting married Wednesday night. I'm the best man."

"So, Jim the best man, where are you from?"

"Originally? Kansas. But I go to school in Miami."

"Kansas? Like Dorothy and Toto Kansas?"

"More like Clark Kent, but yeah. I'm a senior at Miami now."

"College kid, eh?" I teased.

"Definitely not a kid. And who are you to talk?"

"I'm twenty-eight. My undergrad was a long time ago." I poured another glass of wine, finishing off the bottle.

A wicked grin dashed across his face. "An older woman, huh? Looks like I sat at the right table."

"Looks like you did, kiddo. But I really need to be getting back to my friends. See you around." I gathered my purse and left Jim from Kansas at the table.

As I walked back to the room, I stopped at the small bar to thank Wes for the aloe.

"It was no problem." He flashed a grin at me as he mixed a pink cocktail for a cougar at the end of the bar.

"I know, but it was really nice of you. Maybe I could repay you. Buy you a drink?"

"At an all-inclusive?"

"Right." I glanced down at my feet. "Well, then, I'll see you around. Maybe I can listen to your relationship problems or something."

"Maybe, Caroline from New Jersey. I look forward to it." Wes winked at me and I headed back to the room with thoughts of hot bartenders, sexy dimples, and one night stands swirling around in my head.

The next day was spent providing Sarah and Mel with lotion, aspirin, and more water than I thought any person could handle. Thankfully, the burns weren't bad enough to blister, and it seemed as though Melody got the brunt of it. We left the room for the cover of tables with umbrellas and then some shopping at the two boutiques at the resort. I didn't venture out much on my own other than to procure a few items from the convenience store.

By Wednesday, they were back in action, albeit covered up with newly purchased gauzy bathing suit covers, wide-brimmed straw hats, and sunglasses to cover the awful raccoon eyes on their faces. Thankfully, I hadn't spent enough time in the sun to color much more than a soft base tan.

"What do you want to do tonight?" Melody asked from a tree-covered hammock.

"Dinner at the French place?" Sarah offered.

"As long as I don't have to eat snails."

"There's much more to French food than snails!" I laughed as I sipped on the Dirty Banana Wes had made for me.

"Do we have to dress up?"

"I think so. No big deal. We leave in two days and you two have spent the last two in bed with sunburn. We're getting dressed up."

"Bossy! Fine, I'll get dressed up. Can I at least wear my sunglasses?"

"Yes, you can wear your sunglasses."

"Thank you. Can you get me one of those banana thingies you're drinking?"

"Yup. Be right back."

Keeping to the cobblestone path, I walked up to Wes's bar and asked for three Dirty Bananas.

"Caroline from New Jersey!" Jim waved me over from a table. He was sitting with three other guys.

I grabbed the drinks, carefully balancing three between my hands, and walked over. "Jim from Kansas. Fancy meeting you here."

"I didn't see you around yesterday."

"I was with my friends." I pointed with both hands to the area where the girls sat and nodded. "They got really bad sunburn on Monday."

"That sucks. What're you doing later?"

"Probably just relaxing. Don't you have that wedding tonight?"

"Yeah. This is my brother Tom and his two friends Alex and Joe."

"Hi."

"If you and your friends aren't busy, maybe we could all meet up after."

"Yeah, maybe. Well, good luck tonight. Congratulations. Nice to meet all of you." I started walking away when Jim jumped up.

"Let me get that for you." He took two of the drinks from my hands and walked over to the girls with me, handing each of them their drink.

"Well, Caroline, I'll see you around."

"Thank you. See you."

Melody pulled her sunglasses down to the tip of her nose as she watched shirtless Jim walk away. "Who"—she paused dramatically—"was that?"

"That's Jim from Kansas. He goes to the University of Miami and his brother is getting married tonight."

"He's a baby!" Sarah laughed.

"He's hot!" Melody declared.

"He's a child!" I countered.

"Who cares? He's hot, seems to be available, and is totally into you."

"Whatever." The last thing on my mind was getting to know someone. I was not in the frame of mind to get to know anyone.

"I know exactly what you're thinking, Care. You don't want to get wrapped up in any nonsense. You feel like you have some sort of moral code that you'd like to keep intact, even if you busted through it the other night." Sarah pushed a lock of hair out of my face. "What you don't understand is that you don't have to deal with nonsense. You don't have to worry about breaking any rules. Do you know why?"

"Because I'm on vacation." Injecting boredom into my voice did nothing to quell her spirit.

"And what happens in Jamaica stays in Jamaica!" Melody cheered.

"I thought it was what happens in Vegas stays in Vegas?"

"I have it on good authority that the message is transferrable. Wherever you are, it applies."

I looked over at Jim, laughing with his brother and friends. He caught me looking and waved.

"Isn't that a bit much? I mean sex with two guys in less than a week?"

"Time stops when you're on vacation. Everything gets pulled into the black hole. And besides, there aren't as many sluts as you'd like to think. Most are just women with very welcoming vaginas," Melody said, obviously pleased with herself.

"Look, Melody and I can't score now. We look like lobster raccoons. We need you to take one for the team and bang the baby over there. Do it for all womankind, Care. Do it for us."

"He invited us to hang out after the wedding tonight."

"Us?" Melody perked up.

"I thought you were a lobster raccoon?" I laughed.

"Maybe one of his friends is into that kind of thing."

Were they really trying to talk me into having sex with Jim just so they could live vicariously through me? I'd lived vicariously through them enough for twelve lifetimes. I'd listened to their stories, pined over the sexual freedom afforded to them by their mind-set. I never thought I could be that girl. I never thought I could have random sex. But I can and I did. And it was kind of awesome.

But didn't I already do just that? And was it really a one night stand if he and I were seeing each other again next week? Could Jim be the real and true one nighter I'd been hoping for? No strings? No awkward running into each other at the gym? No ridiculously hot roommate to lust after?

"I'll do it."

"You'll what?"

"I said I'll do it. I need to prep a bit though. We need lunch and I need drinks."

I'd avoided Jim the rest of the day, hoping for a bit of spontaneity.

At sundown, the girls and I headed out for our fancy French dinner. We were dressed to kill. We watched the wedding from the terrace. It was beautiful. I saw Jim in the requisite island wedding attire—khaki shorts and a white button down—standing beside his brother. I watched as the bride and groom kissed and my belly dropped. I used to want marriage with Steven. I used to want children, a house in the suburbs, and a minivan. At that moment, on Thanksgiving eve, watching two people get married on the shores of Jamaica at sunset, I had no idea what I wanted anymore.

Melody and Sarah kept sneaking not so subtle glances in my direction, probably wondering if I would go through with it. When I saw the bridal party begin walking off the beach, I summoned the lady balls I'd grown last Saturday and chugged back a half glass of wine. I waited until I saw Jim semialone, eyeballed the girls, and made my way over to him. I not so accidentally brushed up against him.

"Oh, excuse me."

"Caroline!"

"Jim?" I pretended I didn't know what I'd done.

"You look—wow. You look great." He took my hand before kissing me on the cheek. From the smell of it, he was half in the bag with me.

"So do you. So, your brother got married, huh?" I looked around at the intimate gathering of what I assumed to be family and a few very close friends.

"Yeah."

"I don't want to intrude. I'll let you get back to them." I turned to walk away and he grabbed my wrist. I played coy, but inside my stomach was doing somersaults.

"You aren't intruding. As a matter of fact, my brother and his wife are probably going back to their room. And everyone here is just going to continue drinking."

"Oh, well—"

"Are your friends here? I can introduce them to my friends."

I looked around and noticed the two girls were already laughing with the pair of young men I'd met earlier.

"Looks like they've introduced themselves."

I made sure to make steady eye contact and slow blinked the way Melody taught me. It felt dumb and uncomfortable but it seemed to work.

"Looks like it, huh? Wanna go somewhere?"

"We're on an island, there aren't many places to go."

"We could just, I don't know, go for a walk and see where that takes us."

"I'd like that. Let me just let my friends know."

"I'll grab you a drink. What would you like?"

"Wine is good. White, please."

I hurried over to Sarah and Melody, who were half watching with obvious interest.

"We're going for a walk. Don't wait up. Is there anything in my teeth?"

Sarah inspected. "Nope. You're good."

I handed her my shoes and kissed each one on the head before hurrying back over to Jim.

"Thanks," I said as he handed me a plastic cup, full to the top, of wine. I looked at him and cocked my head.

"I figured plastic was better than walking around with glass. I can change it for you."

I took a sip. "Nope, this is fine."

We stood in front of each other for minutes in silence. The longer the silence stretched, the more I drank.

Just as the situation was about to get awkward, he downed his cup of liquid courage, grabbed a towel from a beach bag, and took my hand, sliding his fingers between mine and tilting his head toward the beach.

Finding a semisecluded spot on the beach under a tree, we laid out the towel and flopped down. I stretched out my legs, flexing my feet. Jim scooched forward, took my right foot in his hand, and began massaging it.

He dragged his fingers between my toes, pushed his thumbs into the arch of my foot, and kneaded the pad of my heel with his knuckles. I leaned back against the tree and closed my eyes. It was heaven. Until my eyes shot open when he put my toes in his mouth.

I didn't know whether to cringe or moan in excitement. I couldn't pull it away. There was nothing I could do but shift uncomfortably, lean back, and close my eyes again.

I felt his tongue slowly leave my toes and move along the top of my foot. Much better. That was something I could get used to. His mouth played along my shin as his hands massaged my calf. Definitely something I could get used to.

His mouth reached my knee and the butterflies returned to my stomach. With every lick, the tingling between my legs grew. As his hands gently pushed up my dress and found their way to my inner thighs, I exhaled the breath I'd been holding. I could feel the scruff on his chin delicately rub against me. Tangling my hands in his hair, I pushed his head farther into me. His breath was cool against my rising heat. His tongue was soft against my firm clit. He licked and sucked until I all but passed out.

Quickly, he grabbed me by the hips and pulled me down underneath him. His mouth crashed on mine and the tongue that had explored my leg now explored my mouth. With one hand behind my head, he used the other to unbutton his pants. I reached down and pulled my dress up to my waist then gripped him, guided him where I wanted him to go. Shifting my panties over, he pushed deep into me and I cried out.

He was insatiable. The rhythm was quick, our mouths moved, frenzied with want. He bit my lip and pulled as I sank my nails into his firm ass, pulling him farther into me. He pulled the straps of my dress down so my breasts were exposed. Hungrily he took a nipple in his mouth and sucked hard until I thought I would scream in pleasurable pain.

I felt the familiar vibration rise inside me and I came harder than I ever had before. Gripping my hair, he thrust more forcefully until he emptied himself.

Breathing heavily, we lay still for a long while. He nuzzled my neck and nibbled on my earlobe. I was still quivering from the after-shocks when he suggested we go to his room.

The next morning, I tiptoed back into my room, hoping to make a quiet entrance. No such luck.

"Well, look who's rolling in. Did the walk of shame, did we?" Sarah wiggled her eyebrows.

"Looks like she's the only one of us who got lucky last night."

"Shut it. I'm starving. Let's get some breakfast."

At the small café, I saw Jim and his family having breakfast. We locked eyes over coffee, fruit, and a dozen people I'd never met. He took a sip of his coffee, tilted his head toward the beach like he did the night before, excused himself from the table, and walked away.

"I'll be right back. Or not."

"Where are you going? You're not going to finish eating?" Sarah asked.

Melody looked toward Jim and smiled. "Just don't forget we leave tomorrow."

Chapter Nine

On Monday, I woke up before my alarm. I rolled out of bed, looked out my window, noticing a thin dusting of snow covering the sidewalk, and sighed. The sun of Jamaica suddenly seemed so long ago. Thankfully the throbbing between my legs had all but disappeared. First-day jitters were on high alert. I fell asleep the night before alternating my thoughts between Jim, Ryan, Brian, and my new job. Maybe Sarah was right; there was more to life than singular focus.

In time, I thought to myself. I'd spent the better part of the past five years lost in what I thought was a perfect relationship. It wasn't until I took a step back, wallowed in vats of hot fudge sundaes, and shed tears over every chick flick and romantic comedy that my vision had cleared.

Steven and I weren't perfect. Far from it. But we projected perfection and that, in the end, is what kept us together. Our relationship made his family happy. Honestly? I think the breakup was a rebellion on both our parts. I was tired of dinner parties and galas and client meetings. Steven was tired of holding his daddy's expectations on his shoulders. Of course, that still doesn't excuse him from shoving his dick in the nearest undergrad he could find and screwing her in the bed where I slept.

I shuffled, still tired from tossing and turning all night, into the bathroom. The water, a few degrees below scalding, cleansed extraneous gunk from my thoughts. Jim. Ryan. Brian. Sex. Steven. Sore vaginas. Everything slowly slipped down the drain, at least for the time being. Train schedules and anxiety—but good anxiety—took over. *Where would this job take me? Who would I meet? Will I love it?*

I shook my head. None of it mattered. *Today*, I thought, *I am starting over.*

"Care!" Sarah's banging on the bathroom door slammed me back to reality. "Don't use up all the hot water!"

"Sorry!" I called back before quickly rinsing out my conditioner and forgoing the armpit shave. It was winter, it wasn't like I was going sleeveless.

I stepped out, wrapped a towel around myself, and opened the door.

"You know, ten minutes means you're clean, any more than that and you're jerking off," Sarah said as we did the enter-exit dance.

"Girls don't jerk off!" I yelled back as I walked to my room.

"Okay, technically they jill off. Your battery-operated boyfriend proves that." Sarah giggled before closing the door.

I stood staring at the clothes hanging in my closet. Pretty much everything I owned was business attire. I wasn't sure if the new job was as strict in their company dress code. I wasn't a lawyer at the law firm but I certainly dressed like one. An assistant editor job spoke, to me, of something more laid back, casual but not sloppy. Stylish, not stuffy.

I threw shirts and dresses and pants and suits all over my room until I settled on a pair of very cool gray skinny jeans, a blousy white top, and a black blazer. I popped my thick black frames on my face after I'd applied enough makeup to sufficiently erase the lack of sleep the weekend provided.

In the kitchen, I found Sarah sitting at the table with dry toast and a huge cup of black coffee. I grabbed my mug from the dish drainer and filled up. After copious amounts of sugar and cream, I sat across from her, reaching for a piece of toast from her plate.

"Morning. You're up early."

"Morning. I have to meet with the science department before school starts. I think they're changing the curriculum. Again." She shrugged.

"The trials and tribulations of a high school science teacher."

I loved the fact that we were so different. In college, my nose was stuck in the classics like Voltaire, Dickinson, and Shakespeare, while Sarah was memorizing the periodic table and dissecting pigs.

She lifted her eyes from the notes she was looking over. "The *hot* high school science teacher. You look cute."

"Thanks. I didn't want to look too stuffy. You think this is okay?"

"I don't see why not. What are you going to be doing all day? Reading manuscripts and fixing them up to become best sellers? I figured all you'd need is some comfy jammies and my grampa's recliner."

"I am pretty sure there is more to it than that. Eventually. Right now, I think I'm basically a secretary to the editor."

Sarah looked down at my bare feet. "What shoes are you wearing?"

"I don't know. What do you think? Heels? Boots?"

"Well, not that you're an intern"—I cringed at the word—"but you'll be working with some kids right out of college, right?"

"Not sure."

"Well, sweetie, I think assistant is just a formality. You have loads of experience working PR at the law firm, writing briefs, all kinds of things. I think you need to walk in there with shoes that say 'That's right, bitches. I will own this joint.' I say heels. Ooh, maybe that cute patent leather pair you bought right before we left for Jamaica."

I stared at her a beat. "I'm going to have to concur."

I downed the last of my coffee and jumped up from the table. I heard Sarah mutter as I walked away, "That's right, bitches."

Chapter Ten

The train ride into the city was not uncomfortable, unless of course you count the stale smell of sweat, resignation, and exhaustion. Normally, I'd people-watch, but I was too preoccupied with new beginnings. I dug my e-reader out of my bag, hoping to refresh myself with the manuscript I'd been assigned. There was nothing I loved more than reading and I wasn't a genre snob. Give me a shampoo bottle and I'd read it. Magazine? Cover to cover. Brand-spankin'-new manuscript that the rest of the world had never seen? All day long.

Lost in the author's impeccable world building, I barely registered the text message that chimed on my phone. Melody.

Kick some publishing ass! You'll do great!

I smiled. I honestly had the best friends in the world. My circle was small but I couldn't imagine my life without either Melody or Sarah. It was like the universe knew no one else could tolerate us.

Before I could reply, a new message chimed through.

Good luck on your first day.

I smiled a bit but I had no idea who the message was from.

Thank you. Who is this?

I stared at my phone. It was two more stops before I received an answer.

Someone who loves checking out your ass.

Brian. I had no idea how he got my number. I could only assume Ryan gave it to him. I couldn't help but wonder why Ryan would give my number to his roommate.

I didn't have much time to ruminate; my stop was next. I packed up my things, pulled on my gloves, and checked out my face in my mirror. I was pale but it was nothing a little lipstick and a text from Brian couldn't brighten up.

I shuffled off the train, herded like cattle through tight corridors and powerless escalators. It felt like hours before I finally emerged from the massive building into the sun. I lined up with the rest of the worker bees for a taxi. I was really going to have to figure out the subway system but, at that moment, I didn't want to go back underground. It wasn't that far of a walk, but I hadn't thought much about sensible footwear when I got ready earlier. Plus, trudging through the slushy sidewalks was not my idea of a good time. I was grateful to hop somewhat quickly into a cab.

It wasn't long before I was dropped off in front of the building. Taking it in, I nearly pinched myself. Finally, a dream job I wouldn't have to sell my soul for. Double-checking my bag and fully confident I'd make my mark with this job, I walked in through the heavy glass doors.

"Hi. Good morning. My name is Caroline Frost. Today's my first day. I am supposed to meet with Oscar Little."

The receptionist picked up the phone and announced my arrival.

"Mr. Little is expecting you. Take the elevator to the twelfth floor. He'll meet you there."

"Thanks."

"Good luck."

I smiled, thankful she wasn't a twenty-year-old intern. I'd had enough of those in my life.

The twelfth floor pinged my arrival as the doors slid open and the most beautiful man I'd ever seen stood in front of the open doors talking with Mr. Little. Mr. Little reminded me of my grandfather—tall, gray, and dressed in a well-tailored suit. The other man wore Vans, a pair of distressed jeans that probably cost more than my entire outfit, an untucked white button-down, and a peacoat. I couldn't tell his age, other than he was maybe my age or possibly a little older. With a mess of blond wavy hair, he looked as though he belonged on a beach somewhere instead of standing in an office building in the middle of the city. He reminded me, a bit, of Jim from Kansas. My lady parts woke up at the thought.

I hesitated a moment before stepping into the reception area of the floor. Standing there, a little self-conscious, I wondered how I should make my presence known, since both men seemed to be deep in conversation. So I did what anyone would do, I stepped closer and cringed as my phone went off. I shoved my hand in my bag to silence it but not before both men turned toward me.

Mortified, I kept my face down until Mr. Little said my name. "Caroline Frost?"

Straightening myself out, I tried to recover but only squeaked out a tiny "yes." Certain my face was a million shades of red, I stuck out my hand. "Hi, Mr. Little."

"Hello, dear. Glad to see you again. So happy you're joining us.

This"—he gestured to the Adonis to my right—"is Michael Mortimer."

I shook his hand, lost for a moment in his piercing chocolate brown eyes, while wondering why his name sounded so familiar.

"Nice to meet you, Mr. Mortimer."

His laugh was genuine. "Please, call me Michael. So, how'd you like my book?"

That was it! He wrote the manuscript I'd been reading.

"I thought it was great, actually. I didn't know I'd be meeting you today." I snuck a side glance at Mr. Little.

"Well, Mr. Little here knows I am completely hands-on when it comes to my work. I couldn't let the opportunity to meet the person editing it pass me by since I was in town. I do have to say, I didn't think you'd be so young."

What was he talking about? He looked about the same age as me!

"Well, I guess that makes two of us, Mister, uh, Michael. I will do my best to take care of your book. I've been in contact with Ms. Page, learning the ropes."

"Well, I am looking forward to working with you."

"Caroline," said Mr. Little, "we'll have Holly show you around. She'll get you squared away with human resources. Why don't we meet back up at lunchtime, my office, and we'll go over your first project? Yolanda has been on a much needed vacation. But I am glad to hear you've been in touch since the interview."

"Sounds excellent. I'm looking forward to it."

Holly was a well-put-together woman who was, if I had to guess, in her early sixties. With auburn hair, flawless skin, and sharp brown eyes, she motioned for me to walk with her.

"Until we meet again, Ms. Frost. I'd love to read your notes on my book." Michael nodded toward me and winked. I had the distinct impression that he was checking me out. So I added a little swing to my step.

"I'll have those to you soon."

Leaving the two men, I felt both overwhelmed and at home. It was the first time since college that I felt as though I had some say over my direction.

Holly walked next to me as we made our way down the hall. She opened a door at the end and motioned for me to enter. A large desk topped with a fabulous flat computer screen was the only item, besides a couple of chairs, in the room. Mostly empty bookshelves lined one of the walls.

"This"—Holly waved her arm—"is your office."

"Office? I think there is some mistake." I stepped through the room to the window. Below, cars and taxis played chicken with pedestrians.

"Mr. Mortimer is an important client. He expects the best from the people that work with him. And since you were handpicked—"

"Handpicked? I just got the job!"

"I only know what I'm told, dear. You can place your things in here. Later you and I can go over what else you'll need to make the space workable for you. For now, there are a few trade books on the shelves, copies of Mr. Mortimer's first two novels and a few other things that were left here by the last assistant editor."

"But I don't understand."

Holly's eyes warmed. "I've learned over the years, sweetie, that when something wonderful and unexpected happens, you should never question it. Now, you can leave your things here. I'll take you to human resources."

The rest of the morning passed like a whirlwind. Books and files were brought into my office, I met and shook hands with everyone I'd be working with. It was the most amazing place I'd ever worked. And I hadn't even clocked in a full day!

I had about a half hour before I had to meet Mr. Little in his office. I picked up the phone and dialed Melody's office.

"Melody Ashford."

"Mel, I swear to God I work in Bizarro World. Everyone here is so freaking happy, so nice."

"Well, that's unfortunate."

"I know, right? I honestly am not sure if any of these people speak sarcasm or snark."

"Imagine working in a place where people are nice. I feel bad for you."

"See! That comment right there! I know you're being sarcastic but the people here, I honestly think they're too nice to see that."

I could tell Melody thought I was off my rocker. I wasn't complaining, not in the least. I think I was more surprised than anything else.

"Oh! And I met Michael Mortimer today."

"And Michael Mortimer is…"

"The guy who wrote the manuscript I've been reading. And Mel, he's hot."

"Then put a bull's-eye on his ass and make him a target!"

"I can't do that. I work with him, or will be working with him. And besides, it's not the point. I have an office, too!"

"No cubicle?"

"Nope."

"Are they hiring?"

"I can check."

"Kidding. Look I have to run to a meeting with my boss to discuss the financials of the merger. Have fun and fill me in later. Drinks at Murphy's?"

Murphy's? "Sure, yeah. I guess. See you then. We can discuss my date with Ryan on Friday."

"I almost forgot about that. Yes. We will discuss. Talk later, doll face."

"Later."

I could feel my cheeks flush and butterflies rouse to life in my stomach. I wasn't sure I was ready to go back to Murphy's. I would undoubtedly see Brian. Then again, what did it really matter?

Making my way to Mr. Little's office, I took my time and absorbed everything around me. People were laughing, smiling, and having fun. A complete one-eighty from my previous job. Working at the law firm, looking back, was like dealing with a different crisis every other minute. Always so serious, always so cold. Everyone there was looking for someone else to stand on while they climbed their way to the top. That was never my style and I should have seen it. Unfortunately I was so blinded by my relationship with Steven that I failed to see the job was slowly sucking the life out of me. I have no idea how anyone could live and thrive in that environment.

Holly waved me into Mr. Little's office. He was on the phone but motioned for me to take a seat across from him. As soon as he clicked off, all his attention was on me.

"So, Caroline, it's been only a few hours but how's your first day been so far?"

"It's been great. Better than great, actually. Everyone is so nice and helpful. And I had no idea I'd have my own office."

"Well, it's a small office. We try to make everyone feel at home. We like to treat everyone so they feel like part of a family. The office is just a way of our saying thank you. You came highly recommended and anything I can do to make your transition easier, let me know. And of course you'll be assisting Mortimer's editor. As a matter of fact, she'll be joining us for lunch."

"I can't wait to go over my notes with her."

"Why don't you go get your coat and we'll meet at the elevator? Mr. Mortimer will be joining us as well."

"We aren't eating here?"

"No. Since it's your first day, I figured somewhere special was called for."

Waiting at the elevator, I heard someone call my name.

"Yes?"

A slight woman who looked as though she was barely old enough to drive ran up to me. "Hi, these arrived for you a few minutes ago."

In the woman's hands was a huge vase filled with a bouquet of wildflowers, my favorite. The first name that popped into my head was Brian. I shook off the stupid thought.

"They're beautiful," the woman commented.

"Well, thank you, um—"

"Erica."

"Thank you, Erica. I'll just put these in my office."

"I can do that for you. There's a card." Excitement radiated in her voice.

It was obvious she was interested to know who sent them and probably wouldn't let me leave unless I opened the card in front of her. I pulled it out and read it.

Beautiful flowers for a beautiful girl. Good luck on your first day. Call me. ~Steven

Anger and annoyance vibrated through me.

"So, who're they from? Your boyfriend? I wish my boyfriend would send me flowers."

"What? Oh, no one. Thanks. You can keep them if you want." I crumbled the card in my fist.

"Oh, I just couldn't. Someone put a lot of thought into these."

"No, really. Keep them. I'm allergic." I felt bad lying to her, she seemed so nice. But the last thing I wanted was for my past to collide with my present and future.

"Caroline, are you ready?"

Mr. Little walked toward me. I stifled a giggle when I saw him pull on a wool Jets hat. Definitely not the look I was expecting from him.

"Absolutely. Let's go."

"Erica, the flowers are beautiful!"

"Oh, Mr. Little, they aren't—" Erica responded, looking at me.

"Aren't they? Gorgeous." I winked at her as Mr. Little and I entered the elevator. The last thing I saw was her face break into a huge smile as the doors closed.

Chapter Eleven

On our way to the small restaurant, Mr. Little walked as if he wasn't in a hurry, a departure from the hustle and bustle surrounding us. He made a point to comment on window decor, street vendors, and random people who caught his eye. He was certainly an interesting man.

He spoke about the company, the clients, and, more fondly, about the people who worked for him. He liked to know what was going on in his company but liked to keep distance enough that people didn't feel as though they were being watched. A strategy that was foreign to me, coming from a work environment where movement, in and out the door, was constant and almost expected from those who worked there.

We turned the corner and, as we were passing a bus stop, I halted in my tracks. My gloved hand flew to my mouth and I gasped loud enough to cause passersby to turn their heads as they moved on. On a poster, in the middle of the city, on the side of a bus stop shelter, in his underwear, advertising some men's brand of clothing I hadn't heard of, was Ryan. I was so thrown off I stumbled and dropped my phone, cracking the glass face.

I'd seen this man naked. I'd done unspeakable, albeit memorable both mentally and physically, things with this man. And there he was. Full-size on a poster, in the middle of the city, on the side of a bus stop shelter, in his underwear. The facts repeated over and over in my head like a scratched vinyl record. A pair of underwear that he obviously filled out in ways many others could not stretched across his groin.

I caught myself staring, open mouthed, head tilted, with my eyes zeroing in on every muscle that, only a week ago, had stretched across my body. At hands that had touched me in ways I'd never been touched. At the mouth that...I shook my head to dispel the direction my brain was taking.

"Caroline? Caroline? Are you okay?"

A muffled voice was calling my name. It was a moment before I rejoined the present. Mr. Little had a look of concern on his face. With the Jets hat inching up his head and his face reddened from the cold air, it should have been comical. But it wasn't.

"Caroline? Are you all right? Do you need to sit down? You look very pale."

"No, no. Thank you. I'm okay. I just thought, I wasn't, um, sure if I turned off the coffeemaker this morning. Then I remembered it has an auto-off function." I hoped my stuttering lie didn't alarm Mr. Little. Sneaking a sideways glance as I bent down and fumbled my phone back into my hands, I saw his face morph back to calm.

I wanted, more than anything, to run home and dive under the covers and refuse to emerge until Ryan was a distant memory. But I couldn't. The butterflies in my stomach, the throbbing memory in my panties, and the perspiration sliding between my breasts told me there was no way Ryan would be forgotten so easily. The fact that I was standing in the middle of the sidewalk with my new boss staring at me kept me from bolting.

Why couldn't I have picked up a nice, normal man? Why couldn't I have homed in on a target that was obscure, unknown, and didn't look so damned good in—and out—of his underwear? I decided to throw caution to the wind and planned out my first one night stand. My first true act of irresponsibility and I bring home a fucking underwear model.

Go big or go home.

Thankfully, Mr. Little was quietly whistling to himself the rest of the short walk to the restaurant. As he held the door for me, I thought I would normally be thankful for the warmth of the indoors but, truthfully, I was warm enough from my photographic run-in with my very own, honest to goodness sex god.

Michael Mortimer was sitting at a window table chatting on the phone. To his left was a thin black woman with her hair pulled severely back into the tightest bun I'd ever seen. It gave me a headache just looking at it. Her attire commanded respect. Wearing a deep navy pants suit with matching heels and a pair of wire-rimmed glasses perched on her nose, the woman studied the menu with intensity. Despite the severe outer shell, she emanated warmth and approachability. From just the one time we'd met, she made me feel welcome and comfortable. It was because of her that I knew this was the job for me.

"Yolanda!" Mr. Little called to the woman as the maître d' took his coat.

The woman stood and stepped toward him.

"Oscar, how lovely to see you."

She kissed the air on either side of his cheeks.

"You remember"—Mr. Little motioned for me to step forward—"Caroline Frost. She'll be your new editorial assistant."

I held out my hand. "Nice to see you again. I hope your vacation was restful."

She smiled. "It wasn't quite as restful as it should have been, but then again, when is it ever? Have you read the manuscript?"

"Yes. I brought the notes with me if you'd like to go over them."

"Don't be silly. We"—she motioned toward the table—"are at lunch. We will go over them when we return to the office."

She turned from me and resumed her position at the table studying the menu.

The waiter held my chair out for me and I ended up sitting between Michael and Mr. Little, with Yolanda directly across from me. She snuck a glance at me over the menu. I smiled but her brow furrowed and she went back to the menu.

Michael put down his phone and looked at Mr. Little. "Sorry, Oscar. That was my agent. Something about foreign rights and some production company snooping around. Caroline, nice to see you could join us. Have any notes for me?"

"Oh, let's not make this a working lunch." Yolanda didn't make eye contact. You'd think with the way she was scrutinizing the menu she'd have the thing memorized already.

"Oh, Yolanda. You're no fun. I'd like to hear what Caroline thinks."

"I really liked it." I began, careful not to give too much information. I'd rather not piss off the woman I'd be spending the next however many months with editing a manuscript.

"You liked it? How pedestrian, darling. Are you sure you read it thoroughly?" I did a double take. Where did the nice Yolanda go?

"Not everyone can be as hard-nosed as you, my dear Ms. Page."

If I didn't know any better, and I probably didn't, I'd have thought Michael was flirting with her. I had the feeling he flirted with everyone.

"If she is going to work with me, Michael, she'd better learn to be."

Nothing like having someone talk about you as if you weren't in the room. Mr. Little was looking at me with an expectant look on his face. What did I have to lose?

"Actually, Ms. Page—"

"For goodness sake, call me Yolanda." She waved me off with her hand, bracelets clinking as she did. At least the smile reached her eyes.

"Okay. I did notice a small plot hole in the story. The protagonist's wife could not have been a witness to the crime. She was out of the country. In addition, there are a few other issues I've taken note of and you and I can discuss those after lunch. Back at the office." I added the last part to let her know she and I were on the same page. I would be working closely with the woman and I certainly didn't want to start things off on the wrong footing.

I held my breath. Mr. Little was beaming at me and Michael was watching me with his chin resting on his hand. His long fingers stretched up the side of his cheek and for a moment I could focus on nothing but those fingers. They reminded me of Ryan's.

"Well, Caroline." Yolanda placed her napkin in her lap. "I look forward to speaking with you, at length, about the manuscript. For now, however, I think we need to order."

I slowly blew out the breath I was holding.

"Yes. I am starving. What'll it be?" Michael picked up his menu for the first time since I arrived. I followed suit as the waiter arrived at our table.

Yolanda ordered first. "I'll have a cup of the vegetable soup with the grilled Brie and pear panini. Half sandwich, please."

"Make that two." I figured if she thought we had similar interests, even if it was just a lunch order, she might warm up to me.

Mr. Little ordered the lobster bisque and steak sandwich. I was surprised to find Michael order nothing but a plate of French fries.

"French fries?"

"What can I say? I love them. And they aren't your regular plate of potatoes. These are smothered in cheddar, horseradish, and roast beef au jus. Of course, I have to run five miles a day in order to keep eating them."

I took a sip of my water and Michael winked at me. I swallowed wrong and felt like I was coughing up a lung. I excused myself and choked the whole way to the bathroom. Slamming the stall door shut, I finally gained control of myself, pulled out my phone, and texted Sarah.

Change of plans. Forget Murphy's. Meet me in front of my office building. Tell Mel.

She replied: *K.*

Fixing my lipstick in the mirror, I thought about all the changes in my life over the past few months. I decided then and there that I would learn as much from Yolanda Page as I could, no matter what it took.

As soon as I stepped out of the bathroom I ran into Michael.

"Hi." God, he was close.

"Hi."

He smelled like coconut.

"Hi." I already said that.

"Listen, I hope you didn't get the wrong impression about me back there." He rubbed his thumb across his lower lip. I wanted to reach up and bite it.

Wow. He was really close. I pressed my back against the wall and shook my head to loosen the dirty thoughts swirling through.

"Good, because, well, Yolanda is an amazing editor and Mr. Little has been great to me. I wouldn't want them to get the wrong impression about our…"—he trailed his long fingers down my arm—"relationship." *That was confusing.*

I watched his mouth as he spoke with perfect pronunciation. His lips were full, giving way to beautiful white teeth. A small dimple formed at the corner of his mouth whenever he smiled. I knew he was saying more, talking more, but I couldn't concentrate. My knees wobbled and he caught me when I buckled.

Stepping back, he looked at me and smirked. "So, it's a date? See you at the table."

He retreated into the men's room and I was relegated to what felt like the walk of shame back to the table. A date? What did I miss? I really needed to rein in my sex brain when people were talking to me. Thankfully, Yolanda and Mr. Little were talking, so I was left to sit in silence. I wasn't sure what, if anything, I would say. Was I just sexually harassed? Was Michael Mortimer just full of himself? Did I really care? After five years of being the good girl, the quiet girl, the responsible girl, was I really too terribly concerned that not one but two very good-looking men showed interest? Okay, three if you counted Jim from Kansas. And I did.

Michael arrived back at the table just as the food arrived. He was right, he did not order an ordinary plate of French fries. They were the most addictive things I'd ever tried. For the most part, I ignored his subtle—and not so subtle—come-ons. I think Yolanda, on the other hand, caught on to each.

Other than that, lunch was pleasant and I was growing more and more excited about my role in the company. I must've lucked out. Apparently, it was the goal of most to work with Yolanda in some capacity. And there I was, the new girl, and the opportunity fell right into my lap. I knew I had a lot to learn and I had no doubt she'd show me the ropes, even if her demeanor flip-flopped between warm and severe. But then again, work was work and I made a promise to myself not to let it overtake my life ever again. I just hoped that thought process would fly with Yolanda Page.

Of course that remained to be seen. What was really weighing on my mind was getting the girls here and taking them to see Ryan on a billboard in his underwear. And that image beat any amount of flirting Michael Mortimer could toss my way.

Chapter Twelve

I met Sarah and Melody in front of my building at six. I needed to show them what I had seen. Words would never be able to do it justice and I needed them to have the same reaction I had. I needed to know I wasn't crazy.

"I have to show you something." There was no time for greetings. I grabbed both girls by the arms and herded them up the street. I walked quickly, keeping the conversation to a minimum. I didn't want to give it away. I needed them to see it like I had seen it.

"It's just up here."

"Care, really. You make us hike all the way into the city? We didn't have to go to Murphy's, you know. We were just busting your balls."

"I don't have balls." Fewer words more walking. I was focused; I had a mission not unlike Operation One Night Stand. This was Operation Whatthefuck.

"Don't be so literal. I'm just saying if you're too scared to run into Ryan—"

"Or can't handle being around Bartender Brian—"

"It's just around this corner." It was all I could do not to break into a run.

We turned the corner and there he was. Life-size, in his underwear, on a bus shelter, in the middle of the city. The girls, behind me talking in hushed tones, didn't notice that I had stopped. They both ran into me.

"Care! What the hell?" Sarah questioned in her this-better-be-good voice as she knelt down to pick up her purse.

I said nothing. Instead, I pointed.

I turned to them and watched the realization form in their eyes, surprise contort their faces, and their mouths gape open. Operation Whatthefuck was a rousing success.

"Holy fuck!" Melody squealed as she wobbled on her heels.

"No way!" Sarah ran up to the poster, touching it as if she could somehow feel the hardness of his abs, the smooth lines of his skin, the girth of his dick. "I could wash my panties on those abs!"

"Right? So I'm not crazy? That's Ryan."

"Goddamn Caroline! You banged *this* guy?"

"It's like when Satan decided to put the alphabet in math. Terrifying and curious at the same time." Melody stepped toward the poster, her jaw dropped in wonder.

"Yeah."

"He's in his underwear," Sarah mentioned quietly.

"I know."

"On a bus shelter," she continued.

"No kidding!"

"In the middle of the fucking city!" Melody exclaimed.

My thoughts exactly. Thank God we're friends.

"When shit like this happens, Care, you *do not* keep calm and carry on. You call in sick and celebrate by getting a tattoo."

Melody joined Sarah at the poster, inspecting every pixilated inch. Their eyes wide, they took a synchronized step back, cocking their heads to the side. They took him in. They took in their surroundings. The gravity of this turn of events was not lost on them.

I fucked an underwear model. I fucked him until my vagina was bruised enough to need an ice pack the next morning. For a moment, I felt like a celebrity, even if it was only among my friends.

"Caroline, do you know what this means?"

"Yeah, that Ryan is a model."

"No. Well, yeah but no. It means that not only is he an underwear model, but you Caroline, *you*, as opposed to every other woman that passes this advertisement, have seen what's under the briefs. The rest of us can only imagine, fantasize even, about whether or not that right there"—Mel placed her hand over his package—"is stuffed."

I broke out in a fit of laughter. The seriousness of her tone was priceless. I could have sworn she was going to point out some cosmic fate–type piece of wisdom. Instead, she waxed poetic about the importance of whether or not Ryan's junk was Photoshopped.

"Cucumber big," Sarah whispered the words.

"Wait!" Melody spun around and grabbed my arms. The proximity of her face to mine was a bit unnerving. "You're going out with him on Friday."

Reality crashed down and I thought my heart would stop. Backing up with my hands raised in front of me in defense, I shook my head. "I can't go out with him on Friday. I can't go out with him ever!"

"Why not?" Sarah stopped ogling the poster long enough to ask.

"Well, because look! He's a fucking underwear model! What the hell would he want with me? That's too much pressure." I bent down with my hands on my knees and forced myself to breathe. I'd never had a panic attack before and I wondered briefly if I was about to experience one.

"Um, earth to Caroline. Didn't potato pants willingly go home with you the other night? Didn't he call you and ask you out again?"

"Yeah, but he probably didn't mean it. I mean, I ran into him at the gym, he probably felt bad and—"

"Stop it. Stop it right now. Knock that shit off. I don't get the problem." Melody truly sounded confused. I wasn't sure I would be able to explain my newly developed sense of reticence.

"Mel, don't try to figure me out. You'll honestly just exhaust yourself." Hell, I was exhausted trying to figure me out myself.

"Fuckety fuck, Care. Here we go. You know there's a thin line between silly and stupid. Stop fucking border hopping." Sarah jabbed her finger at me before stepping away.

"Listen, sweets, I want you to repeat after me. I am good enough."

"Mel, you don't get it." I didn't get it.

"Repeat after me. I am good enough." She stood in front of me and placed my face between her hands, staring at me in a way that made me uncomfortable.

I shook my head.

"Jesus Christ, Caroline! You hit the fucking jackpot with this guy as far as physical specimens go. I can't speak to his intelligence, but fuck! Look at him! Who the hell cares! Let him share your bed for a while. What's the harm?" Melody threw her hands up in obvious frustration.

"I just don't understand what a guy like him would see in someone like me."

"Someone like?" Melody's eyes bugged out of her head and I thought they'd roll onto the sidewalk. "Unfuckingbelievable. Have you seen yourself?"

Sarah grabbed my shoulders and spun me around so I was looking at myself in the glass reflection of a small store window.

I wasn't ugly. I knew that. I wasn't particularly tall. I wasn't a size zero. But I was in great shape. My hair was shiny, my teeth were white. My jeans hugged my ass; I never needed to wear a bra if I didn't want to. The sprinkle of freckles across my nose wasn't annoying. The freckles were fun. I had my mother's bone structure. I had my father's eyes. I was pretty.

"I am good enough," I whispered so only I could hear.

What the hell was I thinking? Where did that moment of self-doubt come from? Was it a residual scar from dating Steven all those years? From working in a thankless, boring job? From never having the balls to follow my heart? Why would *Ryan* want *me*? No, no, no.

"I am good enough," I said with more force.

"What was that?" Melody leaned in closer.

"I am good enough."

It felt good to say the words.

"Thank God, Care. I thought I was gonna have to get you some syrup to go along with that twat waffle attitude."

"Twat waffle what?"

"Twat waffle attitude. Basically when a woman acts like a douche."

"Nice."

"Care, you have to realize who you are, what you are, and all the good that goes along with it." Sarah grabbed my hand. "We love you and it kills us when you don't see what we see. And, truth be told, you didn't see anything but Steven for five years. We sat by and watched as you disappeared. We know it will take time, but we can see the old Caroline coming back."

I smiled. "You're right. I don't know what I was thinking."

"Well," Melody began, "it's not every day you see your most recent bang in his underwear, on a poster, on the side of a bus shelter, in the middle of the city."

Both women were back to staring at Ryan, heads cocked to the side.

"No shit." I was still tingling from the discovery. I pulled out my broken phone.

Looking forward to Friday.

I shoved my phone in my purse and stared at the backs of my friends' tilted heads. I swear it was like an epiphany proving, once again, that I needed those two women in my life. They were brought to me by some random divine intervention.

"Come on. I need a drink."

"I'm starving."

"You're always starving. How the hell are you still a size four?"

Melody grinned wickedly. "Lots and lots of sex."

I laughed. "I think I'm beginning to know a thing or two about that."

Chapter Thirteen

The week sailed on. By Friday, I'd learned more about the publishing industry and revising and editing manuscripts and contracts than I thought my brain could process. It was wonderful. Yolanda, though quite terse when she was engrossed in work, was a great mentor. Of course, her remarks would have weakened my knees a few months prior but I was able to see she was molding me. And I was determined to use the woman for everything she could teach me. I was happy to stay on her good side.

Fortunately, it wasn't hard to figure out how to do that. I'd learned quickly that a big ego needed stroking and positive reinforcement and if that's what it took to make Yolanda happy then that's just what I'd do.

Michael, on the other hand, was a bit harder to read. And I couldn't quite figure out why he was hanging around the office. One minute he was sullen and short, fitting the moody author stereotype and the next minute he was full of ego and self-confidence. When he was the latter, he was sure to hit on me in what had become typical Michael Mortimer fashion—crude, crass, and direct. There was no beating around the bush with him. He'd taken an interest in me and he was sure to let me know when the mood suited him.

Michael was a good-looking guy, and had the brains to match the exterior package, but I still didn't know what was going on with Ryan. Not that I wanted a relationship. *God!* It was the last thing I needed. But if I was going to sleep around, I needed it to be with one person at a time.

By late Friday afternoon, I was at my desk packing up my things for the weekend. Streaming my favorite radio station kept my mood light, and considering I had quite a bit of reading to do between then and the following Monday, I was in a great mood. I'd hoped for an easy few days off but Yolanda wasn't having it. It was a good thing I enjoyed the work. And at least I had a date later that night. Sarah and Melody had slammed the door on my self-doubt, effectively helping me to see excitement in new possibilities.

I kicked off my shoes and started dancing to an upbeat song. Using my pencil, I began singing into it like a microphone.

A small knock at the door interrupted me.

"Come in."

"I'm already in."

"Michael. I was just, uh…" I dropped my pencil on my desk and willed myself to remain calm.

"Getting ready to leave?"

"Yeah. I have a lot of stuff to go over this weekend. Just making sure I have everything."

"Did you think any more about what we talked about on Monday?"

Monday. Monday. Monday. I wracked my brain trying to remember if there was anything I missed.

Noticing my struggle with the topic, Michael laughed easily. "I asked if you could accompany me to a dinner next Saturday evening."

I felt like a deer in the headlights. When the hell did he ask me that?

Walking around my desk, Michael leaned in and whispered, "I asked you when we were at the restaurant. I'll be out of town until then and I was hoping to get your answer before I left."

My knees weakened and I remembered. He'd asked when we ran into each other by the bathrooms. And if I remembered correctly, I'd agreed to think about it. Unfortunately I didn't remember until that moment, so I hadn't done much thinking.

"Um, well, where is it again?"

"At some restaurant downtown. I'm supposed to do a reading or something. You don't have to go. I mean, if you have plans. But I spoke with Yolanda and Oscar and they both agreed it would be good for you to represent the company."

"I don't have plans. I mean, if Yolanda and Mr. Little think I should go—"

"Well, then. Good. It's a date."

"Not a date."

"I'm sorry?" A smile played mischievously across his lips.

"It's not a date. I mean, I can't date you."

"Do you want to date me?" He was unbelievably close. I swore he could hear my heart speed up.

"That's not what I meant. I meant, well, I'm pretty sure Yolanda wouldn't like it."

"And you care what Yolanda thinks?"

"Of course I do. Plus, I'm not really a fan of office romances. They don't generally end well for me."

I visibly shivered as he ran his hand down my arm.

"Calm down, Caroline. It's just dinner, and a work-related dinner at that. I swear I'll be on my best behavior. I'll text you the address. Better yet, I'll make sure a car picks you up. And wear a dress."

He pressed his thumb against my bottom lip, grazed his teeth along his, and hesitated a moment before walking out, closing the door behind him.

I fell into my chair. I'd barricaded his advances all week and it suddenly hit me how exhausting it was. The moment I dropped the barrier, he turned my knees to gelatin. I'd have to figure out how to avoid that from happening again. I didn't need pent-up sexual frustration at the workplace. I had enough of that every time I thought about Brian. I mean Ryan. Whatever. You know what I mean.

The train ride home was uneventful. I read some of the manuscript changes Michael had delivered to Yolanda earlier that day. I couldn't help but feel like there was something missing in Michael's writing. Something didn't quite click. It was fantastic writing and he deserved the accolades he'd received but I just couldn't put my finger on what was wrong. I shoved papers back into my bag. Maybe I needed time away from it. Plus, every time I read the damn thing a new word that was obviously spelled correctly but looked so damn wrong popped out at me and I spent what seemed like an eternity staring at it, questioning its very existence.

I hung my bag on my shoulder and got off at the next stop. Wrapping my scarf tighter around my face, I walked the two blocks back to my apartment. On the way, Ryan texted me.

Running late. Murphy's @ 9. Rain check on dinner. Sorry.

That sucked. I was starving and I wasn't especially interested in returning to Murphy's. Not that I didn't want to see Brian, but just that if I was going to be there with Ryan, I didn't want to be distracted by the butterflies that swarmed whenever I was around him.

Sliding my key into the lock, I was met with Sarah and Melody, who were parked at the kitchen counter, full glasses of red between them.

"Hey! Pour me one." I placed my bag on the floor and threw my coat over the stained arm of the couch I called my friend.

"Don't you need to get ready for your date?" Sarah grabbed a glass from the top cabinet and poured me some wine.

"Rain check on dinner. I'm supposed to meet him at Murphy's at nine." I took a long swallow. The alcohol warmed me to my toes. "Thanks," I said, raising my glass. "I needed this."

"So what are we doing for dinner?" Melody asked, riffling through our stack of take-out menus.

"I thought you had a date with Nick the Dick?"

"I did but we're playing it by ear. He isn't a dick, Care. I just had a moment. All women have crazy moments."

"Crazy? I think you were a step beyond crazy."

Finishing off the bottle, Melody replied, "Don't judge me. I was born to be awesome. Not perfect. And besides, you should talk. Weren't you in a relationship with that couch for a few weeks?"

"Ha ha. Shut up. Sometimes even I question my sanity. Occasionally it replies. And smacks me across the face." I threw a balled-up napkin at her.

"Dude! You almost spilled. Don't commit a party foul just because your date got put on hold."

"So." I hopped up and opened the fridge. "What are we going to do for dinner? I'm starving."

"Why don't we just go to Murphy's? They have great sandwiches and their French onion soup is to die for."

I turned and closed the fridge. "I guess we can do that. Why not? I have to meet Ryan there later anyway. Let me change my clothes. Be ready in five."

"Care, I want to borrow something to wear. I came straight here from work."

"Sure. Come on."

"Don't worry! I'll just sit here and keep the wine company," Sarah yelled through the apartment.

Melody ran back to the kitchen, grabbed her glass, and met me back in my room.

"So how was work?" I asked as I stripped off my shirt and walked to my closet.

"Oh, you know. We're all falling into financial ruin. The economy is going to collapse and only those with stockpiles of gold and bitcoins will make it through the apocalypse. You know, normal stuff."

"Sounds like fun."

"It will be."

"What do you want to wear?"

"I don't know. I'm hoping Nick will get off work early."

"What does he do again?" I asked as I riffled through my closet, throwing everything that caught my eye on the bed.

"He's in a band."

I froze and had to mentally talk myself out of a sarcastic response. "A band?" I closed my eyes and hoped I didn't sound judgmental.

"Yeah. He plays guitar."

"That's cool." I finally collected myself enough to face her. "We should go see him sometime."

"Maybe." Melody held up a burgundy long-sleeved, low-cut cashmere sweater. "How's this?"

"With your boobs? It will be perfect."

"I do have great boobs. My plastic surgeon is a genius. Look, I know Nick isn't anyone's dream man but I've had enough relationship lemons thrown at me that I now know when to grab the tequila and salt." She unbuttoned her shirt and threw it on my floor before pulling the sweater over her head. Stepping over to my full-length mirror, she turned to the side and sucked in her nonexistent gut. "Good?"

"It looks great."

"I wish it covered my ass a bit more. Not everyone can have a tight butt like you." She walked over and slapped my ass.

"Good genes. Should I wear this?" I held up an off the shoulder baby blue tunic sweater. It was fuzzy and soft. Kind of like jammies.

"Didn't we just talk about your ass? That will cover it up."

"Ryan's already seen my ass. Besides, I'll keep on the jeans and I can flip it up if I think he forgot what it looks like."

"True. I like it."

"Care! You got a text message. Who's Michael?" Sarah called through the door.

"Michael?" Melody raised her eyebrows.

I opened the door and grabbed the phone.

Looking forward to next Saturday. Don't forget—wear a dress. You have great legs.

"Michael. I'll need at least another two or three drinks to explain about Michael. Let's go and I swear I will fill you two in at dinner. I want your perspective anyway."

"Why does he want you to wear a dress? Where are you going?"

"He's an author. There's a dinner. Let's get out of here. I need to eat."

"That bad, huh?" Sarah whispered.

"Um, yeah. That bad."

Chapter Fourteen

At six thirty on a Friday night, Murphy's was packed for happy hour. Brian was busy behind the bar and when he turned and noticed the three of us walking in, he stopped mid martini shake and winked.

"Dinner or just drinks?" he shouted over the din of people in work attire.

"Both!" Sarah shouted back.

I would have answered but I was momentarily awed. Who knew so many arm muscles flexed when shaking a martini shaker?

"Hold on! I have a table in the back for special guests."

"Special guests, huh? I bet he's sending us to the back so he can check out your ass."

"Not funny. I'm meeting up with Ryan later."

"At least you remember his name."

"That's not funny."

"It's a little funny."

Dropping my shoulders, I acquiesced. "Yeah, I guess you're right."

We followed one of the waitresses to the back of the bar, and off to the corner was a huge table for ten. It was just secluded enough to avoid most of the asshattery that was par for the course in a bar on a Friday night but close enough to the pool table to still feel like part of the crowd.

"Drinks?"

"Two bottles of Cab."

"No problem. Specials are on the board."

The girls had their noses stuffed into their menus. I was starving but for some reason my attention was on the bar. There were two bartenders to keep up with the drink orders. Brian had his sleeves pushed up to his elbows and I noticed the bar towel tucked into his distressed jeans. I watched as he hopped up on a stool and reached for a bottle on the top shelf. Our waitress was standing off to the side talking to a customer with our two bottles and three glasses on a tray.

"I'm having the French onion. Like I said, it's so good." Melody leaned back and stretched her arms over her head.

"Chicken Caesar salad." Sarah folded her menu and pushed it off to the side of our table.

I hadn't even looked at the menu. I picked it up quickly, but not before catching the two exchange a look.

"What?"

"I don't know why you didn't just go for Brian to begin with," Sarah offered.

"He wasn't the target." I leaned back and crossed my arms over my chest.

"Maybe not. But he is hot."

"So?"

"So? You haven't stopped checking him out since we got here."

"Oh, please. I'm just looking around for our waitress. She's over there talking to some customer. Not sure what she's waiting for."

"Testy much?"

"I'm not testy."

"I think we still need to hear all about this Michael character."

"I second that!" Melody raised her hand.

The waitress came just in time to pour the first glass of wine. I suddenly felt like I needed the drink.

I spent the next bottle and a half explaining Michael Mortimer. I described every come-on, every subtle and not so subtle cue, and every reaction from Yolanda. By the time I was finished, I felt like I'd told a life story, and the events were only from the past week!

"So, what do you guys think?"

"You already agreed to go to the dinner thing with him?" Sarah poured another glass as I nodded.

"And he's hot?" Melody piped in.

"Well, yeah. But is that really the point? Yolanda and Mr. Little want me to go, anyway."

"Of course it is. Listen, Care." Melody leaned in. It was Serious Mel time. "Take advantage of the opportunity. So what if this guy's a weirdo? As long as he's a decent guy, what do you have to lose? It's not like you're promising him anything. It's a night out with a good-looking guy."

"But he's a client!" Sarah chimed in. "That alone should keep her away. Caroline doesn't want to lose her job over this. It's like I told you, Mel. Your boss may be hot but, for one, he's your boss and, two, he's married." She ticked off her points on outstretched fingers.

"True. Both of you have valid points. I think, though, this dinner

I agreed to would fall under work. Especially since my boss is sending me to represent the company. I mean, Michael's getting some literary award and if I accompany him to the event in the name of the house then I can chalk it up to work, right?"

"Exactly."

"Be careful."

My friends spoke at once. At the same time, a young guy stumbled in our direction and plopped down in the chair next to Sarah.

Though he was dressed nicely, he reeked of alcohol.

"Hey, baby doll," he slurred, his eyes half closed, as he sidled up to Sarah. Way too drunk to have been drinking only during happy hour.

"Uh, hey." Sarah pushed his hand off her thigh. Melody leaned over and draped her arm around Sarah's shoulders.

"What's up, buddy?" Melody softly rubbed her nose along Sarah's cheek.

"Just hangin'. Came over to see what you hot chicks are doing tonight."

"Her." Melody licked Sarah's ear.

Sarah turned a lovely shade of crimson as she tried not to laugh.

"Oh, yeah. I'm down with that." The guy leaned closer and his hand started kneading his crotch. Thankfully my stomach was empty or I would have vomited all over him.

"You might be but we aren't. I'm strictly into pussy." The way Melody overpronounced her "p" was actually kind of sexy. I emptied the bottle into my glass, sat back, and watched the show.

The guy's eyes widened as Melody caressed Sarah's breasts. Sarah was about to fall into a fit of laughter. Melody, on the other hand, looked as serious as a heart attack.

"Come on. There's you, me, her. It's a no-brainer."

Wine actually came out of my nose. I busied myself cleaning off my face and tried not to break out into a hysterical fit of laughter.

"You know what else is a no-brainer?" Melody leaned in and ran her hands through his hair.

"What?"

Melody whispered in his ear loud enough for the rest of us to hear. "You."

"Damn straight!" He banged his fist on the table. I think he thought she was complimenting him.

"So," Melody continued as she licked Sarah's face, "when the voices speak to you, do you poke them with cotton swabs?"

"Huh?" Horny butterface looked confused.

"There are some ladies over there who'd probably be more into dick than we are." Melody nodded toward a gaggle of college girls. "Why don't you go hit them up? Your cock won't get wet over here, *baby doll.*"

The guy looked over to where Melody directed him and plastered a huge smile on his face. "Well, if you ladies change your minds, you know where to find me." He dropped his business card on the table and walked away.

"Hey!" Melody called out to him.

"Yeah?"

"Don't forget to be awesome, man!"

His face broke out into a lewd smile and, as he turned and walked away, the three of us broke into loud fits of laughter.

"What the fuck, Mel?" Sarah snorted as she shoved her hand in her shirt, putting her boobs back into her bra, then grabbed a napkin to wipe off her face.

"What? As your best friend it's my duty to always pretend to be your lesbian lover whenever you are getting hit on by an ugly asshole at a bar."

"You're awfully convincing."

"Aw, Care. You jealous? Next time, it's your turn." She wiggled her eyebrows and ran her tongue across her lips.

"Weirdo."

The waitress came by with another two bottles and a martini glass with a pink drink, which she handed to me.

"What's this?" I lifted the glass, smelled it, and took a sip.

"Wet Pussy."

I spit out the sip.

"What?"

The waitress looked bored. "Yeah. Brian sent it over. Said you liked kinky drinks. So, you ready to order?"

Melody and Sarah peeked around the corner and waved to Brian, laughing hysterically.

"Well, uh, tell him I said thanks. I'll have the cheeseburger, medium rare."

"Fries?"

"Huh?" I was distracted by the view I had of Brian's ass as he once again climbed the stool to reach the top shelf.

"Do you want French fries?"

"Yeah, sure."

"Chicken Caesar salad."

"French onion soup."

"I'll be back with your orders. Enjoy your pussy." I am pretty sure that was sarcasm.

It was Sarah's turn to spit out her drink.

"Oh my God, Care!"

"He's just being silly from the other weekend."

"I don't know."

"What time is it?" I pushed to change the topic.

Sarah looked at her phone. "Seven fifteen. Why?"

"Ryan won't be here until nine."

"So?"

"So nothing. Just making conversation." I sipped my Wet Pussy.

Sarah stared at me. "So that's what our conversations are reduced to? Commentary of the comings and goings of who you're dating?"

"No. Don't be an ass."

"Care, it's Friday night. Relax. Party on," Sarah reasoned.

"I like to party," I mused.

"And by party," Mel interrupted, "she means take naps."

"Shut up!" I laughed. They were right. I needed to be less socially awkward.

Thankfully, the waitress brought our food relatively quickly. I was starving. As I took a large bite of burger, Brian walked over, pulled out the chair next to me, and sat down.

"What's up, ladies? Finally, the crowd is thinning out."

I couldn't talk. I had too much food in my mouth. I couldn't even chew. I was sure a glob of ketchup, or mayonnaise, had made its home at the corner of my mouth. The juice of the tomato squirted onto the table. I averted my eyes, turned my head, stared wide eyed at Melody and Sarah—anything to avoid the painfully embarrassing cavewoman display of my eating a cheeseburger in front of Brian.

"You okay, Care?" Melody asked with a sweet smile on her face. I wanted to punch her. In the face. With a chair.

"That's an awfully big bite. I didn't know that much could fit in there." Brian smiled at me. "Good to know."

My response was unintelligible and ended with a spray of hamburger meat on Brian's shirt. I wanted to crawl under the table and die.

"No one likes a spitter, Care." Sarah pointed out. How lovely of her. I began to choke on my food.

Brian smacked me on the back and laughed.

"Drink something." He poured a glass of wine from the bottle on the table and pushed it over to me before pulling out his towel and wiping his shirt.

I shook my head, took a sip, and managed to melt the food small enough to fit down my throat.

"Thank you," I squeaked out.

"Anytime. So you're meeting Ryan later?" he asked as he pilfered a fry from my plate.

"Yeah. How late are you working?"

"Closing. Fridays are always busy."

"I can see that. Nice drink choice by the way." I nodded to my empty glass.

"You like that? I have plenty more where that came from, in case, you know, you need someone to help you pick up your target." He wiggled his eyebrows at me.

It was official. I was going to die of embarrassment.

"So Brian." Thankfully Sarah realized I was sinking and rescued me. "What do you do when you aren't tending bar and passing along liquid sexual innuendo to our girl Caroline?"

"You know, I'm trying to give up sexual innuendos. But it's hard. So hard."

Thankfully my mouth was not full of cheesy meat when I laughed.

"If you leave the sexual innuendo door open, even the slightest bit, I'll come crashing through like the Kool-Aid man," Melody quipped.

"Then remind me to always keep the door locked!" Brian laughed.

"You're pretty funny, Bartender Brian. It's a scientific fact that dirty talk and sexual innuendo are the strongest foundations of friendship." Melody was definitely on board. Anyone expert in dirty banter was tops in her mind.

"Then I'm the best friend one could ever have. Having the ability to turn any thought into a sexual innuendo is a mark of the truly talented."

"Who knew," Sarah asked, "the bartender was not only hot but fully entertaining?"

"I just work here. I took it over when my dad died and left it to me. It's been mine about a year now."

"So you're Murphy."

"Yep. Brian Murphy, at your service. Look, the bar's heating up again. Need anything, let me know. I'll stop back later. Oh, yeah, I'll be sending a few friends back here, too. It's my only reserved station. You ladies don't mind, do you?" He looked at me when he asked.

"No. Not at all. The more the merrier." Melody looked happy. She was probably hoping a guy would come back here and rescue her from Nick the Dick the Guitar-Playing Douche.

As if on cue, three guys walked to the back table.

"Shouldn't you be working?" A tall man with easy blue eyes and ruffled red hair high-fived Brian.

"I'll send some pitchers over. Sit, the ladies don't mind."

Another one of Brian's friends, this one with dark eyes, stubble, and short dark hair, smiled.

"You must be Caroline. I'm Dan, this is Drew," he said, pointing at the redhead, "and this is Berk."

Berk wore a cardigan, tight white T-shirt, black jeans, and superthick black plastic frames. I liked him already.

"Nice to meet you. How do you know *I'm* Caroline?" I teased.

"Ryan and Brian talk so much about you, I feel like I could pick you out in a lineup. Stand up for a minute."

I stood.

"Turn around."

I turned around.

Dan lifted my sweater a little bit. "Yup. It's you."

I stiffened and turned to face Brian. "So you've been talking about me?"

Brian smiled. "Well, I kept going on and on about your personality, then I realized how much of a bonus that ass was."

Sarah snickered.

"We keep telling her she has a great ass but she doesn't believe us."

Dan put his arm around my shoulders. "Well, if you need reminding, just let me know. I feel it's a public service I provide."

"And what kind of public service is that?" Melody's eyes were shining. Maybe Dan would be the one to untie her from Nick.

"Well, pretty lady," Dan walked around the table and grabbed Melody's hand, "I think it's my duty, as a man, to point out the best features of all the beautiful women I meet."

Gag me. Sarah and I rolled our eyes at each other but it seemed Melody was taking it all in.

"That's quite a service you provide."

"And may I say, you fill out that sweater very nicely."

I prayed that Melody wasn't falling for his lines. I cringed as she ran her fingers down into her cleavage and Dan stared like he'd never seen tits before.

Then she leaned in closer to him and said, "You know, New Year's is coming up. I think you should save your resolution till next year. You should try out being a douche for another twelve months."

The entire table erupted in laughter. Dan was left with a smirk. Brian clapped him on the back and took off for the bar but not before whispering in my ear, "See you later."

Dan clutched his hand to his chest and fell into the seat next to Melody. "Touché."

Berk stole fries off my plate while discussing the latest in financial reports. Melody was interested in his thoughts considering she worked in that industry. I guessed Dan did as well, since he followed along.

I had no idea what he was talking about. Sarah didn't look quite as bored as I was. She was deep in conversation with Drew the Ginger-Haired Wonder. Something about him was very familiar, but I couldn't put my finger on it.

By the time the second batch of wine and three pitchers were empty, it was a quarter to nine.

"Be right back." I grabbed my purse and headed for the restroom. Unfortunately for me, I bumped into Betsy the Whore and spilled her drink all down her what-might-pass-for-a-dress-if-she-were-a-middle-schooler. I noticed she was with a group of her similarly dressed slut-whore friends.

"Oh. It's you." I started to shrug past her but she put her hand on my arm.

"I'm really sorry, Caroline."

"I don't really care, Betsy."

"I think you do. I think you're upset because your boyfriend liked me better. I'm really sorry about that." She pouted her lips. I visualized punching her in the face.

"Oh! That's right. You fucked my ex. I just ate half a burger. Want those leftovers, too?"

I noticed Brian watching the exchange. I also noticed Steven standing off to the side, looking on with interest.

"You're funny, Caroline. Too bad you weren't good enough for Steve."

Steve? Who the fuck was *Steve?* He hated that.

"You know, when you are dead you don't know that you are dead. It is difficult only for others. It's the same with stupidity."

"Poor Caroline." Betsy had the audacity to laugh along with her friends. Instead of visualizing punching her in the face, I visualized ripping her hair out.

I reached over and took Steven's drink out of his hand, probably a gin and tonic—I was hoping for something with color—poured it over Betsy's head, and walked away.

I didn't look back and instead of heading for the bathroom, I made my way to the bar.

"Caroline, you're going to scare my customers away."

"I need a drink." My hands were shaking. Brian placed his hands over mine to still the vibration.

"Who was that?" He nodded toward Betsy and her supersluts.

"Oh her? That's Betsy the cock-juggling thunder-cunt."

His laugh boomed in my ear. "Well, then. Maybe she's just the type of customer I don't want in my bar. Plus, any girl who can quote a Blade movie is okay in my book."

He placed two shot glasses on the bar and filled each with Jack. "Bottoms up."

"Another," I said as I slammed the glass down. He filled it up. Three shots later, I really had to pee.

"I have to go to the bathroom." There was a slur in my words that wasn't there ten minutes ago.

"You okay?" I pulled my hand away as he tried to place his on it again. I was so pent up I wasn't sure that physical contact was a good idea.

"Yeah. Are you?" My tone had more bite in it than intended.

"I'm good." Brian stood and backed up. "Ryan's here." He nodded toward the door.

I didn't know what I felt. Was I happy Ryan showed up? Was I annoyed? Was I frustrated about Brian? Steven? Betsy?

Ryan walked over and kissed me on the cheek before shaking hands with Brian.

"Be right back. I have to pee."

I left the two of them at the bar and felt both sets of eyes watching me as I walked away.

Chapter Fifteen

I stared in the mirror, hands clutching either side of the sink to stop them from shaking. Why did I care so much? What the hell was it that left me feeling raw and exposed every single time I thought of Steven and Betsy? Leaning my head against the mirror, I stared down at the water flowing from the faucet and wondered why I couldn't be more like the flowing stream. It was never in one place for longer than a millisecond, new fresh water followed in constant movement. Until it was frozen. Ice didn't move much. Doomed to view the same scenery until, mercifully, it melted and moved away. Maybe that's what it was. Maybe I was frozen in time. Maybe I was melting little by little, moment by moment, until I was free. Maybe it would just take longer than two months and a one night stand.

"You okay?" Melody walked into the small bathroom.

"Yeah. I'm fine. I will be fine."

"I saw what happened. You want to talk about it?"

"Not really." I pulled a few paper towels from the dispenser, wet them, and patted my face.

Melody pulled a compact out of her purse and handed it to me. "Okay. You don't have to."

Opening the small metal tin, I used the pad to swipe the redness from my face. "Who the hell does she think she is?"

Mel leaned back against the wall with her arms crossed over her chest.

I continued swiping away the evidence of tears and dark circles. "I mean, fuck her, right? She's the one who fucked up. Not me. And where the fuck does she get off calling him Steve? He hates that. He always preferred to be called Steven."

Reaching into her bag, Melody produced a small tube of cream blush and some mascara. I took the items and continued to fix my face.

"He fucking broke me. He fucking hid me away, and I allowed it."

Mel stepped to the sink and handed me nude lip gloss. I painted my lips until they were too shiny.

"How the hell did I allow that? How the hell didn't I *see*?" I blotted my lips with a square of toilet paper and turned to face my friend.

"How am I supposed to become the new me if I don't know how I became the old me?"

She pursed her lips, thinking of what to say. Mel could be crass and over the top but when it came down to it, she was thoughtful when it came to what really mattered.

"I think," she began, "that maybe you didn't really know who you were then, either. I think you were sheltered—"

"I wasn't—"

"Let me finish. I think that maybe you were more sheltered than you think you were. And that's not a bad thing."

"I can see that. But I don't think I should have to apologize for growing up in a great family. I shouldn't have to be ashamed of having parents and a brother who love me." My stomach dropped and I felt anger beginning to bubble up.

"Oh goodness no! Please don't misunderstand me." She reached out and placed her hand on my arm. "I think that you began to see what was out there and maybe you pulled away from his shadow a bit. I don't think he liked that. And I think Betsy is more than willing to allow a sugar daddy to take care of her. You, on the other hand, whether you realized it or not, wanted more. You still want more."

I turned back to face the mirror. Melody was right. Both she and Sarah have been right about all this mess. I hated that I needed the push but I was grateful for it. Every day I felt more independent, more in control of what I want.

"I think you flipped today because you hadn't had the opportunity to flip before this. Of course it's still raw. You were together for five years. And he broke your heart. You have every right to react. Just don't let it consume you. React and move on."

"React and move on," I repeated.

"Yes. Now. You have a superhot guy waiting out there for you. A great night of fun and debauchery. Are you going to let trivial people like Betsy and Steven ruin that for you?"

"No."

"That's my girl."

"No," I said with more force. "Absolutely not. I am starting over. I am taking control of my life. Fuck them."

"Exactly!"

"Thank you."

"Oh sweetie, no thanks needed."

I hugged Melody tighter than I thought possible. She was wrong. I didn't just have a brother. I had two sisters as well, and who cared if they weren't blood? They were sisters to me—more even, just the same.

Chapter Sixteen

Melody left the bathroom before me, giving me an extra minute to make sure I was composed. Stepping out, I made my way to the bar first.

"I'm sorry."

"For what?" Brian pulled three beers, obviously busy with the nighttime crowd that had begun to trickle in.

"For my earlier display of idiocy. I shouldn't have done that and I'm sorry."

Brian stopped for a minute and placed his hands on the bar. "You have nothing to be sorry about. I mean, it probably wouldn't be good for business if you made dumping perfectly good drinks, which I made by the way, on the heads of my customers. Everyone has something that sets them off. I get it."

"Thank you." I placed my hand on his and he looked down at it before pulling his away.

"Yeah, well. Like I said. Don't make it a habit. I have to go get these drinks out before there's a riot." He laughed easily and walked away to serve the customers.

Looking around, I saw Betsy and Steven had decided to leave. I didn't feel remorse toward Betsy. I didn't feel anything toward either of them. I knew it would take time for it all to go away but the least I could do was take Mel's advice. React and move on.

I looked over at the table: my two friends and a group of guys we pretty much just met were sitting around, chatting, laughing, and having the good time I deserved. Smiling, I joined them.

Sitting next to Ryan, I looked over to find him smiling at me. He leaned in to whisper, "Everything okay?"

"Perfect," I whispered back and kissed him on the cheek.

I wasn't sure where this *whatever* was going with Ryan but I was more than happy to find out. So maybe he wasn't going to be my forever. I was content to have him as a right now. Besides, a little voice inside my head told me relationships were off limits until I was used to functioning without one.

I leaned back and took everything in. It looked as though Melody and Dan were at it again.

"You sound reasonable. I think it might be time to up my medication." Melody rifled through her purse as the rest of the table laughed.

"I'm just saying. When it comes to people in your life, you need to share certain things. For example, if 'Don't Stop Believin'' comes on and the person you're with doesn't join you in the sing along, you need to remove them from your life. Everyone knows that song. And if the person you're with isn't down you have to wonder if you need that kind of negativity in your life? Am I right?"

Melody laughed easily. "You're right. Hard to argue with that kind of rationality."

"Speaking of music." Drew stood up and walked over to the juke-box, popped in a five-dollar bill, and started pressing buttons. I jumped up to join him.

"What's your poison?" Drew scanned the list of available songs.

"This one." I typed in the corresponding code.

"Awesome! I haven't heard that one in years!"

"Mel, Sarah, and I used to sing this all the time."

"College?"

"Yeah."

"So"—Drew turned to face me after he inputted all the song requests—"what's the deal with Sarah?"

"The deal?"

"Yeah." He leaned closer. "Is she, like, seeing anyone?"

"Oh!" I glanced over at Sarah, who was laughing at the conversation at the table. "No, she isn't actually."

"Cool. Thanks. So, uh, what's up with you and Ryan?"

"Why do you ask?"

"I don't know. It's not really my place to say anything."

What did they always say? Curiosity killed the cat?

"What isn't your place to say?"

"Oh nothing. It's just odd that both Brian and Ryan talk about you so much. Didn't you just meet them?"

"Yeah and?"

"Well, look. You seem like a nice girl but Ryan and Brian are my friends. I just don't want them to get hurt if you can't make up your mind."

I had to shake my head and clear it of everything just to make sense of what he was saying.

"I'm not sure what you heard, but Brian and I don't have anything going on other than meeting him a couple weeks ago and a brief run in at the gym. As for Ryan and me, well, that isn't really your business."

Drew held up his hands. "I'm sorry. I didn't mean to assume. I just thought—"

"Never assume. It just makes an ass out of you."

"And me," he replied.

"That's what I said. Look, not that *this* is any of my business but Sarah's my friend and if you fuck with her, I will hunt you down and crush your balls with the heel of my stiletto. M'kay?"

"Ha! Understood. I think you and I just might get along after all." He put up his hand and I slapped him a high five.

Berk walked by with a tray of shots. "I couldn't wait for the waitress anymore. I took it upon myself to get these."

"What is it?" Sarah asked as she sniffed the drink.

"It's called an Erection."

"What?" Dan held up the glass between his two fingers and inspected it.

"Like you've never had one!" Melody piped up.

"I've just never had one in my mouth," Dan replied.

"Don't knock it till you try it!" Berk shouted over the din of the bar. He downed the shot and ran his tongue across his lips. "Oh, Danny boy! You don't know what you're missing!"

"Get the fuck out of here! Go find yourself a fuck buddy!"

Berk laughed and walked over to a group of guys standing by the bar.

I leaned forward. "Is he gay?"

"You can't tell?" Sarah asked.

"No, I mean, it didn't even cross my mind."

"Ha! Well, ladies, Berk is as handsome as they come but unfortunately for you, you aren't his type." Drew raised his shot before pouring it into his mouth.

"Well, that's too bad," Melody purred. "Looks like I won't be having any fun tonight." She looked at Dan with hooded eyes and he took the bait.

"Oh, darlin'. We wouldn't want that now, would we?"

"You know anyone who's interested in having some fun?" Melody ran her fingers along his hand. I loved watching her in action. I don't think she's ever been turned down.

"They don't call me the kamikaze king for nothing."

"Kamikaze king?" I had to ask.

Ryan, Dan, and Drew laughed as Dan explained, "Sixty-nine is the kamikaze of sex. If I'm goin' down, she's comin' with me."

I was laughing so hard I couldn't breathe. Sarah's wine actually shot out of her nose. We did that a lot. Melody smiled as if she'd won the lottery.

We were drunk. After countless bottles of wine, numerous pitchers of beer, and shots with names like Stumble Fuck and Dirty Whore's Bath Water, it was a wonder any of us could stand. And then it happened.

The song I'd plugged into the jukebox started playing. I watched with glee as my friend's eyes widened and piercing screams of remembrance echoed against the walls.

Melody was the first to jump up and start dancing. Sarah grabbed Drew's beer and drained it.

"I love this song!"

"I have no idea what he's saying!"

"I Believe in a Thing Called Love" by the Darkness played loudly throughout the bar. Patrons actually stopped and stared as the three of us jumped around and tried to keep up with the high-pitched, fast-paced lyrics of the song that reminded us of freshman year of college.

I grabbed Ryan's hands and pulled him out of his chair. Melody took the opportunity to bump and grind on Dan like it was her job. Sarah climbed on top of the table and crawled over to Drew while singing the song at the top of her lungs.

Berk ran back to the group screaming, "I love this song!"

He got in on the action by climbing on top of the table with Sarah.

Brian stopped what he was doing and looked on from behind the bar with a smile on his face.

By the time the song was half done, most of the bar was singing and dancing along.

Ryan twirled me around until I was dizzy. It didn't take much; I was half in the bag to begin with.

Drew ran over to the jukebox and added more money.

"Time to test Dan's theory."

As soon as our song ended, "Don't Stop Believin'" pounded through the speakers. The entire bar let out a huge cheer and sang along.

"See? Was I right? That's how you know Brian's bar is the place to hang."

"You were right!" I shouted.

Ryan wrapped his arms around my waist and pulled me in closer. "You wanna get out of here?"

I looked around at my friends. Sarah was singing along with Drew. Melody and Dan were lip-locked as he pinned her up against the wall. Even Berk had found himself a hottie.

I kissed Ryan quickly on the lips. "Let's go."

I reached to grab my coat and purse.

"Leave them." His voice was forceful and the hunger in his eyes was apparent.

We raced through the bar, through a door at the back. He pulled his keys out of his pocket as we made our way through the stock-room space.

"Your place?"

He nodded as he pulled the door open and shoved me through. He pushed me up against the wall at the base of the stairs, his lips on my neck.

"I want you."

I grabbed his face. "I want you, too."

"Let's go."

We raced up the stairs to his apartment above the bar. I figured my friends would be okay without me for a while.

By the time we hit the top of the stairs, his shirt was off and my pants were unbuttoned. Clumsily I kicked my shoes off and pulled my shirt over my head. Ryan pulled his shoes off before reaching for me again.

I slid my tongue down his jawline as his hands reached for and cupped my breasts, his thumbs tracing circles around my hard nipples. He pinched them between his fingers and I moaned.

I fumbled the zipper and edged his jeans to the floor. I pushed him onto his leather couch before dropping to my knees. I pulled down his boxers and he breathed out. I hadn't realized we were both holding our breath.

Never in my life had I been forward enough to take the lead. Never in my life had I felt more comfortable than I did in that moment.

He moaned quietly as my tongue licked his tip. He slowly brought his hands to my hair and his fingers knotted themselves in my curls as I took him in my mouth, slowly at first.

My hand stroked him as my mouth slid up and down his length. His moans grew louder as I increased the friction and scraped my teeth gently along his engorged cock. When I took him all, my hand moved to his balls and I massaged them lightly.

"Oh shit, Caroline." Ryan's head fell back and he squeezed his eyes tight. His fingers tightened their grip on my hair and for a moment I was afraid he'd rip it out by the roots. But the harder he pulled, the more I responded. As his eyes glazed over, I shifted to the balls of my feet.

I knew he was almost ready and pushed him closer to the edge by squeezing my hand along him as I stroked. In a frenzy, I couldn't get enough of him and I took him in and out of my mouth, sucking hard. He tried to push my head away but I held on, taking him deeper as he exploded at the back of my throat. Swallowing every last drop, I felt good in knowing I satisfied him.

I laid my head against his thighs as he caught his breath.

"Caroline, that was"—he lifted my head and looked me in the eyes—"amazing."

"Well, thanks. I aim to please." I giggled into the palm of his hand as I kissed it.

Suddenly, he reached down, grabbing me by my waist and lifting me off the floor.

"Your turn," he breathed into my ear as he spun me around and threw me on the spot he'd just vacated on the couch. Slowly easing my jeans down over my hips, he pulled them off and threw them over my head. Placing a hand on either side of my naked thighs, he kissed me deeply.

As his tongue explored my mouth, his hands reached around and unhooked my bra. The ferocity of his kiss pushed me back into the couch cushions and I moaned into his mouth.

He tugged at my thin silk panties until they tore. His fingers found me, already slick with want, and massaged the inside of my folds. When I felt the current rise in my belly, he pinched me and I called out in anticipation as he slid a finger inside.

His tongue danced with mine and he slipped another finger inside me. His touch was like nothing I'd ever experienced before. It was urgent and gentle. Ferocious and calm. A lesson in opposites. He had to know I would come quickly and he fingered me until I screamed and came.

"Ry—"

Before I finished yelling his name, he brought his face to me. Pressing his tongue on me, he continued to explore me with his fingers. It was as if he knew every inch of me and was committing it to memory.

As he buried his face in me, I pushed his head deeper into me. Every lick, every suck, threw me closer to the edge again. When his finger moved to my ass and teased the rim, I tried to prepare myself. It was no use.

I screamed in pleasure as another orgasm rocked me to my core. He wouldn't let up.

His tongue dove inside me as his finger entered again. He ate and licked and sucked until he was out of air. His mouth, his face, was covered in me.

I pulled his head up and licked his mouth, tasting myself.

I felt free. It was like nothing I'd ever experienced before.

Sliding my ass closer to the edge of the couch, I needed his fingers to fill me faster. I quickly shoved his head back down and tightened my legs around his shoulders. Within seconds, I came harder than the last time, if that was even possible.

Slowly removing his finger from my ass, he lifted himself up and pressed his forehead to mine.

"That was…" He tried to catch his breath.

"Amazing?" I tried to still my racing heart.

"Yeah." His head flopped on the couch beside me as his arm hung heavy across my lap.

"Unbelievable."

"Yeah."

"Where did you learn how to do that?"

He laughed as he looked up at me, his eyes still glazed over. "Oh that? Just something I picked up along the way."

I couldn't focus. Besides being drunk, I hadn't yet begun to descend from the orgasmic high I'd just experienced.

"Well," I began, "you should do that more often."

"Ditto."

He slowly rocked back to his heels and reached for his shirt.

"You okay?"

I smiled. "I'm perfect."

"Pretty damn close if you ask me."

"You know, about what happened earlier"—I pulled my tunic over my head—"sorry you had to see that."

"What?" He turned to face me as he pulled on his boxer briefs. It was like the advertisement live and in living color. I couldn't stop staring.

"Earth to Caroline." He smirked.

"Sorry. I just, uh, was reminded of something I saw earlier this week."

"What?"

"Well, if you must know"—I slid into my jeans—"I just so happened to see something on the side of a bus stop when I was in the city."

He visibly blushed and looked away. "Oh that."

"Yeah, that," I teased. "Why didn't you tell me?"

"When would I have had the opportunity? Not like there was much talking going on the night we first met."

"True."

"And besides, I try not to make it a point of telling everyone I meet. I mean, I get a hard enough time from the guys."

"Well, just to let you know, I defended your honor." I cocked an eyebrow.

"My honor?" Confusion spread across his face.

"Yeah, Mel and Sarah weren't convinced that it was all you in the picture, if you catch my drift."

His face reddened even more. "Oh, well. Yeah. That's me."

"I know."

"I know you know." He pulled me closer and nibbled on my earlobes. I'd always heard about people having "a spot" but I'd never been able to find mine. I knew then that I could very likely have another orgasm if he continued to bite and suck on my earlobes.

"I'm glad you know."

"Care, I think you and I are going to be great friends."

The world screeched to a halt. I mean, I knew I didn't want a relationship. If I was being logical, I wasn't in any shape to have one.

But come on! This was probably not the best time for him to point out what great friends we'll be. So I took it a step further.

"Friends, huh? With benefits, I take it?"

"Yeah." He must've seen something in my face. "Care, you okay? I'm sorry if I led you to believe something else would go on with us. I mean, I just moved to the city, I have this cool new job. It's just nice to be able to, you know, ground myself with someone like you."

"Someone like me?" I wasn't sure if that was a backhanded compliment.

"Well, yeah. You're cool. You're pretty." He kissed my neck. "You're great in the sack. And, as opposed to many of the other people I've met lately, you're normal. And I need a little normal once in a while."

I chewed on a fingernail; something my grandmother always chastised me for. "Perfect. Friends is perfect as long as you do *that*"—I pointed to the couch—"more often."

Friends with benefits. You know what? I was more than okay with that and since it was out in the open, a wave of relaxation and acceptance washed over me.

"You got it. Let's go back downstairs before we're missed."

He grabbed my hand and we made our way back to the others.

Friends with benefits. Never had one of those before. Always a first time, right?

Ryan left to use the bathroom and I sat at the table with the others. They were still in celebration mode. The kind of celebration you get when you click with people you've never met before. It was perfect.

Brian sat down next to me. "'Bout to call last call. You need anything?"

I checked my phone. I had no idea it was that late.

"Um, no thanks. I'm good."

Brian tapped his fingers on the table and bounced his knee until I placed my hand on it, signaling him to stop.

"Anxious much?"

"So, you and Ryan—"

"Are just friends."

"With benefits." It wasn't a question.

"I guess you could say that."

"That's too bad." He threw his towel on the table and got up to make his rounds among those at the table. It was last call after all.

Chapter Seventeen

The next morning I was thanking the weekend gods it was Saturday as I sat at the kitchen counter reading Michael's manuscript, drinking a cup of coffee. I had just finished writing a page full of notes on my computer when Sarah walked through the front door.

"Holy hell! You look like shit!" I rushed over to help her with her coat. I pulled my face away. "Jesus, you stink!"

"I honestly don't think I'm sober yet. I haven't had a night like that in years. I might be too old to drink like that." She backed up against the door and leaned her head back.

Kicking off her shoes, she toed on the slippers she kept by the door, shuffling over to the wall and clicking off the light switch.

Her eyes were swollen, with dark circles from a long night of partying, and she reeked of a mixture of sweat, booze, and sex.

"You got laid!" I jumped back and pointed at her accusingly.

"Please don't shout. I feel like I have a mini construction crew drilling for oil in my head."

"How was it?"

"How was what?" She covered her eyes with her hand and navigated slowly to the couch, where she proceeded to lay down and pull a throw pillow over her face.

"Getting laid?"

"You talk as though you never have."

"Oh, shut up. Not my fault you drank until your body called for a time-out."

"How the hell aren't you hung over? Didn't you drink as much as I did?"

"I was drunk, sure. But I sobered up."

I remembered the exact time I sobered up.

Friends.

With benefits.

Too bad.

I walked to the kitchen and grabbed a sports drink from the fridge and a couple of aspirin from the cabinet.

"Here. Take these."

Sarah peeked out from under the pillow before sitting up and dutifully taking the medicine.

"Thank you," she said as she handed the bottle back to me.

"Come on, let's get you to bed."

I pulled her up and she crashed into me. I pulled my face away and crinkled my nose.

"But first, you need a shower. Did you at least have fun?"

"Yeah. Drew is great. Drew the awesome screw!" She giggled before burping up whatever greasy after-hours diner food she must have consumed.

"And I think we'll brush your teeth, too."

I turned on the water in the shower while Sarah sat naked on the toilet picking her toenails. Putting toothpaste on her toothbrush, I handed it to her and steered her into the shower, closing the curtain and taking her place on the lid of the toilet.

"Oh my God! The water feels so awesome!"

"That's right. Scrub, scrub, scrub. Brush, brush, brush."

"So, you and Ryan disappeared last night for a bit. Where did you go?"

"Upstairs. He lives above the bar, Brian's place."

"Oh, right. Brian was none too happy when he saw you two were gone."

"Why would he care?" I held up my close-up mirror and cringed at the blackhead forming next to my nose.

"You really are clueless sometimes. Brian really likes you. But, I mean, Ryan's great, too. Maybe you guys will go somewhere with all this."

I snorted. "Not likely."

"Why do you say that? Hey, do we have any more of that lavender body wash?"

I reached under the cabinet to retrieve the extra bottle. "Oh, no reason. I mean, other than Ryan told me we'd be great friends. *After*, of course, I sucked his dick and he went down on me. We'll be great friends with benefits."

"Friends with benefits, huh?"

"That's what he said."

"That's bullshit. Why can't people call it what it is? I need another razor. This one's too dull."

Again I ventured under the cabinet to grab a fresh razor. She handed me the dull one as I gave her the new one. I dropped the old one in the garbage.

I began making faces at myself in the mirror over the vanity. Opening and closing my mouth so that I looked like a freak. Squinting, stretching my face back, checking for nose hairs.

"I think I am getting wrinkles. And what do you mean, 'call it what it is'?" I yelled to her as I peered closer into the reflection. Sure enough, when I moved my mouth a certain way, wrinkles appeared near my eyes. Opening my tube of eye cream, I found I was out. I definitely needed to make a trip to Sephora.

"You are not getting wrinkles! And I mean, look at it this way. You and I are friends, right?"

"Yeah." Ugh. More wrinkles. This time encroaching on my forehead.

"Well, you do stuff for me and I do stuff for you, right? I mean stuff that benefits each of us."

"Yeah, so?" *Ohmygod!* I raked through the hair at my temple. Was that a gray hair?

"Well, wouldn't that make *us* friends with benefits? I mean, you make dinner, I do the dishes. You vacuum, I dust. I come home with a wicked hangover—feeling a little better by the way—and you take care of me. So, by definition, you and I are friends with benefits."

"Huh." I'd never thought of it that way. I guess she was right.

"So, I think you should call what is going on between you and Ryan what it actually is."

Not a gray hair. Blond highlight. Thank God. "Which is?"

"Friends who fuck."

"Friends who fuck?"

"Yeah. Do you go bowling together? No. Do you do your taxes together? No. What do you do? You fuck. You are friends who fuck." She punctuated the last word by turning off the water and reaching toward the towel rack for a towel.

Stepping out of the shower, she looked at me. Her eyes were more open than they had been when she first came home but they were still bloodshot. She looked tired but not gross. And she smelled better. "Am I right?"

"I guess you are." I plopped back down on the toilet and put the mirror away. I'd done enough scrutinizing of my old lady wrinkles for one day. "So I should call it what it is. But friends who fuck sounds so—"

"Vile? Degrading? Pornographic?" She giggled as she dried herself off and wrapped another towel around her head.

"For lack of better adjectives, yeah."

"Then call it something you're comfortable with. Friends who bang. Friends who do it. Friends who have sex. Whatever. But, from what you told me, there is no better verb for what you two do than fuck."

"Yeah." I handed her the deodorant. "You aren't wrong."

"Thanks." She smeared the clear gel under her arms. "Well, then. Just own it. Know what it is. Embrace it. You're not a little kid anymore. You're a grown-ass woman and if you want to have a relationship based on nothing more than meaningless sex, then do so. I'm sure it's loads better than Steven's fabled missionary position." Sarah pumped lotion into her hands and smoothed it over her arms and legs. I handed her the face lotion after she used the towel to remove the remnants of the body lotion from her hands.

She was right. Steven and I rarely ever had sex that wasn't missionary. Him on top, me on the bottom. Him dominant, me submissive. I shuddered.

Anything was better than that. No wonder I'd gone through so many batteries in the past five years.

"So"—I took the lotion she handed me and placed it back in the vanity—"what are you doing the rest of the day?"

"What time is it?" She stood towel-drying her hair, the rest of her dripping onto the bath mat.

"I'm not sure. Almost eleven?" Walking out into the hallway, I tried to peek around the corner and catch the time on the clock in the kitchen.

"Doesn't really matter. I'm going to bed. Not going out tonight. You?" Sarah started toward her bedroom.

"Nope."

"So we'll order in Chinese and watch a movie?"

"I can do that if you don't mind me reviewing a manuscript while we eat and watch."

"Fine with me. What are you doing now?"

"I'll probably try to hit that yoga class that starts at noon. Then I need to run out and pick up some things. Need anything?"

"Maybe a bottle of wine? White. Sweet."

"You got it." I threw my wallet into my gym bag, grabbed a bottle of water from the fridge, and headed out the door.

Chapter Eighteen

With my gym bag slung over my shoulder, I pulled my scarf tighter around my neck. It was a pleasant hour of stretching and clear-headed focus followed by a ridiculously long shower that worked out the rest of the tension that weighed me down.

Knowing I needed a dress, according to Michael, for the dinner the following week, I left the gym and made the brisk walk to the department store. Pushing through the revolving doors, I was reminded of my need for a few items from the makeup counter. I busied myself with the saleswoman discussing the benefits of an eye cream that hid visible lines, something I hadn't yet had the opportunity to discover, but she swore that early prevention was the best policy. I was about to lay out the arm and leg it cost for a tube the size of my pinky, but instead decided on purchasing a new tube of mascara, a new tinted lip gloss, and facial cleanser. As I handed the girl my card I spotted Yolanda. I dropped to the floor in a squat. It wasn't that I didn't like her. I really did like her, when she wasn't in full-on work mode. I just wasn't in the mind-set to deal with her outside the office. She was judgmental enough about my work; I didn't need her beady eyes perusing my latest purchase.

Looking up, I saw confusion spread across the saleswoman's face as she turned to hand me my card and receipt.

"Psst."

She looked down. "What are you doing?"

"My boss is over there." I pointed, feeling like a complete ass.

"Where?" she said a little too loudly as she whipped her head around to look.

"Just hand me my stuff and I'll get out of here."

"You get a free gift with your purchase. What would you like?"

"I don't care."

"Well, we have a free makeup bag with some samples. The bags come in a variety of patterns and colors."

I rolled my eyes when I saw her lift herself onto the counter and look down to where I squatted. "I don't care. You pick. Please. Just give me my stuff and let me get out of here."

"Caroline."

The hair on the back of my neck stood on end and my shoulders involuntarily tensed. So much for yoga and my hot shower.

"Yolanda." I busied myself with my shoelace before standing up.

"In a hurry?"

"Well, not really. Just had to pick up a few things." I turned to the saleswoman, who looked more confused than she had when I disappeared. "Thank you. I'll take the pink bag."

"Are you sure?"

"Yes. Yes. Thank you." I took my bag from her and stood in front of Yolanda. I don't know what it was about her, but I often felt as though I were about to be disciplined for something.

"Well, dear. Do you have something to wear for the dinner next week?"

"Um, well. That's one of the reasons I'm here actually."

"Good. I will help you find something suitable to wear. Heaven knows what you youngsters think will pass for suitable dinner attire. I mean, look at what you're wearing now." She laughed but I wasn't sure how to take it.

My stomach sank to the soles of my new running shoes as I looked down. I was wearing leggings and running shoes. My hair was in a messy, almost dry pony bun and I had no makeup on. She was wearing perfectly tailored pants, smart flats, and an ivory turtleneck sweater that peaked out from the collar of her navy peacoat. I wrung my hands together. "I just came from the gym."

"You should always take pride in your appearance, Caroline. Even if you are running to the grocery store for milk, you should always present yourself as you want others to see you. Let's go. Third floor."

With my head down, I followed Yolanda to the escalator. Out of the corner of my eye, I saw the saleswoman mouth, "I'm sorry." Yeah, *you're* sorry.

Yolanda didn't look back at me the entire way to the third floor. She walked swiftly, weaving in and out of racks until she stopped in front of a section of cocktail dresses. I watched as she methodically began sifting through the dresses. Stopping for only a moment to scan me from head to toe, Yolanda tossed dress after dress in my direction. Just as I thought I couldn't hold any more, she turned on her heel, crooked her finger at me to follow, and headed toward the dressing rooms.

She spoke quietly to a saleswoman; they both turned their heads to look at me before continuing with their hushed conversation. I stood there feeling like an awkward outsider. It seemed like hours before they included me in their little chat.

"Size two, that's just what I thought, Kelly. Thank you."

"Anything for you Ms. Page. Caroline, please step in here." She took the items from my arms and motioned for me to enter an open dressing room that was roughly half the size of my bedroom.

Surrounded by mirrors, I saw my mouth drop open when Yolanda's reflection entered the room with me and took a seat on a plush white chair in the corner of the fitting room.

"Don't look so surprised, my dear. It's nothing I haven't seen before. Drop the unsightly gym bag. Don't you have anything less tattered? No matter. Try on this one first." She handed me a black beaded, sleeveless number that looked entirely too small.

I shyly undressed, attempting to keep myself covered at all times. It was not an easy task and I thanked goodness for all the time I spent at the gym. At least my body wasn't—couldn't be—something with which she could find fault.

Keeping on my bra and giant cotton panties—thank God they were clean—I slipped the slinky material over my head and felt the light material skim down the rest of my body. It fell a couple inches above my knees. Sleeveless and fitted at the top, I admired the soft A-line of the skirt.

I was slowly running my hands along the fabric when Yolanda cut in. "No. Next."

"But—"

"Trust me. Next." She stood, took a cream-colored swatch of material off its hanger, and handed it to me as I gave her the black beaded dress.

For an hour I played dress up with Yolanda Page. Every now

and then, she'd sniff "maybe" and place the dress on the designated maybe hook. More often than not, I was faced with a short "no" as I was handed another dress. I lost count of how many I'd tried on, lost count of how often poor Kelly rushed in and out of the dressing room at Yolanda's order.

And then it happened. Over the top of the dressing room door, Kelly handed over a deep charcoal wool dress. I stepped into it and pulled it over my hips. Slipping my arms in, Yolanda zipped up the back for me. The off-the-shoulder dress had a four-inch fold that lay nicely on my arms and a thick strip of fabric that rested above my breast. It was fitted and fell mid-thigh. Yolanda gasped when I lazily turned to face her, waiting for yet another veto.

"This is it. This is the dress."

I gave myself permission to look in the mirror, something I hadn't done for the last forty or so dresses. It seemed everything I liked, Yolanda didn't. I wasn't expecting much.

"Wow." I whispered, turning around to check out all of the dress. I was expecting the dark gray to wash out my pale skin and drown me in shadows, but something about the dress made me feel like I was in a spotlight.

"Kelly!" Yolanda called. "We've found the dress. As we discussed."

Busy admiring myself in the mirror, I barely felt Yolanda tug on the zipper. I stepped out of the dress, careful not to wrinkle it, when I caught sight of the price tag. It was more than I made in a single paycheck. Of course, I could always charge it on Dad's card, but I made a point to be as self-sufficient as I could.

"Yolanda, I can't afford this."

"Don't be silly. I am purchasing this for you. It is a work dinner, after all. Do not worry about it. If you are going to represent this company, if you are going to represent me, you will dress as such."

Kelly opened the door and handed Yolanda a few small items.

"Take off your bra."

"What?"

"We need to see which of these undergarments fit you best. We have two strapless bras and a body slimmer." She spoke as if I should know what she was talking about.

"A body slimmer?"

"Oh, dear. There is nothing wrong with your body. The slimmer will just make sure everything stays where it ought to at all times, as well as hide the lines from your other undergarments. Now, it may be a tad uncomfortable in the beginning but trust me. It will be fabulous. I'll be out here."

I thanked God Yolanda stepped out as I dropped my bra on the floor and fastened the strapless bra that, surprisingly, fit better than most of the bras I owned. Thankfully I was able to keep my own underwear on as I slithered my way into what must've been designed by a man, because I cannot for the life of me understand why any woman would invent such a torturous piece of clothing.

I was barely able to fit into the body slimmer without crying. But Christ, I had a hard time breathing. At least it was short enough to allow me to step back into the dress. When Yolanda zipped it up and told me to take a step back, I realized she was right. I couldn't quite put my finger on what was different but the dress fit even better than it had before.

"Kelly! Shoes! What size are you, dear?"

"Um, eight."

"Size eight! Nothing too strappy. Or shiny!" Yolanda looked at me. "Try sitting in that dress."

I tiptoed over to the chair she'd vacated and sat. The fabric moved with me and didn't tighten or slide up as many other dresses would. The body slimmer constricted me in a way I wasn't used to but I didn't want to say anything to her. I looked at her expectantly.

"Good. Do you have a proper coat?"

I mentally riffled through my closet. "Yes! I have a long red wool coat. It has black buttons and an embellished collar."

"It sounds like it would work. Clutch?"

I nodded.

"Okay, let's get some shoes and be on our way. I have things to do." The almost friendly Yolanda that had appeared over the past hour and a half was disappearing and I wondered if I'd see her again.

Kelly came to the door with another saleswoman, their faces were barely visible over the stack of boxes they each carried.

"It would be better to try them on out here," Kelly said as she lifted her gaze over the boxes.

I made my way to the small foyer of the dressing area and sat on the white linen chaise. Looking around, I realized this was an area of the store where my mother would shop. It wasn't that I shunned my parents' money. They taught me to be self-sufficient and I think it made my father, at least, proud that I was able to fend for myself. They, of course, never let me want for anything. I just never asked for anything anymore. I liked being a grown-up. Then again, Yolanda was pulling me back into the world of having someone else provide for me. I wasn't sure how I felt about it.

After the sixth pair of shoes, I was sure I'd found the pair I was looking for. I'd been so wrapped up in slipping my feet in and out of designer shoes that I'd failed to notice I'd been left alone. I couldn't figure out where Yolanda and Kelly had gone off to, so I took the opportunity to make my own shoe decision.

I stood in the four-inch understated black platform pumps and walked toward the three-way mirror at the end of the hall. I was admiring my silhouette and how the heels helped my butt pop a little more than normal when I saw Brian in the reflection. I spun around and almost fell, catching myself only when I shot out my arm and steadied myself on the mirror.

"Hi."

"Hi." He smiled and my stomach flopped.

"What are you doing here?"

"Just hanging out."

I smirked and rolled my eyes. "I mean what are you doing standing among women's dresses?"

"Oh! You should have been more specific. I'm here shopping with my sister."

I craned my neck looking for a female version of Brian. He laughed. "She's in the dressing room."

I hadn't noticed anyone walk through, but then again I hadn't noticed Yolanda and Kelly were absent, either.

"You look, uh, nice." He scratched the back of his head, causing his already tussled hair to poof out a bit more. It was cute.

I smiled. "Nice? You think this dress"—I walked toward him slowly—"is just *nice*?"

I liked how the height of my shoes had my line of sight even with his mouth.

His Adam's apple bobbed as he swallowed. "Well, let's see you walk that way." He pointed toward the mirror as he leaned against the wall.

I turned slowly and looked over my shoulder as I tried to sway my ass without looking like a cartoon. When I reached the mirror, I stared at his reflection and smiled.

"Maybe"—he coughed—"that dress is a little bit more than just nice."

"A little, huh?"

"Yeah. I wouldn't want your head to get all big and whatnot." He rubbed his thumb along his lip before shoving his hands in his pockets and shrugging.

I stepped out of my heels and placed them back in the box as I heard a woman calling Brian's name. I turned my head around so fast I thought I'd get whiplash. Standing before me in the very first black beaded dress I'd tried on was a slight woman with long wavy red hair, full lips, and Brian's baby blues.

"Who is this?" She stepped forward with her hand extended while she looked at Brian.

"This is Caroline Frost. The one I was telling you about. Caroline, this is my sister Siobhan."

I whipped my head in his direction. *He was telling his sister about me?*

"Oh! You're the one who works with Yolanda Page! Is it true what they say about her? Is she really a dragon lady? I heard she's impossible to work with."

Siobhan leaned in like she was trading secrets with a girlfriend. Since I was never one to gossip, I didn't quite know how to answer.

"Well, she's tough for sure, but I'm learning so much from her. I think those things are said by people who don't know her."

Siobhan's face fell like I'd popped her last party balloon. "Oh, well. That's great. I didn't mean that, you know—"

I placed my hand on her arm. "It's okay. I was scared of her at first. She's really a great person."

A warm smile spread across Siobhan's face. "So, are you working with Michael Mortimer? What's he like?"

"Don't mind her," Brian said. "She's just looking for dirt. All the great journalists look for dirt."

"Oh, shut up! Brian's just jealous because I get to meet all the fabulous celebrities and he's stuck running a bar."

"I meet some interesting people, right, Caroline?" He winked at me. It made me feel slightly flustered.

"You're a journalist?"

"Well, trying to be. I've been assigned some literary dinner next week and I heard Michael would be there. I'd love to bring an interview to my editor."

"Well, then you should join Caroline." Yolanda walked into the foyer in standard Yolanda fashion. She owned the room. Siobhan blushed, obviously flustered.

"I will have the car pick you up after Caroline next Saturday. You'll sit with them and after, Caroline will make sure you get a few minutes with Michael. Will you be joining her, dear?" She turned her attention to Brian.

"Um, I don't, well, I wasn't planning on it."

"Well, of course you should. You can keep Caroline out of trouble while your sister interviews Michael." She turned to me. "Which shoes did you choose, Caroline?" I pointed at the box on the chair and she nodded. "Fine. Kelly knows what to do. Give everything to her. I will see you at work on Monday. With your *completed* notes. Am I clear?"

"Crystal."

"Good. I expect nothing less." She turned back after she'd begun walking away. "Oh, and Siobhan, you would do well to ask Michael if he thinks I am a dragon lady. I'd be interested to know what he thinks."

The three of us froze for minutes after she'd left before Brian finally let out a booming laugh. "I told you your big mouth would get you in trouble!"

"I am not in trouble! She invited me to the dinner! As her guest." She sat next to me after I'd plopped on the chaise. "You don't think I am in trouble, do you?"

I shook my head. At least I didn't think Siobhan was in trouble. I'd seen a glimpse of Yolanda that made me appreciate her even more.

Siobhan and I changed in the dressing rooms and I handed my things to Kelly.

"Well, I'll see you later. Nice to meet you, Siobhan."

"Wait! Caroline! What are you doing for dinner? I'd love to pick your brain about Michael and Yolanda. I promise, nothing inappropriate. I just want to be prepared."

"Shiv, I am sure she has plans."

"Oh, right. You probably have a date or something."

I caught a look in Brian's eyes. Was it regret? Disappointment?

"Actually, no. It's just me and Sarah sitting around eating Chinese. You're more than welcome to join us."

"Oh thank you!" She hugged me. "We'll see you then!"

"We?"

"Yeah, silly. I can't leave my baby brother home on a Saturday night, now can I?"

I smiled as Brian looked uncomfortable. "No. I guess you can't."

Siobhan grabbed for her purse. "You should get Brian's number so you can text him the address. I'm always losing my phone." She raised her eyebrows and looked toward Brian.

Always losing her phone, my ass. "I think I have it already." I raised an eyebrow when I saw Brian smile at my words.

"Yeah. I guess you do." He rubbed the side of his cheek. "Just, um, text me the address. What time?"

"Six." I took a few steps backward before turning. As I walked away I heard Siobhan whisper, "You're right. She is very pretty."

"Yeah, she is."

Chapter Nineteen

Sarah buzzed them in at six. She and I had just wiped out a bottle of Pinot and were perusing the take-out menu.

Siobhan and Brian entered through the open apartment door with a dusting of snow on their shoulders.

"Hey! Your apartment is great!" Siobhan unzipped her coat and handed it to me.

"Great to see you. This is my roommate, Sarah."

"I've heard so much about you." Sarah's eyes widened when Siobhan hugged her tight.

"Let me take your coat, Brian," Sarah said when she finally released herself from Siobhan's grip.

He'd changed his clothes from earlier, replacing the V-neck sweater with a tight thermal long-sleeved shirt in navy. I was momentarily hypnotized by the outline of his pectorals. His pants were the same distressed designer jeans I'd seen him in earlier, with a wide, aged brown belt holding them up. It was a casual look. Casual and fucking sexy as hell. He pulled off his hat to reveal the disheveled blond mop I'd often thought about running my fingers through. But that would be inappropriate. As would rubbing my face along his ever present five o'clock shadow. Damn, he was yummy. And off-limits. Not for the first time, I regretted not taking my friends' advice and abandoning the target for the bartender.

Sarah left to put the coats on the bed with Siobhan in tow and Brian handed me two bottles of Cabernet. Following me to the kitchen, I handed him the bottle opener as I reached for two more wineglasses.

"Nice slippers."

I looked down at my feet. I'd forgotten I was wearing them.

"They're comfy. And I wasn't going anywhere."

"No need to defend them."

I ducked my head. "Right. So, no work tonight?"

He poured four glasses, emptying the first bottle. "Nope. My brother's taking care of it. I needed to take the night off." He took a sip. "You smell good. What is that? Vanilla?"

"Yeah. Um, thank you. Vanilla." I stammered and mentally kicked myself for the sudden inability to take a compliment. "Your brother?" I asked, looking at him over the rim of my glass as I took a large sip.

"Yeah. Patrick. His wife is out of town and he needed something to do. He's staying at my place while he's here since Ryan's gone for a few days."

"Ryan's gone for a few days?"

"Yeah. Why? He didn't tell you?"

I shook my head. "Why would he tell me something like that?"

Brian smiled and shifted in his seat at the counter. "I don't know, maybe because you two are—"

"Friends." I cut him off.

"That's what I was going to say."

"Right. So your brother Patrick, he doesn't live here?" I climbed on top of the counter and took up my crisscross applesauce position with my back up against the wall.

"Nope. He lives in Connecticut with his doctor wife, two point five kids, Labrador retriever, and state-of-the-art minivan."

"What does he do?"

"He runs his own computer software company."

"Nice."

"Yep. So that's why I am here taking over the bar. No one else wanted to do it."

"What did you do before this?"

"Lawyer. I was in ROTC all through college, did my time, got out. Started working in the private sector. Dad died. Poof. I'm here."

"Did you want to leave your job?"

"Didn't matter. Didn't love it."

"Do you love the bar?"

"Sometimes." He gave me a look that made my heart pound before he got up and walked to the window. "The snow's really coming down outside, huh?"

"Huh?" I really needed to stop staring at his ass. "Yeah. Supposed to get a lot tonight." I joined him at the window as Sarah and Siobhan returned. "Wine's on the counter."

"I was just telling Sarah how you saved the family business." Siobhan curled up in my spot on the couch. There was still a hint of chocolate stain on the arm. No matter how many times I tried to clean it, it remained, I'm sure, to mock me.

"No one needs to hear that." Brian turned a slight shade of red.

"We were going to have to sell it. Too many violations. But Brian came in and saved the day."

"That was nice of you," I whispered.

"I didn't do it to be nice." He walked back to his seat at the kitchen counter and picked up the take-out menu.

"Oh, he's just modest."

"Siobhan, enough. Come on. I'm starving."

"Fine. Fine. I was just making conversation." She plopped down on the stool next to her brother and took the menu from him.

Their dynamic was fascinating. They were obviously close, though Siobhan was more of a free spirit. They balanced each other out.

My brother and I were close but we were so much alike, there was no balancing act. When we were together, we were as competitive as foes. And when we had to, we joined forces to hold the other up. But when we fought, it was a blowup. Two people so much alike, it was hard to distinguish one from the other. Which was why we made it a point to keep our visits with each other to a minimum. Didn't mean I didn't love him more than anyone else in the world, it just meant that I knew where our boundaries fell.

Once we settled on the food, Brian called for delivery. Looking out the window, I kind of felt bad for the delivery guy because the snow was really starting to pile up, but the pity didn't last once my stomach rumbled loud enough to be heard across the room.

"Was that your stomach?" Leave it to Sarah to call attention to the embarrassing.

"Yes. Yes it was. Shall I give you a dollar for guessing correctly on your first try?"

"Um, maybe we should put out some snacks?"

"Oh please! I am starving!" I poked my head in the fridge and pulled out a wedge of Brie and a couple of pears. Sarah grabbed a box of crackers.

"Want me to make a drink or something?" Brian offered.

"Yes!" Sarah and I said together.

"Where's your liquor?"

I pointed.

"What would you like to drink, Care?" As soon as he said it, I realized it was the first time he'd used my nickname.

"Yeah, well, you know. Anything. I'm easy."

"Are you now?" He chuckled as he pulled bottles from the shelf.

Thirty minutes of small talk, stolen glances in Brian's direction, and a myriad of questions, rapid-fire style, from Siobhan followed the awkward moment. Thankfully she was interrupted by a long buzz.

"Food's here!" Sarah jumped up to get her purse.

"I got it." Brian held out his hand and left the apartment to head downstairs.

"Care, I think he likes you!" Sarah must've forgotten Siobhan was in the room because we both froze when she said it and slowly turned our heads in his sister's direction.

"What? You aren't wrong." She poured another glass of wine and plopped back on the sofa.

"Spill." Sarah sat on the couch next to her.

"Sarah, no. I'm sorry, Shiv, she's off her meds."

"Oh, no. I don't mind. Honestly, I haven't seen him light up around anyone in a long time. And pardon me for mentioning it, but I think I feel a vibe coming off you, too. Why don't you guys, you know, just try it out? See where it goes?"

I was being put on the spot by the sister of the guy I'd passed over. I kind of hoped the floor would open up and swallow me away from the hell that was that moment.

"You see, there was a target and Brian kind of helped me and then there was the gym…" I stared at Sarah, silently imploring her to help me.

"Oh no. You're doing great."

"Well, I am sure Ryan would understand. It's not like you two are a thing, right?"

Yup. Hell.

"What do you know about Ryan?"

"That you two are friends with benefits or whatever."

"No. Siobhan, if we're going to move on here you need to know. I am her friend with benefits. You are her friend with benefits. Ryan is her friend whom she fucks. Nothing more. Nothing less."

"That makes more sense. Now, if only social media would allow you to classify relationships like that. You know, 'One Night Stand,' 'Do It Yourself,' which, by the way, would be my status, 'Friends with Benefits,' 'Friends Who Fuck.' I should really write a piece on this. Let me get my notebook."

Siobhan ran to Sarah's room to grab her purse and I plopped down in front of Sarah.

"What the fuck?"

"What? I was just getting intel you won't ask for."

"I don't need you to do that for me. I am more than capable of finding out information on Brian if I want to. And I have more than enough on my plate. I can't be in a relationship right now and I think taking the path of Brian would take me there. Ryan is uncomplicated. It's just sex."

"If you think sex is uncomplicated—"

"No, I mean Ryan isn't the type of guy I would want to be in a relationship with. With Brian, that's all I see. Brian is safe. And I've had enough safe for now."

"Well, wait too long and Brian won't be around. Care, he's a catch."

"I know. I just—I don't know."

"Who's hungry?" Brian walked in with a huge bag of Chinese takeout. The smell made my stomach growl again.

"Let's make sure Caroline gets fed first before we all lose fingers." Brian handed me my quart of chicken and broccoli and a pair of chopsticks.

I pulled up a floor pillow to the coffee table in the living room and didn't wait for everyone else before I dug in. Brian pulled up a pillow next to me after refilling my wineglass.

"Floor, huh?"

"I like it. Plus it's usually just me, Sarah, and Mel. What'd you order?" I popped open his container with my chopstick.

"Orange beef."

"Is it good?"

"Try some." He offered me some of his food while he plucked a piece of chicken from my take-out box.

"Are there mushrooms?"

"I don't think so. You don't like them?"

"Allergic. Hives, stomach issues. Not pleasant."

"Good to know. I'll never make you anything with mushrooms in it."

I should have glossed over the comment but the thought of him cooking me something to eat was kind of hot.

"And nothing too spicy."

"Stomach?"

"Yeah." I crinkled my nose and he laughed.

"All right. No mushrooms, no spicy food. I'll remember that."

"Whatcha talking about?" Siobhan made herself comfortable on the couch next to Sarah.

"Caroline was just telling me about her aversion to food."

"Shut up!" I playfully punched him in the arm.

"Sorry, she was telling me how much time she spends in the bathroom after she eats mushrooms and spicy foods."

"Asshole!" I laughed hard enough to spew food on the table.

"What?" He spread his arms out in front of him. "Being an asshole is part of my manly essence."

"You, my friend"—Sarah poked her utensil at him—"are not an asshole."

"You're right. I'm too *safe*"—he cocked his eyebrow at me—"to be an asshole."

I immediately began choking. Sarah jumped up. "Are you okay?"

"Yeah." I coughed. "Something. Wrong pipe," I managed to squeak out.

"Was it something I said?" Brian laughed as I threw my napkin at him.

"Eavesdropper."

Sarah doubled over with laughter. Siobhan got up to retrieve another bottle of wine. "I certainly don't think we're drunk enough."

The rest of the night continued as if we'd known one another our whole lives. Siobhan asked a million questions about Yolanda and Michael, jotting each answer down in her well-worn notebook. Sarah and Brian teased each other easily and chatted a bit about her job as a high school science teacher. And even though my stomach flopped every time I caught Brian looking at me, it was easy. Easier than when I was around Ryan. He made my skin crawl in a way that would lead only to an orgasm. Both good feelings, but it was like I couldn't relax around him. With Brian, I don't know. It felt simple. Like I said, easy.

Before we knew it, it was almost two in the morning and we'd polished off a little more than a half dozen bottles of wine between us. I was certainly feeling it. Siobhan had passed out on the couch, curled up in a tiny red-headed ball.

"When did she fall asleep?"

"I have no idea." We laughed because at that point, everything was funny. Another bottle and the giggles wouldn't come as easily. We were at the point where if we stopped, maybe we wouldn't embarrass ourselves.

"I need to wake her up. We should really get going." Brian started toward his sister.

"No. Leave her there. You guys can stay here. You don't want to walk home in this." Sarah pulled back the curtain to reveal the several inches of snow that had fallen.

"I wouldn't want to put you out. I can come back in the morning and get her."

"No. Really. It's no problem. You can sleep in my room."

Brian raised his eyebrows at me.

"Not like that. I can bunk with Sarah."

"Not what I had in mind as far as a bedmate, but beggars can't be choosers. I'm beat. Good night, Brian."

"Good night, Sarah."

Brian and I stood by the window, both feeling the effects of a night of wine and Chinese food. I watched as he licked his lips and remembered how they felt last week at the bar. I wanted nothing more than to kiss him again.

"So, this is awkward." He snapped his fingers before clapping a hand over a fist. He rocked back and forth on his heels.

"I don't think it's awkward." Liquid bravery set in as I stepped closer to him and tugged lightly on his shirt.

"Well, we should get to bed." He wrapped his hand around mine and pulled it away from his shirt.

"Right. I think I have a pair of Steven's pajama pants that I never returned to him. You can wear them if you don't mind wearing douche pants."

"I don't mind at all. I've always wanted a pair."

I opened the door to my bedroom and saw that Sarah had already put his coat on my chair. Brian stood at the threshold.

"You can come in, silly. I won't bite."

"Oh, well then I'm not sure I want to come in now."

He walked around my room, stopping to look at photos and flip through my books.

"You read a lot?"

"All the time. You?" *Please say yes. Please say yes.*

"I do, actually. *A Separate Peace* by John Knowles was always a favorite. You probably think that's weird."

"No! I love that story. How Gene was unable to get past his own shortcomings and how envious he was of Phineas. Phineas was such a free spirit. I loved how real he was."

"You don't think he was pretentious?"

I flopped on my bed. "Pretentious? Absolutely not. He embraced goodness. Gene, to me, represented the darkness we all have inside."

"All? Including Phineas?" He sat on the bed next to me and placed his hand on my knee.

"Well, I guess so." I lay back and stared at the ceiling. My head was all over the place. Forget the fact that I was a little drunk. I hadn't felt like this since I was sixteen. It felt new and scary and right.

"Care. You know. I know I'm not the wild and crazy *whatever* you're looking for. I'm okay with that. But I'll have you know, I'm not *safe*, as you say."

"I didn't mean it that way. I just meant, I mean, I just got out of a five-year black hole. I can't do that again."

"Who says I'm looking for a relationship?"

"No one. I didn't mean it how you're taking it. It was supposed to be a compliment."

Brian eased back until he was lying next to me, staring at the ceiling with me. His hand reached for me and he intertwined his fingers with mine. Rubbing his thumb along mine, he sighed.

"You don't have to sleep in Sarah's room if you don't want to. I don't want to put you out."

"It's okay. I don't mind."

"I meant, you could sleep here, too, unless you think something will happen that you don't want to happen."

My eyes felt like they were going to pop out of their sockets. "Um, yeah sure."

"How about you give me those pajama pants and I'll go get changed in the bathroom?"

I shot up and rifled through my bottom drawer. He took the bottoms, pushed a curl out of my eye, and left the room.

As soon as he left, I closed the door and did a quick pit sniff. At least I smelled good. I ran a brush through my hair. Bad idea. Anyone with curly hair knows this. I threw it in a sloppy bun. Taking off my pants, I ran my hands over my legs. Thankfully there wasn't much stubble. I threw off my shirt and reached for my favorite Dave Matthews Band T-shirt. I had just unhooked my bra and tossed it on the floor and was slipping the tee over my head when Brian walked in the room. His eyes widened.

"I'm sorry. I thought I gave you enough time to—"

It would have been enough time had I not stopped to check out my personal hygiene first.

"No, it's okay. I'm just on autopilot. I wasn't thinking. Go ahead. Pick a side."

A sexy smirk played on his lips. "Are you going to put on some pants?"

I looked down. I totally wasn't thinking. The T-shirt barely scraped my hips and I was standing in the middle of my room, in front of Brian, in my underwear. Thank Jesus they were at least a cute pair I'd picked up last week when I was preparing for Operation One Night Stand.

I quickly grabbed for a pair of tiny shorts. I tripped as I tried to put them on and fell into Brian's grip. His hands were firmly on my upper arms and I carefully stood and looked up at him. His eyes sparkled in the lamplight. Bending down slightly, he smiled as his hands rubbed my shoulders. As he softly brushed his lips against mine, I was brought back to last weekend at the bar when I first met him and—

Ryan. Shit.

"What's wrong? I was kidding. You can sleep in that if you want to. I mean, I really don't mind."

"It's not that. It's just—"

"Ryan." He took a step back and dropped his hands from my body. The flicker of light I saw in his eyes moments ago dimmed.

"Yeah." Suddenly a tiny stain on the carpet grabbed my focus.

"Hey look. You said it yourself. Ryan's your guy. I'm the safe one here. So it's *safe* to say nothing's going to happen tonight."

He climbed into bed, settled in, and pulled back the covers.

"Stop saying you're safe."

"Well, that's what I am, right? Now get some sleep, Care. And don't think so much."

I put on my shorts and climbed in next to him. The inches that separated us may as well have been miles. Clicking off the light, he rolled over so his back was to me and I was relegated, once again, to staring at the ceiling; this time alone. Since when did life get so complicated?

Chapter Twenty

Brian was gone by the time my eyes snapped open at 6:03 the next morning. His coat was gone and the pajama pants were carefully folded on top of my dresser. The only indication he had been there was that the mattress was still warm. He hadn't left that long ago.

I threw the covers off, pulled on the oversize pajama pants that he'd worn the night before, and tiptoed out into the hallway.

"Come on, Siobhan, let's go." I heard Brian's voice.

"I'm so tired! Why couldn't we have just slept in a bit longer?" Siobhan's voice took on the whiny tone of someone who clearly wasn't ready to be out of bed.

"I'll get you coffee on the way."

"I didn't get to thank them for letting us stay over."

"Call later." Brian was obviously in a hurry to get out of Dodge. I could hear him juggle his keys.

"Fine. I don't know why you're in such a hurry. Did something happen last night?"

"No. Nothing happened."

"Did you want it to?"

"Shiv, I'm tired. I have a lot to do today. We can talk about it later."

"You like her."

"Who?"

"Who? Caroline."

"You're crazy."

I held my breath. Even from the hallway I could hear the lie in his voice.

"Crazy intuitive. Why don't you just tell her?"

"Because she's with Ryan. I don't have time for this." The lock unlatched and opened.

"I don't think she is. And I don't think you think she is, either. You always do this."

"Do what?"

I didn't hear her answer because the door closed behind them. I blew out the breath I was holding and unclenched my hands. Leaning back against the wall, I slowly banged my head a few times. What did it matter if he liked me or not? Not like we knew each other or anything. He probably just wanted what Ryan had gotten, a romp in the sack.

Making my way to the kitchen, I prepped the coffeemaker and pulled down my favorite polka-dotted mug. I had just turned to the cabinet to get the sugar when the door opened. Standing in the door staring at me was Brian.

"I didn't know you were awake."

"I always wake up this early. It's some sort of punishment for something terrible I did in a previous life, I'm sure of it."

"How long have you been up?" He was still standing in the doorway, looking unsure of himself. It was a different look for him.

"A couple of minutes. Did you forget something?" I turned away and took the coffee creamer from the refrigerator.

"My sister, she um, forgot her notebook."

"Oh. Well, I can help you look."

I motioned for him to come in and began looking under the sofa cushions while he checked the tables.

"Found it." I held up the small pink notebook.

"Thanks." He walked over and I handed it to him.

"You're welcome."

We stood in front of each other not making eye contact.

"Look, Care. About last night—"

"What about it? Nothing happened."

"I know. Ryan's my friend."

"He's mine, too." I turned and walked back to the kitchen.

"I just don't want to step on anyone's toes."

"I get it. Look, no big deal."

He shoved his empty hand into the pocket of his navy peacoat.

"You're interesting."

"Interesting?" I looked at him over the rim of my coffee mug. "Isn't that the compliment of the century."

"Yeah. And well, I like getting to know you."

"I like getting to know you, too." I put the mug on the counter.

"Well, okay then."

"Okay then." I repeated.

"Brian! Did you find it?" Siobhan walked into the apartment and stopped cold when she saw the two of us looking at each other. "Oh. Good morning, Caroline."

"Good morning." I didn't take my eyes off Brian.

"We should really be going." Brian stepped toward the door. "Thanks again for finding this." He held up the notebook before handing it to his sister.

"Anytime."

"See you."

"Yeah. See you." I made eye contact one last time before he closed the door.

I dropped my head to the counter.

"What the hell was that?" Sarah yawned as she made her way to the coffeemaker and poured herself a cup of coffee.

"What did you hear?"

"All of it."

"Then you know."

"You two slept together last night?"

"Slept together as in slept. Nothing else happened. Well, we kind of kissed."

"Kind of kissed? What does that even mean?"

"Yeah. It was barely a kiss. Then we fell asleep. Well, he slept. I stared at the ceiling all night."

I tucked my legs under me as I took up my spot in the couch. I was glad to find my ass still settled into the cushion perfectly. Sarah sank into her chair.

"So what does that mean?"

"Nothing. He doesn't want to step on any toes."

"I got that part. What does that mean for you?"

"I don't know? Nothing?"

"Something?" Sarah called me on my bullshit.

"Maybe. Who knows? I've been out of the game for so long—"

"Don't make excuses. If you like him, you like him. Doesn't make you a bad person because you slept with his roommate. You didn't even know him then."

I placed my mug on the side table. "Exactly. I still don't know him. And he doesn't know me. So why all the weirdness?"

"Because I don't think he wants what you think he wants."

"Which is?"

"A good romp. I think this guy is into you for more than sex and I don't think you're in the mind-set to expect that from anyone. But you're into him, too. And I think it scares you a little."

I leaned my head back on the sofa cushion and closed my eyes. Sarah was right. After Steven, I wasn't sure I was in the right frame of mind to be in any kind of relationship that required emotions. I was wrung out and wasn't sure I could handle any more.

"Look," she continued, "Ryan wasn't even supposed to be part of the equation. He was supposed to be a one night stand. What you need to decide is if you would be as conflicted if he and Brian didn't know each other."

Her words rang true. I needed to look at things from a different angle. The new me would take the time to think things out before writing them off. I owed it to the old me.

"You're right. I'll think about it."

"You do that. I'm going to get dressed. Early gym today. I have a lunch date with Drew."

I thought about Brian and what he'd said, what I'd heard him say. I kept going back to the same thought. The best feeling was when I'd look at him and find him already looking. That had to count for something.

"Melody's meeting us here before spin." Sarah interrupted my thoughts. "She had a date with Danny last night. I'm hoping he's the one that finally erases Nick the Dick from her mind."

"We'll see. She's pretty fickle."

"True, but I think, kind of like you were, maybe she's finally decided that being treated like a thing, like a fuck buddy, isn't really a relationship."

"Is that all I'll be to Ryan? And does it matter? What if I want to get to know Brian?"

"I don't know. And if it's what you want, it isn't necessarily a bad thing. You just have to decide what would make you happy. Ryan and his promise to be your fuck buddy friend or Brian and whatever that brings. You certainly can't have both."

Chapter Twenty-One

The week flew by without a call from Ryan or, for that matter, Brian. Instead of obsessing over the lack of contact, I threw myself into my work, much to Yolanda's pleasure. We were nearly done with Michael's book and looked to be on schedule with the release date, a mere six months away. In the publishing world, six months was quick. Of course, the manuscript was edited multiple times long before I arrived to work on the final round. I was happy that Yolanda was pleased with my work and even happier that she'd expressed that happiness with Mr. Little.

I woke up Saturday morning ready for a day of preparation. I'd come to learn the dinner I was attending was actually a pretty big deal for Michael and the publisher. What had slipped past me was the novel had been optioned for a movie and the screenplay was nearly finished. It was exciting to be part of something so big, especially for a first project.

There would be numerous media outlets attending and I was being trusted as the face of the publisher. No stress or anything.

Staring in the mirror, my face freshly washed, I leaned in only to find a long scraggly gray hair protruding from my eyebrow. Mortified, I grabbed the tweezers from the drawer and plucked the rogue old-lady hair from my face. Somewhat satisfied but still aghast at the fact that I was getting gray hair, even if it was only in my eyebrows, I pulled my hair into a ponytail and walked to the kitchen to refill my empty coffee mug.

Sarah still wasn't home. She'd spent the night at Drew's apartment. As a matter of fact, she'd spent three nights at his place during the past week. I was happy that she'd hit it off with someone so quickly. As a general rule, Sarah was ridiculously picky when it came to guys and usually liked the freedom the single life afforded her. But, according to our conversation the day before, none of us was getting any younger. The thought of turning thirty freaked her out and Drew came along just in time to ease the blow, or at least muddy the view of the big three-oh.

As for me? I still had a year and a half until I had to meet my next decade, a small victory for being the youngest in my tiny group of three. I didn't have too much time to mull over life changes. I had a date with a personal trainer before I plopped myself in the chair of my hairdresser, who had agreed to do something fun with my continuously out-of-control curls.

It wasn't until three on the afternoon of the party slash dinner slash whatever it was that I found myself back in my apartment. Sarah was emptying grocery bags and dancing to the newest pop station. Bouncing around the kitchen singing about being happy, she was startled to see me standing across the counter with an amused grin on my face.

"Welcome back."

"Jesus, you scared me."

"Imagine how I felt. I haven't seen you much over the past week. I wasn't sure if I was seeing a ghost."

"Ha ha. Funny, Care. Your hair looks great!" She reached over and ran her fingers through the front. My hairdresser had trimmed my hair and spent two hours straightening it. Now, instead of falling to my shoulders, my hair reached down to the middle of my back. I had to admit, I loved it. But then again, what curly-haired girl doesn't dream of straight hair? I resigned myself to the fact that once I showered, it would kink back up. At least for one night, I could feel like a princess.

Sarah returned to emptying the grocery bags. "What time are you leaving for that dinner thing?"

"The car is picking me up at six. I told Yolanda to have the driver pick up Brian and Siobhan first, just to give me a bit of extra time to get ready."

"Speaking of Brian, have you talked to him?" Sarah asked over her shoulder as she put a carton of almond milk in the fridge. I crinkled my nose a bit; almond milk was gross.

"Nope." I hung my coat on the hook. "Haven't talked to Ryan, either. Michael, of course, has been in constant contact."

"Isn't he away?"

"Yep. Well, he was. He got in last night, I think." Hopping up on the stool, I grabbed a handful of grapes and popped them in my mouth. "Didn't stop him from e-mailing, texting, calling. You know, normal weirdo author stuff. I think he's OCD or something. He kept making sure the plans were on schedule."

"Will you be driving with him, too?"

"No. He'll meet us there. He lives in the city, so I think it makes the most sense."

"You'll be back late?"

"Not sure. I think so. I'll call you and let you know. You staying here tonight?"

"Yeah. I miss my bed. Drew's is nice but I don't get much sleep when I'm there. Almost a week of fugglesnucking has worn me out."

"Fugglesnucking?"

"Yeah, you know. When all the snuggling and fucking are over and you're back to snuggling and thinking of sneaking in another quickie. And then you do it instead of thinking about it."

Leave it to Sarah to add another word to the dictionary. "Sounds tiring."

Sarah smiled. "It is."

"I bet." Wiggling my eyebrows, I hopped off the stool and grabbed the makeup bag I'd just purchased and filled. "I gotta go rest up before I put on my face."

Looking at the clock on the stove, Sarah replied, "Yeah. It'll take you three hours to do that."

"I want to take my time. What if I mess up? You remember the last time I tried to do a smoky eye?"

Sarah made a face and shivered. "You're right. Better start now."

I heard her giggle before turning up the music and I imagined her bouncing along to the newest boy band release. Shaking my head, I closed my bedroom door.

Flopping on my unmade bed, I stared at the ceiling and finally took notice of the knots in my belly. I was excited to see Brian, to see him all dressed up. I was nervous about the fact that I was tapped to introduce Michael to the attendees. Reaching down, I shuffled my hand blindly through my purse, looking for the index cards that held the small introduction Yolanda had written for me. Finding them, I brought them to my face and read them over and over until I was sure I had the words memorized. The clock read 3:55 before I decided it was time to start getting ready. Grabbing my makeup bag, I made my way to the bathroom and got to work on my face.

Thankfully, the girl at the makeup counter had understood my need for understated. On a regular day, my routine involved little more than pressed powder, mascara, and lip gloss. Of course, that wouldn't do for the event, so I purchased new blush, eye shadow, and lipstick. Considering I couldn't remember the last time I used such things, I was wary of painting my face with the items I already owned.

It took three tries and quite a bit of makeup remover before I got my eyes right. Adding in a bit of blush and fluffing my hair a bit, I was pleased with the final results.

In my room, I pulled out the body slimmer Yolanda had chosen. Off my body, it looked about five sizes too small. I stared at it lying on my bed while I fastened my strapless bra. The tags were still on the slimmer, and reading the directions, I saw I was supposed to step into it "for better results." Not sure what that meant, I figured I might as well do as instructed. I had it pulled halfway up my thighs before yelling to Sarah for help.

"What are you doing?" she asked as she walked into my room.

"I think it's twisted."

"I think you're right." She laughed at my predicament.

"Shut up and just help me pull it up."

Sarah and I grabbed and tugged for a few minutes, untwisting the thing before we were able to stretch it up to the bottom of my bra.

I tried to take a deep breath but only managed to squeak out what little air was left in my lungs. It felt tighter than it had when I bought it. Stupid morning croissants. "Jesus. People wear these things?"

"Um, yeah. It smooths you out. You've really never worn one before?"

"That's what Yolanda said. And no. Never." I turned side to side to look at myself in the full-length mirror. "It had to be a man who invented these things."

"Give it a little bit. You'll forget it's on."

"Can I even eat in this?" I splayed my hands across my stomach; I couldn't imagine stretching out the fabric any further. As it was, I thought I would split a seam.

"Yeah. A few peas and a sip of water." Sarah plopped onto my chair. "Where's the dress?"

I took it down from the back of my closet door and unzipped it from its plastic encasement. "All this trouble for a dress." I smoothed my hands down the silky fabric of the undergarment. "I feel like I'm stuffed in a fucking sausage casing."

Sarah grabbed the tag. "For a dress that cost almost as much as your half of the rent! Put it on." She took the dress off the hanger and held it out.

I stepped into the dress and slipped my arms in the small holes until it settled off my shoulders. "Can you zip me?"

Sarah zipped the dress and I stood back and admired myself in the mirror. I was shocked to see that I didn't look like the young kid I was sure everyone took me as. I looked professional. Sexy. "Wow."

"Yeah. Wow." Sarah stepped back. "You know it's going to be twenty degrees out tonight?"

"So?"

"So, your legs are bare."

"Huh?"

"You need pantyhose."

"What the fuck. Now I have to do this all again? I don't think I have the strength to peel this slimmer thing off then put it back on."

"Hold on." Sarah ran out of my room and returned a few minutes later with a slim envelope of cardboard.

"What's that?"

"Thigh highs."

"Get the fuck out of here! I can't wear those! I'm not a hooker!"

"God, Care! Relax. No one will know you're wearing them, unless, of course, you want them to know." She pulled them out of the package and handed one to me. "Pull them halfway up then I'll help you shift the dress and the slimmer so we can pull them up the rest of the way."

Between the two of us, it took only another twenty minutes to fit the black thigh high stockings under the dress and slimmer.

"That was fun." No it wasn't.

"If your friends don't help you put on your pantyhose, you don't need them in your life, right?"

"Ha! I guess. Thank you." I riffled through my closet looking for the box my shoes came in before remembering they were under my bed. "What time is it?"

"Five till six."

"Can you get the red clutch from the top shelf for me and fill it with my stuff?"

I shoved on my shoes, which lifted me a good four inches higher than normal, and walked to the hall closet to retrieve my red coat, black leather gloves, and black-and-white-checked scarf.

"How do I look?"

"Perfect. Here, put on some lipstick."

I swept the color on my lips before placing the tube in the clutch Sarah handed me. I had just finished blotting when the doorbell rang.

Sarah buzzed Brian up and I took one last look in the mirror.

She opened the door and, I swear, time stood still. Brian was dressed in a black suit, gray shirt, and red tie. His wavy hair was slicked back but still looked as though I could run my fingers through it. The stubble on his face was trimmed but not gone. His eyes were hidden by aviator shades.

"You look, just wow, Caroline." His smile told me I definitely had his attention.

"Thank you. So do you." I cocked my head to the side. "What's with the sunglasses?"

"Oh." A sheepish look was plastered across his face before he ducked his head and took them off. When he looked at me again, I gasped.

"What happened?" I rushed across the space and investigated the yellowish bruise encircling his left eye.

"Well, Ryan and I kind of got into a fight. He punched me."

"What?" I was mortified. What the hell could they possibly have fought over? "Why?"

"Don't worry about it. It isn't important. You ready?" He offered me his arm and slipped his sunglasses back on.

I looked back at Sarah, who had her teacher face on and mouthed, "What the fuck?"

She shook her head as we walked out the door.

Chapter Twenty-Two

Brian opened the rear door of the black sedan and I slid in next to his sister, Siobhan. Brian sat up front with the driver.

"Love your coat!" Siobhan looked like a kid in a candy store with unlimited funds. "So, Yolanda e-mailed me and said I could have ten minutes with Michael. Do you think that will be enough time?"

"I think so. Let me see your questions."

Siobhan handed over her notebook. "You can't ask him this." I pointed to her question about the rumors of his playboy image. I pulled a pen from her bag that sat between us and crossed the question out.

"That's all anyone wants to know! He's one of the most eligible bachelors in the city. My editor will be pissed if I don't get some dirt."

Pouting was not a good look for Siobhan. It made her look even younger than her twenty-six years. And really? Michael was considered one of the city's most eligible bachelors? I didn't see it.

"Look, ask him the other questions and I'll see what I can do about getting you some dirt. Just don't go about it that way. Yolanda will have both our heads."

The rest of the drive was spent in silence as Siobhan reworded her approach, Brian made quiet small talk with the driver, and I alternated between reviewing my note cards and looking out the window. Tiny snowflakes twinkled in the overhead lights. I smoothed out my hair and sighed. At least it would be straight for a little while. I secretly thanked Sarah for the thigh highs. She was right. It was cold outside and even if the thin nylon material gave only minimal comfort against the chilly air, it was better than nothing.

The car slid in front of the restaurant. Brian opened my door to help me out as the driver held Siobhan's hand as she clumsily stepped out of the car.

"Shoot!" I heard her say as she crouched down in the street. The driver crouched next to her to gather the items that had fallen from her purse. Brian stepped to her side of the car to help out.

"Caroline. You look beautiful." Michael approached under the flash of a few cameras and grabbed my hands, kissing me on either cheek. "Let's go in, shall we?"

"My friends—" I trailed off as he steered me toward the entrance with his hand dangerously low on my back.

"They can meet us inside."

I looked back as Brian helped his sister to the curb. The height of her heels made my feet hurt and I wondered how on earth she'd stay upright for the remainder of the evening.

Shoving my gloves into the pockets of my coat, I allowed Michael to slip it off and hand it, and my scarf, to the girl at the coat check closet.

"Wow, Caroline. You look amazing." Michael looked at me hungrily and slid his hands up and down my arms.

Clean-shaven and dressed impeccably in a suit that matched the color of my dress perfectly, his big brown eyes shone. It wasn't the cold air that rushed in through the open door that was giving me goose bumps.

I had to remind my libido to take the night off. It wouldn't do to give Michael the slightest hint of how his presence affected me. Plus, it wouldn't do to give him the satisfaction. I'd become good at tamping it down and regarding him as a nonsexual being. Brian, on the other hand, was an entirely different story.

Brian and Siobhan walked in. Our eyes met briefly before I watched Brian's gaze drop to my feet and slowly take me in. For a moment, I felt like I was the only woman in the room. I wasn't sure if it was the body slimmer, but I suddenly felt as if I were going to burst out of my skin. There wasn't a wall in the world that would ever erase the tension I felt when Brian was in the room. There was no way to look at him without imagining his hands all over my body.

"Shall we go in?" Michael's hand dropped to my lower back as he whispered in my ear. I could feel my face flush and knew Brian could see it. Not what I wanted.

I stepped away from Michael's touch and said, "Sure. I have someone here that you need to meet. Yolanda cleared her to interview you."

Michael sighed. "You do know how I hate interviews."

"I do know, but I think, and Yolanda agrees, that it would be good for your image. Just a few minutes, a few questions, and you'll be done. It would be good press."

"But how"—he tucked a strand of hair behind my ear—"am I

supposed to maintain an air of mystery if I answer questions about myself?"

Ducking my head, I replied, "You'll still be mysterious."

"Fine. You're going to owe me. Big-time."

"Fine. Whatever. Here she is." Brian and Siobhan walked over. Brian looked Michael up and down as Michael regarded Brian as nothing to be interested in. "Siobhan, this is Michael Mortimer. He's agreed to the interview."

"Nice to meet you, Mr. Mortimer." Siobhan held out her dainty hand. Michael suddenly became very interested in the interview.

"Please call me Michael. Siobhan, was it?" He took her hand and brought it to his lips. Siobhan blushed and giggled. I rolled my eyes.

"Okay, so you two talk. Brian and I will go get a drink. I'll find you in ten minutes."

I grabbed Brian's coat and pulled him away. I wasn't sure if my eyeballs would fall out before his. At least, surely, one of us would lose them with all the rolling.

At the bar, I ordered an amaretto and ginger for myself and a gin and tonic for Brian.

"Who the hell was that?" Brian looked across the room at his sister and Michael. Siobhan was laughing loudly with her hand on Michael's chest. Michael had his hand on top of hers and was caressing it with his thumb.

"That, my friend"—I hopped up on the bar seat and swiveled around to check out the crowd—"is Michael Mortimer, best-selling author of three novels with a fourth in the works. The fourth, soon to be a major motion picture, is the novel Yolanda is working on. She's using this one to teach me."

I looked down, following Brian's gaze. I swear to God, I'd never felt so sexy crossing my legs.

"He seems, uh, like—"

I smiled as I took a drink. Brian couldn't decide where to lay his eyes—on my legs or on his sister.

"Like a, uh—"

"Douche bag?"

"Yeah." Our eyes finally met once again.

"He is but he's harmless. He thinks he's God's gift."

"I noticed he's very hands-on."

"Very touchy-feely. I usually can keep my distance and he can usually read my signal. Tonight, he's liking the freedom."

"I didn't like it." Brian took a deep drink.

"I got that."

"Just so we're clear."

"Crystal. So, you wanna tell me why you have a black eye?"

"Nope." His smile was brilliant but the message it gave off was clear. *Leave it alone.*

I looked through the crowd and saw a few people who looked familiar. Michael and Siobhan, however, were nowhere to be seen.

"Where's my sister?" Brian placed his glass on the bar top and stepped forward.

"They probably went to the back room for the interview. It's a little noisy in here and they were probably being interrupted."

"Yeah, I guess so."

Brian leaned into the bar, brushing up against me as he did, and flagged down the bartender. "Do you need another?"

I could only nod in agreement because his hand was slowly sliding up and down my thigh. Suddenly I felt as though my head would pop off. I began to sweat.

"Are you all right?" Brian grabbed my elbow as I began to slump off the chair. "You're white as a ghost."

"Can't. Breathe." I fanned myself with a napkin and plucked an ice cube from my drink and began to rub it all over my neck.

"Let's get you some air."

The blast of cold air hit me like a ton of bricks as the droplets of sweat froze to my skin. I shivered and Brian took off his coat and wrapped it around my shoulders. "Come on, let's walk."

He and I walked halfway down the block but I still felt like I was being squeezed by a boa constrictor. "Oh fuckety fuck. I think it's the body slimmer."

"The fuckety what?"

"The thing that goes under my dress to make me look skinny."

"But you *are* skinny."

"I don't have time to explain. I need to get out of this thing now." I tugged at my dress and looked around.

"Let's go back in and find you a restroom so you can take it off."

"I can't take it off by myself. I need help."

"What?"

"It's too tight."

"You want me to help you take off your underwear?" The smirk that crossed his lips made my stomach flip.

"Not my underwear. The thing that's over my... Oh, never mind. Fuck. Just come help me."

"You're the boss." Brian chuckled as I trotted back to the restaurant.

Looking around to make sure the coast was clear, I pulled Brian into the single bathroom with me and handed him back his coat. He hung it up on the door hook and clapped his hands together. "So what do I need to do?"

"Unzip me."

"Yes, ma'am."

"No, really, I need to get this fucking thing off me."

"You really have a dirty mouth."

"What? Oh, right. Sorry."

"I wasn't complaining." He unzipped my dress and slipped it off my shoulders. It fell to the ground.

I stepped out of my dress and handed it to Brian and he hung it up over his coat. I stood in front of him wearing a sausage casing, thigh highs, and heels. I should have felt sexy but it was hard when it felt like my skin was about to peel off.

Caroline, meet humiliation. I think you know each other.

I rolled the slimmer down to my hips and breathed a sigh of relief as Brian watched in obvious amusement.

"Oh, great mother of shit. I can finally breathe." I took large, deep breaths.

Brian pointed at me. "So that's the thing that you were talking about."

"Yes." I huffed as if I'd just run a mile. "I need help getting it over my hips."

"This thing is supposed to make you look skinnier?"

"Yeah. Stupid, right?"

"Well yeah, especially when your waist is as big as my thigh."

Brian stood in front of me as I brought my legs together. He tried to roll the material over my hips as I wiggled from side to side. Both of us tugged at the stretchy material. It snapped back and pinched my skin. "Fuck me! Ouch!"

"I didn't think we were there in our relationship yet. I mean I barely know you." Brian smirked but I was confused.

"What?"

"You said 'fuck me.' I was just stating—"

"Seriously? You make jokes *now* when I am obviously in terrible danger of being suffocated by an undergarment?"

"Turn around." He spun me so my back was to him. My skin tingled as I felt his palms on my waist.

He hooked his thumbs under the fold of the slimmer, stretched it out, and slid it down, effectively coming cheek to cheek with my ass. I watched in the mirror as my face turned cherry red. I held on to the sink as I stepped out of the garment and turned back to face him. He held up the material.

"This is what you were wearing?" It had shrunk back to its original five-times-too-small size. "Kinky."

I snatched it from him. "Give me that." I looked around, trying to figure out where to put it since my clutch was entirely too small.

He took it back from me and threw it in the garbage can.

For a few beats we stood in the small bathroom staring at each other. I had never been so aware of my nakedness.

"I like those." He reached over and snapped the top of my thigh highs.

"Can I, um, have my dress?"

"I don't think you need it."

"Brian!"

"If you say so. I was just trying to help." He pulled the dress off the hook, knelt down in front of me, and motioned for me to step into it.

Sliding the dress slowly up, his hands guided the material and caressed my skin. Tugging it up over my hips, his hands slid around to my rear and his fingers teased the top of my panties. I reached back for the sink as my legs threatened to give out. I tucked my arms into the dress and closed my eyes as I slowly turned around and pulled my hair to the side so he could zip up the back. He turned me back around; our bodies were centimeters apart. I watched as his tongue slid out of his mouth and he licked his lips.

"Did I tell you how good you look tonight?" His voice was huskier than usual. He smelled like summer and it warmed me.

"I, well, I think so." My mouth suddenly felt as dry as the Sahara.

"Think so, huh? You look fucking unbelievable tonight."

He bridged the small gap between us and rested his lips gently on mine. I breathed out as he reached around and cupped my ass in his hands.

"Caroline." I could feel his warm breath on my neck. "I had no idea when I met you that I'd end up thinking about you every day."

"I think about you all the time." I tucked my hands around his waist and pulled him in. He lifted me so I was sitting on top of the sink. My dress rode up to the top of my thighs as I wrapped my legs around him.

"Can I ask you something?"

"Sure." It wasn't the least awkward position to be in when someone wants to ask a question.

"About Ryan—"

"I don't want Ryan." I know the words tumbled out of my mouth but at that moment, I realized I truly meant them.

"No?"

"I want you." And I did.

His kiss was hesitant at first. Sweet and soft. Before long, my bottom lip was between his teeth and his hands were cupping my breasts. He moved down and placed kisses and small bites on my chest along the top of my dress. His body rubbed against me and I could feel my panties dampen. The kisses became furious with want and he pulled me off the sink and held me against the wall. I was on the tips of my toes when he hiked up my dress and hooked his thumbs under the elastic of my thong.

Crouching down, he trailed kisses down my leg as he slowly pulled my panties off. Just when I thought I would orgasm from the anticipation he slowly stood in front of me, breathing heavily, smoothed my dress back down, and tucked my panties in his pocket.

He kissed me quickly on the lips and said, "If you're good, you'll get these back later."

He opened the door and walked out of the bathroom, leaving me to catch my breath and wonder what the fuck had just happened.

I banged my head against the wall and closed my eyes in an attempt to regain my equilibrium. I smoothed down the front of my dress and counted backward from ten before stepping over to the mirror to reapply my lipstick and fluff my hair.

The tingling between my legs graduated to full-on throbbing and I was left to wonder if I was experiencing the lady version of blue balls. Sighing, I pulled down a few paper towels to mop up the moisture that had collected between my legs.

I opened the door and slipped out of the bathroom. I saw Michael and Siobhan walking down the hall from the back of the restaurant.

"Finished with the interview?"

Siobhan turned scarlet and mumbled something about getting a drink before ducking away.

"You're looking positively flushed." Michael twisted a lock of my hair through his fingers.

"Your zipper's down." I frowned at him.

"Oh, well, yes." He made a show of slowly pulling it up.

"What did you do?"

"I didn't do anything. Siobhan and I just chatted a bit. She's very good with her mouth."

At that moment I knew what I felt whenever he was near me and it wasn't sexual. It was slimy. I wasn't getting knots in my stomach because I was sexually attracted to him. I was getting knots in my stomach because I was trying not to vomit.

"Jesus Christ, Michael! What the hell is wrong with you? You know, common sense is so fucking rare it should be classified as a super power." Shaking my head, I pulled him toward the back room.

"What?"

He honestly did not think he'd done anything wrong.

"Look. We have to sit down now and have dinner. Then I have to introduce you and you are supposed to read an excerpt from the novel. Do you think you can keep your dick in your pants long enough to get all that done?"

"Well, that depends on what you're doing now." He winked and pulled me closer.

"Gross! Michael, get off me!" I slapped him.

The flash from a camera temporarily blinded me.

"Seriously?" I yelled at the photographer.

"This is not over, Michael. Keep it in your fucking pants and keep your hands off Siobhan and me. Or I swear—"

"Swear what, Care?" His voice sounded dangerous as he challenged me.

I pulled my arm from his grip. "I'll tell Yolanda."

"Well." Michael straightened his posture and fixed his tie. "There's no need to be hasty. Let's get on with this."

He walked away, leaving me to question my sanity.

"What was that about?" Brian approached with a drink in his hand.

"Nothing I can't handle. Thank you." I took the drink and downed it. "I swear, I am not getting paid enough to babysit this guy."

Brian and I walked over to the table and took our seats. I wanted to get there before Siobhan, but she was already seated next to Michael, something I didn't want. Considering I didn't want to make a scene, I took my place next to her. At least I'd be able to keep her in check.

Throughout dinner, Siobhan and Michael giggled and whispered to each other, much to the dismay, it seemed, of Brian. He was clearly not happy with the company his sister was interested in keeping. I attempted numerous times to get her attention, or at least Michael's, but to no avail.

I was in the middle of torturing my cloth napkin when Brian put his hand on my knee. He looked at me and smiled.

"It's okay. What are they going to do in the middle of the restaurant?"

"You're right. I know you're right."

When it was time for me to introduce Michael, Brian reached under the table, squeezed my hand, and said, "You've got this."

The rest of the evening went well. I successfully managed not to stutter in front of a room full of people and Michael read eloquently—I almost forgot what a dickhead he was. At the end of the night, I made my rounds with Michael, taking care to thank everyone for spending the evening at the event. I even managed to get the photographer to delete the photo he took of me slapping Michael.

When I finally made my way to the front of the restaurant, I saw Brian standing there, holding my coat.

"Ready?"

"Yes." I looked around. "Where's Siobhan?"

"She made plans to stay with her friend Melissa. She already got a cab."

"So it's just us?" I slipped my arms in.

"Yep. That okay?"

"Of course it's okay. I need my panties back anyway." I pulled on my gloves as Brian wrapped my scarf around my neck.

"Not sure if you've been a good girl."

"No?"

"Nope."

"Will I at least get them back before I get home?"

"Home tomorrow. Tonight my place."

"Wouldn't that be awkward?"

"Nope. Ryan's out of town for the week. Los Angeles, I think."

Standing on the sidewalk, we waited for the car to pull up. When it did, Brian pulled me close and kissed me hard and fast. I was left to catch my breath and my balance as he opened the door for me to get in. Reaching in the car, he pulled my seat belt across my chest and across my lap, securing me in.

I watched as he walked around the car and slid in the other side, buckled his seat belt, and smiled. There was a deliberate space between us and after that kiss it was unwanted. I unbuckled my seat belt to slide closer but he just said, "Nope, not yet," and refastened my belt.

Chapter Twenty-Three

The ride back to Brian's place was quiet as I found myself, once again, looking out the window at the passing cars and falling snow. I thought about where everything was all going. I'd finally gotten the true one night stand out of my system when the girls and I were in Jamaica. Sure it was fun, but it wasn't what I was looking for. As fun as Ryan was, he wasn't what I was looking for, either. I had enough friends and I didn't need another one that clouded my judgment. I'd realized Brian was what I wanted. Thinking back, I was pretty sure I knew that the night I first met him.

He was always the one I thought about over the past month, he was the one who tied my stomach in knots. Brian, I was sure, was the one who would give me what I wanted. Needed. What I needed.

I was pulled out of my reverie when Brian opened the car door. I hadn't realized we'd arrived at his apartment. It was barely midnight and the bar was still alive. I took his hand and his fingers closed around mine. The way they fit together made me smile. I lifted our hands up and brought them to my mouth and kissed his knuckles. His smile lit up his face.

"I need to talk to Patrick, make sure everything is okay before we go up. Five minutes?"

Right. I remembered his brother, Patrick, was watching the bar.

"No problem. You want me to wait in the bar for you?"

"You don't have to." He handed me his keys. "You can wait upstairs for me if you want."

"Sure. I can do that."

With his hand still in mine, he steered me to the entrance.

"Before you go up, I want to introduce you to my brother."

Stepping up to the bar, he flagged down a tall good-looking guy with wavy red hair and a swath of freckles across his nose and cheeks.

"Pat!"

Patrick leaned over the bar and gave Brian a hug as I stood back. My hand felt odd since he let it go. Then Brian turned and reached for me.

"This is Caroline."

"Ah. The ever-elusive Caroline. I was beginning to think my brother made you up." He held out his hand and I took it. "It's very nice to meet you."

"It's lovely to meet you, too." I turned to Brian. "Meet you upstairs."

"I'll be up in a few minutes." His smile was brilliant.

I started to turn away but Brian hooked my arm and spun me to him, then planted a heavy kiss on my lips.

I heard him chuckle as I walked away, attempting to keep my balance.

Once upstairs, I kicked my shoes off at the door and draped my coat over the sofa.

Checking out his overstuffed bookshelf, I pulled out a copy of Ray Bradbury's *Fahrenheit 451*, my all-time favorite book. I was standing against the window, flipping through it, when Brian walked through the door.

Both of us froze as our eyes met. His tie was loosened and the top two buttons of his shirt were undone. With his hands in his pockets, he blew out a long breath.

"Hi." He undid his tie the rest of the way and tugged it from around his neck.

"Hi." I slid the book back on the shelf.

"You want a drink?" He walked over to the liquor cabinet.

"Sure."

I watched as he took ice cubes from the freezer and dropped them in two tumblers before taking a ginger ale from the fridge.

I stood rooted to the floor, fascinated as I watched him make the drinks. My stomach flip-flopped when I saw him take off his jacket and roll up his sleeves and turn on the stereo. I wanted to go to him but my legs had decided to stop working. Time slowed down as he turned to me, walked to the window, and handed me my drink. My fingers tingled when they met his.

"Are you cold?" He asked, noticing the goose bumps that littered my arms.

"No." My voice was breathier than usual and I cleared my throat.

Music filled the space. And filled me.

He took my hand, interlocked his fingers between mine, and led me to the couch. Sitting on either side of the vast piece of furniture, I felt like I had in the car. There was too much space between us, but for some reason, my brain turned into that of a girl on the verge of her first time, and I could figure out no way to express myself. I hated that feeling. I was a woman, successful and somewhat experienced. Why couldn't I take charge?

He leaned his head back on the sofa and closed his eyes. I wasn't sure what to say; I wasn't sure if I should make a move. My brain was blank of everything except him. Every dirty thought, every possible scenario of how the night would play out, raced through my head as I watched him relax. My stomach stirred again and heat began to rise from my toes. Suddenly, it clicked. I didn't need to wait for him to make the first move. I had the ability to take what I wanted.

Placing my drink on the end table, I slowly stood and stepped over until I was standing in front of him. Lazily, his eyes opened and he watched as I took the drink from his hand. I took a long sip before placing it on the table. He followed my hands as I hiked up my dress a bit and dropped my knees to the sofa, on either side of him, until I was straddled across his lap.

He massaged the tops of my thighs as I ran my fingers down his shirt, unfastening each button slowly.

"Care..."

Before he could finish his thought, I placed my lips on his, kissing him softly. The restraint was killing me. Every fiber of my body screamed for me to move faster, kiss harder. But the slow and steady pace felt good in my heart.

His tongue explored my mouth as I ran my fingers through his hair. He slipped his hands behind me, cupping my rear and pulling me into him. His hips pushed upward and I could feel him swell against his pants. He unzipped the back of my dress and tucked his hands inside the fabric, against my skin.

I gasped from his touch.

His lips moved to my neck and I let my head fall back as he

shifted on the couch and stood, carrying me to the door. With my back pressed against the door, he continued to kiss and nibble on every bit of my exposed skin.

He slowly slid me down so my feet were barely planted on the floor. My dress pooled around my feet. From his pocket, he pulled out my panties and slipped them on me, carefully sliding them up my legs. Throwing my dress to the side he reached over and picked up my shoes. He knelt down and slipped them onto my feet. He quickly kissed me, biting my lower lip before stepping back and picking his drink up from the table and gulping the liquid down. His eyes were hungry and he was breathing heavily. His eyes fell slowly from my head to my feet before they met mine again.

I stood, barely able to hold myself up against the door, wearing nothing but my bra, panties, thigh highs, and killer shoes. Back at the restaurant, I had felt a twinge of embarrassment, but in this moment, I felt sexier than I ever had in my life. I knew I looked good and his appreciative look boosted my confidence.

Quickly he closed the distance between us and pinned me to the door. His mouth was not gentle. It was as hungry as I was.

I shoved his shirt over his shoulders and he shook it off his arms, leaving it to fly across the room. My hands tugged his belt loose and before I could unbutton his pants, his hand cupped the swell between my legs. My gasp was louder than the last and he smiled as I pressed myself tighter against the door.

His face inches from mine, he kept his gaze glued to my eyes and I watched as he watched me rise until I was about to fall over the edge. Heat rose from inside me and I opened my mouth to draw in more air but all I could do was moan. His fingers worked their way inside me as his other hand pulled my breast out from the fabric of my bra. As he rolled my nipple between his thumb and forefinger, my nerves sang.

"Come for me, Caroline."

His fingers pushed in deeper as his thumb rubbed my clit.

I closed my eyes, anticipating the rush, when I felt his hand gently but firmly press against my neck.

"Look at me when you come."

With one hand working inside me furiously, he pinned me against the door with the other. Eyes locked, I could feel the end. From the pit of my stomach, vibrations racked through me until I yelled out.

"More."

His eyes reflected the pleasure he gave me. And the promise that it was only the beginning.

Another loud moan erupted from my throat and his mouth crashed on mine. He lifted me up and I wrapped my legs around him as he carried me to the back of the apartment.

We tumbled onto his bed with his body pressed on top of mine. He gently pushed my hair from my face and kissed my nose.

"You are so beautiful," he whispered, before gently tugging my earlobe between his teeth.

I could feel my cheeks flush and I smiled. "I feel beautiful with you."

"You should always feel beautiful." His nose grazed mine. "I can't get enough of you, Caroline."

Goose bumps covered me. "You can have as much as you want."

He buried his head in my neck and hugged me tighter. "We don't have to do this. We can hold off a bit."

"Do you want to hold off?"

"No. I just don't want you to think this is all I want from you."
He propped himself up on his elbows and looked me in the eye. "I,
of course, want this, but not *just* this. Does that make sense?"

I nodded. "It does. It was you from the beginning." I kissed the
corner of his mouth.

"From the second you walked in the bar, Caroline. I knew." His
tongue ran along my lower lip.

"I want this, Brian. I want you."

Every touch, every kiss, every breath, made me want him more.
Thoughts of excitement, newness, and surprise stung my eyes.

He lifted himself up, kneeling between my legs. Slowly, he pulled
off my shoes, then each stocking. I lifted my hips as he tucked his fingers into my panties and tugged them off. Leaning over, he reached
behind my back, unhooked my bra, slipped it off, and tossed it on
the floor.

I lay in the middle of his bed with my hair splayed wide and my
arms resting above my head as he stood and stepped back, crossing
his arms over his chest. I was exposed. On full display. And I loved
every second of it.

"Every inch of you is perfect." He shoved his hands in his pockets.

"Perfection is perception," I countered.

"And perception is reality." He pulled off his unbuckled belt and
placed it on his dresser. "Slide down to the edge of the bed."

I sat up, scooted to the edge of his bed, and reached for his pants
when he stood in front of me. But he playfully gripped my wrists
and guided me back down to the bed.

He leaned over me, his hands still gripping my wrists. "Tonight is
all about you, Caroline. Your being here, being mine, is more than
enough for me at the moment. So I want to make you feel good."

"But—"

He placed his finger on my lips. "No, no. Believe me. I will feel everything you feel. Let me do this for you."

It was as if he knew what I wanted as he began his slow trip down the length of my body. He spent time at my neck, kissing and nibbling just above my collarbone.

"Mmm. That's nice." I closed my eyes.

His tongue circled one nipple, then the other. He took his time as his tongue moved slowly and deliberately and his teeth barely scraped the hardened nub as he pulled it into his mouth and sucked. He released me with a pop and gently blew on the moist skin. I shivered and pitched forward.

"Brian." I breathed out his name as I fell back to the mattress.

"Good girl," he murmured between tiny kisses along my rib cage. "Your skin is so smooth."

I could feel the clench between my thighs when his fingers dug into my hips and he pressed his teeth into my flesh. Warmth spread from my center and I could feel the swell between my legs. My thighs quivered in anticipation.

"You have goose bumps." He ran his hands along the tops of my thighs as if he were trying to warm me up.

"Your fault. You're driving me crazy." I smiled and turned my head to look at him.

He bit his bottom lip before saying, "You think *this* is driving you crazy?" His chuckle did me in and I knew I was in for it.

"Awfully confident." I drew up one leg and pressed it against the other, denying him access.

His hands pulled gently and I shook my head. "Caroline."

"Brian." I giggled before I relaxed my legs.

He gently spread them as he knelt between them. He teased and gently kissed each inner thigh as my feeble attempt to steady myself crumbled.

His lips kissed me everywhere. His breath was warm against me. His fingers explored and his tongue teased. I felt his fingers pinch and open me wide before he plunged his tongue inside me. Between his mouth and his fingers, I was brought to the edge over and over, though he didn't let me fall off completely. I fisted his gray down comforter as I twisted and writhed. Each time it became too much and I began to pull away, he dragged me back in until I was finally able to sit up and lean into him.

"More." My voice was hoarse. "Please, Brian. More."

I did all I could to push myself closer against him. Reaching over his back, I hooked my fingers in his belt loops and tugged his body closer. He responded with a growl as he pushed his hands under my legs and lifted them up, flopping me back down on the bed, but not before I raked my nails up his back. He muscled my legs as far apart as he could and continued to suck and lick me until a wave of tremors shook me until I felt dizzy.

My entire body vibrated as I yelled, "Oh my God, Brian!"

My thighs squeezed against his face and my toes curled and cramped. I was mid tremor when he grabbed my hand and lifted me to my feet. My legs felt like they were going to give out and I fell back to the bed. Scooping me up, he stepped to the side of the bed, bent down, and pulled the covers back before placing me back down. My head settled into the pillow as I basked in the afterglow of the orgasm that was still knocking on my lady bits.

"Be right back." He padded out the door.

Be right what?

He returned quickly with a bottle of water, top unscrewed. I took it and gulped down half the bottle before handing it back to him.

He watched me as he drank deeply and smiled as he placed the bottle on the table.

"What are you smiling at?" I fell back on the pillow.

"You."

"Me? I'm funny?" I crossed my eyes and made fish lips at him. I felt comfortable enough to act like a goofball and it felt good.

It felt better than good.

It felt amazing.

He crossed his eyes back at me and laughed. "No. You're awesome. I can't believe you're here."

"I can." I reached for the bottle of water.

"You can?" He cocked his eyebrow with the question.

"Yep. I saw the way you looked at me."

"And how did I look at you?"

"The way you look at someone when you like them."

"I'll have to relearn my poker face."

"Don't do that. I like it."

"Well, in that case—" He leaned in and kissed me. When he pulled away my eyes were still closed and my lips were still puckered. He pinched my lips and I pulled away, laughing.

"Now come in here with me before I get cold." I patted the bed.

"Yes, ma'am." He unbuttoned his pants and they dropped to the floor. His boxer briefs strained for a moment before he slipped those off, too, and slid into the bed next to me.

Both of us lay on our sides, close enough to touch. He trailed his fingers along my skin.

"You okay?" he asked.

"Perfect. Why?"

"I don't know. I sort of feel like I was torturing you for a bit there."

"You sort of were. But I liked it."

"Do you need a break?"

A break? There was more? "You mean I need more of a break than what you've already given me?"

"Yeah. I guess so."

I was quiet a moment as I contemplated him. Smiling, I reached down and fisted my hand around him.

His face broke out into a grin and he said, "I'll take that as a no."

He leaned over and reached behind him to open the nightstand drawer. I heard the foil tear and felt the bed jostle a bit as he rolled on a condom before he positioned himself on top of me, keeping eye contact. I spread my legs apart to help him settle in.

"Ready?" His voice was quiet.

I nodded slightly. "More than."

I felt myself swell around him as he entered me. We each drew in a breath and held still, taking in the first feeling. He leaned down to kiss me. As the kiss deepened he began to move slowly in and out. I moved my hips with him until we fell into a slow, steady rhythm. Dropping to his elbows, he ran his hands along my cheeks and kissed my eyelids. Each thrust was gentle and deliberate. I felt each movement down to my toes.

"Beautiful Caroline." He whispered in my ear and my skin tingled.

Our rhythm matched, we were in total sync. There was no ferocity to the lovemaking, as there had been with the foreplay. The urgency still surrounded us and I wrapped my legs tighter around him and hugged him closer. The need to crawl inside him was overwhelming.

I rocked my hips hard in an attempt to get closer to him. He met my thrust with one of his own. Back and forth we pressed into each other and the feel of him inside me pushed me to my limits until I clenched around him and cried out.

"Oh my God, Brian!" My legs tightened around him as the orgasm crashed over me. "Brian, yes!"

He rocked harder into me until my legs fell limp to the side. Slowing down, he kissed my neck and I nearly jumped out of my skin.

"You okay?"

"Sensitive," I managed to say between haggard breaths and he chuckled before he stilled. He was waiting for me to catch my breath. When I finally calmed down, I smiled and shifted my weight until we rolled and I was on top of him.

"Well, this is nice." He smiled as I leaned down to kiss him, my hair wild and curly curtained around us.

"Nice, huh?" I bit his lip and tugged. I reached back and wrapped my hand around him as I lifted myself up and guided him back inside me. His groan was music to my ears.

"Maybe a little more than nice." He winked, though I could tell he was struggling to gain his composure.

With my hands on his chest, I pushed myself up until I was sitting across him and he was deep inside me. Slowly I rocked back and forth and his hands moved from my thighs up my body to my breasts and back down again.

"Still *nice*?" I asked as I pressed my hands into his chest and grinded into him.

"C-C-Caroline." He stammered. "Oh my God, Care."

My thighs tightened as I felt my climax build. He reached around and grabbed my ass, pulling me in faster, his hips thrusting up and slamming into me. I grabbed his hands and leaned over him, holding them over his head. My breasts pushed into his chest, my lips found his.

He pulled his hands away and wrapped them around me tight, holding me to him. Together we thrust and pushed until I erupted and shook. Two thrusts later and he was the one calling out my name.

I lay on top of him, shuddering and feeling his vibrations. I closed my eyes to gain some semblance of calm and when I did, I realized I'd already found my balance.

Every emotion I felt was raw and exposed. It was like I knew what he felt, what he thought. I was sure my heart showed on my face, as much as his heart shone through. The longer I looked into his eyes, the farther I fell. Instinctively, I knew he would be there to catch me.

* * *

The next morning I zoomed past my usual wake up time and slept until almost nine. Raising my arms over my head, I stretched long and hard, smiling when I thought about the night before. Slowly, I opened my eyes and looked around. Sunlight streamed through the window. My dress was hanging on the closet door. And Brian was nowhere to be found. I flashed back to the morning after he slept at my apartment and frowned.

The frown was short-lived because, as if on cue, he walked into the room carrying a steaming cup of coffee and wearing low-slung pajama pants.

"Good morning." He placed the coffee cup on the table and leaned in to kiss me.

He'd already brushed his teeth. I remembered Steven used to hate it if I didn't get right up and brush my teeth. I had to rein in the panic attack. I had no toothbrush and Brian wasn't Steven.

"Good morning."

"Did you sleep well?"

"I did. Thank you. When did you get up?"

"Like an hour ago. Had to say goodbye to my brother. He went back home."

"So we're alone?" I propped myself up on my elbow.

"We are."

I pulled myself up and planted small kisses on his neck and shoulders.

"So, last night, I had Sarah drop off a bag at the bar."

I pulled back. "You did?"

"Yeah. She packed stuff for you. Extra clothes. A toothbrush."

"That was awfully presumptuous. Did you think I was a sure thing?" I teased and resumed kissing his body.

"Not exactly, but just in case, I didn't want you to have to rush off."

"That was thoughtful." I wanted to pay attention to what he was saying but he was just so damn delicious.

"I thought maybe we could do something today."

"Like what?"

"Go out to breakfast, go to a museum. I don't know."

"Sounds like fun. But first—" I pulled him down to the bed and climbed on top of him until I was straddling him. My fingers teased the top of his pajama pants and it was my turn to watch the goose bumps cover his body. "I have an idea of how we can get this day started."

"Yeah?" A slow, sexy grin spread across his mouth.

"Yep." I leaned down, pressing my mouth to his.

Chapter Twenty-Four

It was just after eleven when Sarah called me. Brian and I were getting ready to head into the city for the afternoon.

"Care, what the hell happened last night?"

"What do you mean? I spent the night at Brian's. Thank you for packing a bag for me by the way."

"You mean you don't know?"

"Don't know what?"

"Does Brian have a computer?"

"Of course he does." I placed my hand over the phone and asked him, "Do you have a computer?"

He nodded and I put her on speaker.

"Search yourself."

"Search my what?"

"Yourself. Go on the computer and search your name."

"Okay."

Brian typed my name into the search engine.

"Did you do it?"

"Yeah, what's all this?"

"Click on any article, make sure it's some sort of tabloid, though."

Brian clicked on the first article. A huge photo of me slapping Michael stared back at me under the heading "Lover's Quarrel."

"Holy shit."

"Do you see what I see?" Sarah was obviously alternating between concern and all out laughter. "Do you see the big red arrow pointing to the big red circle?"

Brian moved closer to the screen. Both of us stared for a moment before we figured out what was highlighted.

Michael had what looked like a pair of white panties sticking out of his pocket, circled in red by the author of the article.

"You weren't wearing white panties," Brian said seriously.

"No shit I wasn't wearing white panties."

"Ha! Care, they think you and Michael are doing it," Sarah yelled. Thank goodness she was on speaker or I was sure I would have lost my hearing.

A call beeped in and I looked at the phone. Yolanda.

"Oh shit, Sarah. I have to go. That's Yolanda."

"Good luck and I want all the deets on your night with Brian's love stick."

Brian suppressed a laugh.

"You're on speaker."

"I know. Later!"

She clicked off and I switched over to Yolanda's call.

"Hi, Yolanda."

"I hope you have an explanation. I thought I told you not to get involved with Michael."

"I didn't."

"Well, it sure as hell looks differently. I want you in my office now. Michael and Mr. Little are already on their way. We need to figure out a way to diffuse this before it goes viral or whatever you kids call it."

She clicked off before I could answer. I plopped into the chair.

"Son of a bitch."

"We both know those aren't your panties."

"Right." I stared off into space, trying to wrap my head around the situation.

"Then whose panties are they?"

I knew whose they were. The question was whether or not I should tell Brian.

"Wait." Brian stood up and walked back to the computer. He studied the screen for a minute before he spoke again. "Wasn't that photo taken after my sister interviewed him?"

I could only nod.

"Are those my—" He brought his hands to his head. "Are those my *sister's* panties?"

I shrugged but the look on my face told him all he needed to know.

"I will fucking kill that guy!"

"Wait, wait. We don't know for sure. You said your sister went to her friend Melissa's? Call your sister and ask her again where she slept."

His phone was out of his pocket before I finished my sentence. Dialing his sister's number, he stalked back to his room and slammed the door. Though most of the conversation was loud and muffled, I did get confirmation that I was right. They were Siobhan's panties. Looked like two of us got lucky last night.

I battled my inner "You go girl!" against two things:

1. I was mentally high-fiving Brian's sister. Though I wasn't sure where he and I were in our relationship, I was pretty sure I needed to side with him on that particular point.

2. I wasn't sure if I could actually proceed with the mental high five because it was Michael she slept with. Then again, we've all slept with worse.

I tried to tamp down the judgment, I really did. I wasn't into slut shaming. Like I mentioned, you go girl! But it was *Michael*. It could have been anyone but him. He was such an icky douche bag, it gave me the heebie-jeebies just thinking about the fact that I'd even entertained the possibility he was sexually attractive. Physically? A fantastic specimen. However, his personality dropped his stock exponentially.

When Brian reentered the living space, I could tell he was not handling whatever information he'd just received from his sister very well.

"She's on her way to your office with him."

"Michael?"

"Who else?" His tone dripped with annoyance.

I held up my hands and stepped back. "Look, don't be mad at me. I didn't do anything."

"Did you know?"

"That she was going to his place? No, of course not."

"Why is she so stupid? I love my sister but, man, she makes some really shitty decisions."

"I know it's not my place but she's an adult, you know. At twenty-six, she can't really be considered a child."

"And I'm thirty-three. Still doesn't give her the right not to use common sense. Anyone could tell that guy was—*is*—bad news."

Funny, I hadn't known how old he was. I'd never thought to ask.

"Look, why don't you come with me? You can sit with her while I lose my job."

"Fine. Let's go."

He threw on his jacket and opened the door, motioning for me to exit.

The train ride there was filled with icy silence. Brian was fuming, texting furiously on his phone. I could only assume Siobhan was on the other end and by the force with which he was stabbing the screen, I was certain she was getting a complete dressing down. I felt bad for her. I knew what it was like to make bad decisions and have to live with the consequences. Hell, I'd made a bad decision that lasted five long years.

The building was eerily quiet, just the way I liked it. I enjoyed staying late at work or coming in on the weekends to get work done in the peace and quiet. I ran my hand along the wall as we waited for the elevator. I wasn't ready to say goodbye to the job. I'd worked there only two weeks, though it felt much longer. I had so much more to learn and I knew I'd learn it from Yolanda. It was a shame I couldn't make it work.

The elevator dinged when we hit our floor and I told Brian to wait in the lobby. His sister was already curled up in one of the chairs looking out the window at the city that never sleeps.

I took a deep breath before opening the door to Yolanda's office. Mr. Little, Yolanda, and Michael were all sitting in the room, deep in discussion.

"Caroline. Please come in. Have a seat." Mr. Little motioned for me to sit next to him.

"Glad you could make it." I didn't like Michael's tone.

"I got here as fast as I could."

"Okay. We've heard what happened from Michael. We want to know what happened from your point of view." Yolanda had her pen poised, ready to take notes. The yellow legal pad did nothing to make me feel any better about the situation.

I spent the next fifteen or so minutes recounting the evening from the time I reached the restaurant to the time I left. I did what I could to keep Siobhan out of the mix but with the photo circulating with her panties sticking out of his pocket and the fact that they already knew she'd spent the night with him, there was no getting around mentioning her.

"So, they were not your, er, um"—Mr. Little stumbled over his words—"panties?"

"No, sir. They weren't."

"What was it exactly that prompted you to slap Michael?"

I closed my eyes and shuddered and retold the conversation he and I had in the hall. I mentioned how he insinuated Siobhan's oral prowess and how he propositioned me.

"I did not proposition you!" Michael leaped from his chair.

"You will sit down, Mr. Mortimer. Right now." Yolanda's tone was icy.

I could feel my job slipping from between my fingers and I figured I had nothing left to lose.

"Truth be told, it isn't the first time, Michael. And I am quite sure, with an ego the size of yours, it won't be the last. Now, don't misunderstand me. I can handle you. I understand you're a slimy horn ball who gets his jollies off on preying on women you consider unable to fight off your advances. You're gross. Your behavior is unacceptable. Unfortunately, you're also a brilliant author. Even more unfortunately, that fact inflates your ego more than I would ever think is humanly possible."

I turned my attention to Yolanda. "Ms. Page, I love this job. I love working here. I know I have a lot to learn. I wish I could erase the photo that's spreading like wildfire all over the Internet. I can't help but feel as though I've let you down in some way. But please know, if I had any idea as to Mr. Mortimer's intentions with Siobhan, I would have put a stop to it one way or another."

I couldn't stop talking. "Mr. Little, I want to thank you for the opportunity to work for you and your wonderful company. I only wish my tenure could have been extended."

The room was silent. I contemplated standing up and leaving, but Michael was blocking my way to the door.

"Are you giving notice?" Mr. Little asked.

"Well, I figured, after all this mess, you wouldn't want me working here anymore."

"That's stupid." Yolanda was blunt. "You're the best assistant editor I've had since I started this business, and that's saying something. Indeed, you do have quite a bit to learn, but I think you have a bright future in this business."

"I don't want her working on my books anymore." Michael pointed at me.

"Well, after this book, that will no longer be an issue." Mr. Little stood and buttoned his jacket. Even at the last minute on a Sunday, he was wearing a suit. "We will not be renewing your contract, nor will we be considering any more of your work. I built this company from the ground up. We have standards. We have morals. And we expect those who work for us to hold the same values. Are we clear?"

My mouth hit the floor. I looked back and forth among Yolanda, Mr. Little, and Michael.

Michael jumped from his seat. "You can't do this to me! I make more money than half your other authors combined! Yolanda, tell him!"

"I have nothing to say." She closed her mouth in a thin line of nude lipstick.

Mr. Little stuffed his Jets hat on his head and pulled on his gloves. "My word is final. You will no longer come into this office. The rest of the work that is completed on your manuscript will be communicated via e-mail, telephone, or post. I've sat back and watched your shenanigans and have had to spend more money on public relations because of you. You make us money? Not after we spend it fixing your shenanigans! It's just not worth it anymore.

"Now, if you'll excuse me, I have some grandkids to visit. Yolanda, as we discussed."

"Thank you, Oscar. Caroline, I expect to see you bright and early tomorrow. We have some things to discuss. Michael, I need one more word with you."

Rooted to my seat, I knew I should get up and leave but I was still in shock with what had gone down.

"Caroline? Tomorrow?"

"Yes, Yolanda. Thank you."

Back in the lobby, I saw Brian rubbing his sister's back. It was such a nice thing to see. I knew the anger he'd displayed earlier was only because of his concern for her. It was endearing and made me feel more than happy with my decision to see where he and I would go.

"Ahem."

Brian looked up and smiled. "You okay?"

"Yeah. I'm good."

"Caroline, I am so sorry I got you fired. He just seemed so nice. I didn't think I was hurting anyone."

"I didn't get fired. He did."

"What?"

"They are not renewing his contract. I get to stay on. As a matter of fact, I am to report bright and early tomorrow morning."

"That's great news." Brian hugged me tight. I never wanted him to let go.

"I know! Crazy. I thought for sure I was getting the boot."

I pulled away from the embrace in time to see Michael stalk toward the elevators, muttering under his breath. Our eyes met.

"You! This is your fault. But you know what? Screw you. Screw this fucking place. I have more talent in my fucking pinky than anyone else you could bring in here. You'll see."

I saw him notice Siobhan. "Oh, here." He threw something at her that landed at her feet. "You can have your fucking panties back. I don't need them anyway."

Siobhan cried out in embarrassment. Brian sent a right hook across Michael's cheek as the elevator door slid open.

"I'm sorry," Brian whispered.

"Don't be." I tiptoed up and kissed him.

The last time I ever saw Michael Mortimer he was holding his cheek with a shocked look on his face as the elevator doors closed.

"Come on," Brian said. "Let's take the stairs."

Chapter Twenty-Five

When I finally made it home, Sarah and Melody were in the kitchen poring over take-out menus. It looked as though we'd be having sushi tonight.

"You're back!" Melody ran over and hugged me, lifting me off the ground. "Now spill! I want to hear all the dirty details about you and Brian. I went with Sarah to drop off your bag at the bar. His brother is cute."

"Easy. He's married."

Melody pouted. "He's still cute."

I hadn't had time to take off my coat or drop my bag, and both of my best friends in the world were sitting side by side on the couch waiting to hear about all of my drama. I'm not ashamed to say it felt good. I'd spent too long living vicariously through them and it was pretty freaking awesome that I finally had dirt to dish.

"Let me take off my coat, get a drink, and order some food. We have a lot to talk about."

The three of us sat cross-legged around the coffee table sharing pints of noodles, spring rolls, and three rolls of sushi. And, of course, wine. We were working on our second bottle when I got to the part where I slept at Brian's apartment.

"Holy shit, girl! He's hot and sexy!" Melody had obviously had more than her share of the two bottles of wine.

"I know, right?" I giggled, downed my glass, and opened a third bottle.

"So I take it you didn't need an ice pack this morning?" Sarah asked.

"No, I didn't." I threw a pillow at her. "It wasn't like that, though. I mean it was. It was hot and sensual and amazing but mostly, it was—"

"Perfect?"

"Yes. Perfect. It's like I woke up and realized where I am supposed to be and it's with him. And then in the next thought I asked myself why it took me so long to figure it out, you know? Like somehow I knew all along it was supposed to be Brian but I didn't let myself go there because he wasn't 'the target' or some stupid shit."

"Well, I for one am very happy you opened your eyes. I mean Ryan, what can I say? He was definitely fuck-me-stupid hot but he wasn't for you. You need more, what's the word?"

"Structure? Stability?" Melody piped in after a loud hiccup.

"Maybe. But you know what I mean."

"I do." And I really did. "Is it weird that I miss him already?"

"Nope. Not at all!"

"It's like you want to write 'I miss you' on a rock and throw it at his face so he knows how much it hurts to miss him."

I shook my head. Only Melody would come up with shit like that.

"Sure, I guess. But that's not even the best part! I have to tell you what happened when I was called into the office."

"Pantygate."

I looked at Melody. "What?"

"That's what they called it on some blog. Pantygate."

"Great. Ugh." I told them all about how I told off Michael. I was pretty proud of myself.

"Love it. It's like I told my principal, I might be a lady but when I get mad I become an evil demon bitch who will make assholes wish they were never born." Sarah always did have a way with the visual.

I continued with the story of how I found out and Brian's reaction. I walked them through the meeting and ended with Brian punching Michael.

"I wish I could have seen your face when Brian hit him. Must've been awesome."

"It kind of was." I spoke through a mouth full of food. "He totally stood up for his sister, you know? She was a bit of a mess. Especially when Michael threw her underwear. I felt bad for her."

"Yeah, she seems like a nice girl. Mel, you'd like her."

Melody cringed. "I'd rather that than the cold shoulder I'm getting from Danny. I swear, I'm off alcohol."

We stared at her as she lifted the wineglass to her lips.

"Well, not *now* but in the future. Alcohol is bad for my legs."

"They swell?" I asked, suddenly concerned.

"No, they fucking spread like soft butter. I haven't heard from Danny since the night at the bar. Whatever. I think my guardian angel drinks enough for the both of us."

"Danny's out of town." I remembered a conversation Brian and I had earlier.

"Well, isn't that great. Doesn't mean he can't call me. Fuck him."

"Sweetie," Sarah began, "did you give him your number?"

The blank stare on Melody's face told us the answer.

"You dipshit! How is he supposed to call if he doesn't know your number?" Sarah threw half a spring roll at Melody.

Melody picked up a noodle and flung it at her.

"Maybe I should stop drinking. When I'm not in my right mind, my left mind gets pretty crowded."

"So, what's up with Brian's black eye?"

Sarah changed the subject. Not that we didn't want to hear Melody's woes but sometimes there were so many. Maybe we were terrible friends.

"You didn't tell me he had a black eye." And Melody was back from her twenty-second trip to her personal black hole of sex partners.

"He didn't want to talk about it."

"Do you think it was about you? I mean, Ryan hit him, right?"

"Wow. How the hell did you go from living in Steven's shadow to having two men fight over you?" Melody stretched out on the floor.

"I don't know. I just know he doesn't want to talk about it." My phone rang and I looked at the screen. "Speak of the devil."

"Brian?" Melody sat up as straight as an arrow.

"Nope. Ryan." I held out my finger. "Hello?"

"Care! How are you? Sorry I didn't call. I'm in Cali meeting with my agent."

"That's okay. So, what's up?"

"I just thought it would be cool if you and I had dinner when I got back. Just to catch up."

"Dinner when you get back?"

Both girls looked like they would pop blood vessels.

"I don't know if that would be a good idea."

"Oh, right. Brian. Well, I mean, we can have dinner as friends. We are friends, right?"

"Yeah, we're friends."

"So dinner on Saturday?"

I didn't know what to say so I blurted out, "Make it lunch."

I shrugged and made a face at the girls. I wasn't sure if dinner was a good idea. Lunch sounded safer.

I heard Ryan laugh on the other end of the phone. "Lunch it is. See you then."

I clicked off and dropped my phone like it was tainted with bubonic plague.

"You really think that's a good idea?" Sarah pulled out her teacher voice again.

"What was I supposed to say?"

"You were supposed to say no. You were supposed to say that you're giving it a go with Brian and that you appreciate the offer and thanks but no thanks."

Sarah stood abruptly and walked to the kitchen.

"It's not like she's going to fuck him at lunch." Melody intervened.

"Of course not. I'll tell Brian. Plus, if I am going to find out how Brian got the black eye, I'm going to have to ask Ryan. And it will give me a chance to make it clear that there will be no more hanky-panky between us. We'll just be friends without the 'who fuck' part of the equation."

"I guess," Sarah said as she put leftovers in the fridge.

She was clearly not happy with my decision. I was a bit put off, truth be told. Wasn't she the one who'd lectured me on taking charge of things and not hiding and running away?

"What's your deal, Sarah?"

"I don't have a deal."

"You have an attitude."

"Uh-oh." Melody curled up on the couch to watch the interaction.

"No, Care. I don't. I just don't want you falling back into your old habits."

"Nothing about this screams 'old habits.' Since when is it a habit of mine to pluck a guy from the bar and bring him home? Bang a complete stranger on vacation? Finally find a guy who likes me for who I am and not what he can mold me into?"

"I'm just saying. I'm your friend. I want you to be careful."

"Well, thanks for the concern but I think I and my lady balls got this one. Maybe you should start paying more attention to your old habits and let me do what's best for me."

"That wasn't called for," Melody piped in.

"Oh, shut up! You two bitch because I'm not happy then you question my motives when I am."

"I didn't bitch." Melody looked sad. I shouldn't have dragged her into the argument.

"Care—"

I didn't give Sarah time to finish her thought. "Don't 'Care' me. I think you like it when I'm a weepy mess. When my life is as pathetic as yours."

"Fuck you!" Sarah yelled.

"Fuck you twice!" I screamed back at her.

I stormed into my room and slammed the door. I barely spoke to her the rest of the week.

Chapter Twenty-Six

The week flew by and I felt like a weight was lifted off my shoulders. I didn't have Michael texting, calling, or e-mailing every five minutes wondering where his edits were. Yolanda was on fire, probably fueled by the fact that without Michael bringing in the revenue, we were going to have to stack up a shitload of fantastic manuscripts. The slush pile was about to become a skyscraper.

Brian took the news of my lunch with Ryan well. Not that I thought he would be mad. Well, maybe just a little, but his reaction was anything but. I let him know about the phone call and the fact that I'd changed it from dinner to lunch. I told him that I'd let Ryan know there would be no more hide the pickle. He didn't need to hear any of that. He understood why I needed to say what I had to say in person. He got it.

Siobhan stopped by during the week to apologize for the millionth time. She and Melody finally had the chance to meet and they hit it off. Apparently they made plans to hang out.

Sarah and I were on polite terms but certainly not like we were. It made me sad that I thought I would lose one of my best friends over something so trivial. Melody swore she knew we would work it out but I knew there had to be some sort of come to Jesus before either of us would budge. I was looking forward to that conversation about as much as I was looking forward to lunch with Ryan later that day. The only silver lining was that I would meet up with Brian at the bar and hang out there with friends until he closed.

For the most part, everything in my life was coming together. I felt more like myself than I ever had. I had a job I loved, a boyfriend who actually cared more about me than what others thought about me. A small part of me was waiting for the other shoe to drop. But since I was more of a glass half full girl anymore, I dismissed the notion and headed out. I figured I'd get a little shopping done before lunch. I needed to update my work wardrobe.

I was in the store trying on blouses when I heard the nasally voice. Betsy was in the next dressing room. I wasn't sure if I should hightail it out of there, hide, or face the music. I chose the latter. After all, what the hell did she have on me? If she was still with Steven, then kudos to her. If leftovers were her thing, then she was more than welcome to sample from the buffet.

I handed the saleswoman a few items I wasn't interested in and started riffling through the racks again. I didn't need much but I was in a great mood and new clothes were always an added perk. Unfortunately, I turned the corner to check out the sales rack and ran right into Steven. The shock on his face was quickly replaced by a condescending smirk as he put his phone in his pocket.

"Well, look who's out and about. You're looking well, Caroline."

"Steven." I nodded and tried to step around him but he blocked my path.

"I mean it. You look good."

"Happiness and self-awareness do that to a person. Excuse me."

He stepped in front of me again. "I miss you."

"Isn't your girlfriend in the dressing room?"

"She isn't my girlfriend. She isn't you."

"Last I checked I wasn't your girlfriend."

"Not anymore."

"Thank God for that. Seriously, Steven. Leave me alone. I don't have anything to say to you."

He gripped my arm. "We never had closure. I think we should talk about what happened."

I pulled away from him. "There is nothing to talk about. I've said all I needed to say."

"What happened to you? You always used to be so accommodating. Look, I was stupid—" He raked his hands through his hair. I used to think that was sexy. Used to.

"Too bad you can't fix stupid." I hung up the clothes I was carrying on a random rack.

"That isn't fair. You're going to throw away five good years because of a *mistake*? Because that's what Betsy was, a mistake."

I pointed to the purse he was holding. "Looks like your mistake is still hanging around. Look, Steven. I'm not mad. I'm really not. I'm happy that your mistake gave me the opportunity to move on, find myself. I've never felt better."

"Well, I'm miserable."

"And I'm not. Look, you didn't fight for me when I was around so don't cry now that I'm gone."

"Caroline. We were engaged. Engaged! Doesn't that mean anything to you?"

I looked at him a moment. "It does, actually. But not in the way it once did."

I turned and headed for the door.

"Care, we were in love. You can't walk away from love."

I looked over my shoulder as I opened the door to the shop. "Steven, love is a blind whore filled with bat-shit crazy and a shitty sense of humor."

I headed toward the restaurant, window-shopping along the way. I still needed clothes but I had to get the hell out of the store before I lost my mind. Not that I wanted Steven back or anything, but I just couldn't continue the conversation. Hopefully he'd gotten the hint. Sometimes people are like clouds. It's a brighter day when they disappear.

My phone rang. As soon as I checked out the display, an insta-smile the size of North Dakota spread across my face.

"Well, hello."

"What are you wearing?" Brian teased.

"Oh nothing. Just the smile you left me with."

"Good. Keep that outfit on later when I see you. What time are you meeting Ryan?"

"Thirty minutes or so."

"Just so you know, he moved out."

"What the hell happened between you two? I would never want to get in the middle of your friendship."

"You didn't."

"Then why do I feel responsible?"

"Because you worry too much. Because you're amazing. Don't worry about it. He and I will patch things up. This isn't the first time we've acted like bitchy schoolgirls and I'm sure it won't be the last.

But it is for the better that he moved out. Now we can have sex anywhere we want."

I totally pictured his smirk and it made me giggle.

"After this past week, I wasn't sure there were any more places in the apartment to christen."

"Oh, you'd be surprised. Look, I've got to get a delivery. You have fun and call me if you need anything."

"I will. See you soon."

"Can't wait."

We clicked off and I noticed a spring in my step that wasn't there before. Brian encouraged me to feel amazing. Who was I to deny the feeling?

A bit later I opened the door to the restaurant and, despite being ten minutes early, I saw Ryan sitting in the corner booth. He stood as soon as he saw me. I approached the table and he leaned in to kiss me. He frowned when I maneuvered in time for his lips to plant on my cheek.

"How've you been?"

"Great. You? How was Los Angeles? You look nice and tanned."

"It was good. Taking a new direction. Apparently I'm getting too old to model in my underwear. David Beckham can do it but I'm too old! My agent set me up with a few calls and I got a walk on role on a detective drama. She thinks it's the direction I should go."

"Well, that's great. I'm sure many women will be disappointed not to see you in your boxer briefs, though." I picked up the menu and realized I was starving. Served me right for not eating breakfast that morning.

"Ha!"

His laugh was light and reminded me why I had been into him in the first place. It was just unfortunate he wasn't what I was looking for.

"How's work for you? I mean, the new job going okay?"

I recounted last weekend's debacle, stealthily leaving out the details about Brian and me. I was sure he knew what was going on by the slow-to-heal shiner Brian was sporting but I didn't think it was necessary to rub it in his face.

"Sounds like a trip! At least you kept your job, right?"

"Absolutely. What are you having? I'm starving!"

After we figured out what we were having and ordered, Ryan leaned back and put his hands behind his head. He looked at me as if he were thinking of what to say.

"What's up?" I asked, knowing he had something to say.

"Nothing."

"Nothing? Brian's black eye doesn't say 'nothing' to me."

It was out there. I'd broached the topic and I hadn't thrown up. Score one for me and my stomach of steel!

"Ahh. I was wondering when that would come up. He and I had a, uh, disagreement."

"About?"

"You."

I knew it! "Me?"

"Yeah. Apparently he was having some sort of feelings for you and asked me what my intentions were."

"Intentions, huh? And what did you say?"

"I told him that I thought you and I could be good friends. He said he wanted more. Words were exchanged. I punched him. End of story."

"That doesn't sound like the whole story to me. There's something in there you aren't telling me."

The waitress brought over a basket of bread and though carbs were my nemesis, I tore off a piece, slathered it with butter, and popped it in my mouth. Ryan watched my every move. It was a bit unsettling.

"Well, there was someone else there."

"Who?"

"I forget her name. Michelle or Maria. It isn't important."

"Wait. What?"

"Look, you and I, I figured, were having fun. I was having fun with another girl, too. Brian wasn't happy. Said I wasn't treating you right."

It was my turn to lean back and contemplate him.

"So I wasn't the only person you were fucking?"

"Well, no. But it wasn't like that. Why, was I the only person *you* were fucking?"

The waitress refilled my iced tea. I ignored the question and whispered, "Then what was it like?"

"I know what was happening the first night we hooked up. It was a one night stand, a fling. Then I saw you the next day. It was weird. How was I supposed to know I'd run into you again?"

"So, you what? Felt *sorry* for me?" Oh hell-fucking-no. "You called *me* and asked *me* out again. You didn't have to do that. You could have left it at awkward. No harm, no foul."

"No. I know. It's just when I saw you, I thought maybe it could be a regular thing, you know?" He was fiddling with his fork but kept eye contact throughout the conversation. This guy was unbelievable. "I just don't really know how to do regular."

I needed to take a breath. Why was I getting so worked up? I knew it was a one night thing. I knew it wasn't going anywhere. I knew we were just "friends." I knew all of it. So why was I insulted?

Because, as much as I hated to admit it, I was a girl who couldn't separate feelings from sex. It sucked, but there it was. I hadn't thought that I felt something, even if it was a fake something that stemmed from bruised lady bits, but I guess I couldn't disconnect the two things. It wasn't his fault.

"So, you wanted to continue to be friends. That doesn't explain why you punched Brian in the face. If you didn't want anything more, why not step aside?"

"Well, that's the thing." The waitress dropped off our lunches. Even as he thanked her, with me sitting in front of him, he couldn't help but check her out and throw out that shit-eating grin that had me eating out of his, well, I'd rather not say.

I snapped my fingers in his face. "Hey. Ryan. Easy boy. Explain all this to me and I'll get her number for you."

"Right. So, like I was saying, the thing is I didn't think I wanted more. Until Brian said he did. Then I thought to myself, if he can like you that way, then why can't I?"

"I seriously doubt you're a relationship kind of guy." I bit into my sandwich.

"I'm not, or I wasn't. I haven't been since my college girlfriend broke my heart. Since then, it's been all one night stands and friends with benefits."

I got where he was coming from. He was lonely. That wasn't going to change overnight.

"But Ryan, maybe you *want* a girlfriend. The fact that you've checked out our waitress a dozen times already shows me that you don't want *me* as a girlfriend. I'm not who you are looking for, just like you aren't what I was looking for."

"I guess. But we had fun together."

"We had fun, twice. And both times, there wasn't much talking."

The tension that crept in at the beginning of the conversation dissipated and it suddenly felt like I was talking to an actual friend.

"You're right. Maybe I'm just feeling too old to keep banging every hot chick I see."

"Glad to know I'm a hot chick, but a little concerned that I'm in the 'every' category."

"You know what I mean."

I did know what he meant and I felt like a weight had been lifted off my shoulders. Sometimes one night stands were meant to remain just that—just one night.

"Anyway, since the morning I punched Brian, I've been in California or staying with friends. I've had a lot of time to think and Brian was right. And knowing him as well as I do, I know he doesn't fall for just anyone. I think the two of you will be great together."

"So you two worked it out?"

"Not really. I kind of moved all my shit out when he wasn't around."

"That's a douche bag move."

"Well, you know what they say, everyone has an asshole friend and if you don't, then you're the asshole. The thing is, none of my friends are assholes so you do the math."

"I don't think you're an asshole. I just think you need to square things away with Brian. I can tell it bothers him and if you're telling me the truth, then it bothers you, too."

"Yeah, you're right. I'll go over there after I leave here. I can't be a dick to him of all people." His eyes lit up. "Hey, maybe you guys can help me find the right girl!"

"Being single is way better than being in the wrong relationship. Trust me. You'll find her when the time is right. Until then, have fun. Nothing wrong with fun."

"How can someone so tiny be so smart? You're like my Yoda."

"First of all, because one has nothing to do with the other. Besides, I'm not tiny, I'm concentrated awesome, and second of all, green isn't my color. Ryan, you and I can be friends. Like real friends. Without all that—"

"Mind-blowing sex?" He laughed easily.

"Yes, mind-blowing sex." I checked the time on my phone. "I've got to go. Melody and I are going to get manicures." I stood and put on my jacket. "Just promise me you'll square it away with Brian?"

"Yeah, I will. Promise." He rolled his eyes when I gave him a questioning look.

"Good. So, you going to the bar tonight?"

"Won't that be weird?"

"Why? We're friends right? You'll fix things with Brian, right? Nothing weird about that."

"But I can picture you naked whenever I want," he joked.

I hit him with my gloves. "Well, don't. Or if you do, don't tell me or Brian about it."

"Deal. Thanks, Caroline."

"Anytime." I gave him a hug.

"Hey, before you go, can you, uh—"

"Get the waitress's number for you? Sure thing."

Before I left I whispered to our waitress and sent her over to Ryan. It was the least I could do.

Chapter Twenty-Seven

Melody was late to the manicurist appointment and, in true Melody fashion, her entrance was dramatic. Sweeping in with her long trench coat, wild hair, designer sunglasses, and handbag, it was hard not to center attention on her.

"So sorry I am late! I had a late-morning fuck date." She wore bed head like no one else. She hung her coat on the chair and dropped her purse, oblivious to the fact that three blue-haired ladies gasped at her words and were whispering in one another's ears about her lack of couth while frowning in her direction.

"No problem. I just got here myself. So who was it?"

"Who was what?"

"Your late-morning fuck date. Who were you with?"

"Oh you don't know him. We, uh, work together." She brushed me off.

I nodded in silence. I loved Melody but sometimes I couldn't keep up with her revolving door of bed buddies.

"So, what color are you doing?"

"This pale pink." I handed her the bottle.

"Oh cute. So you. I think I'm going red this time."

She pointed to a color and said, in perfect Mandarin, what she wanted. Sometimes I forgot how freakishly educated she was. Just goes to show, easy and educated *do* go hand in hand.

"So, have you and Sarah ironed shit out yet?"

"Not yet." I thought back to the advice I'd given Ryan earlier. Maybe it was time to take a teaspoon, or a gallon, of my own medicine, suck it up, and have the conversation I've been dreading. "I don't know what to say. I don't know why she freaked out."

"Then you're an idiot."

"I'm not an idiot."

"Don't you think if I were wrong, I would know it? Of course you're an idiot. And so is she."

At least I wasn't the only one.

"So, oh exalted one, please tell me why *I* am an idiot."

"Sarah doesn't want to lose you. She already feels like she was losing you after you and Steven broke up. You were a zombie, Care. And she kind of did. You were all wrapped up in losing him and forgot to live for a while. Plus, you started to not hang out with us while you were with him. That last year we hardly saw you."

"That's not true!" I cringed, knowing she was right.

"Oh, please. We saw you, what? Every couple months? Whenever you could get away?"

"I took spin class every Sunday with you guys!"

"Whatever." She rolled her eyes. "Look, she wants you to be happy more than anything and she doesn't want you making shitty decisions. She thought having lunch with Ryan was a shitty decision that would fuck up what you've started with Brian. And if that fucked up, you'd be back to eating pints and crying over Nicholas Sparks movies."

I shook my head.

"Tell me I'm wrong."

"You're wrong."

"Now tell me and mean it."

I couldn't. She was right. Goddamn, she was smart.

"Fine. I'll talk to her."

"That's all I want you to do. Look, if I'm going to be stuck in between two people it wouldn't be you two. Don't get me wrong, I love you guys, but you don't have cocks."

"What?"

"Cocks. I need to be in the middle of a cock sandwich, not a girly emotional standoff. And that's all I'm going to say on the matter. Unless you don't talk to her, then I am going to bitch smack both of you."

"You have a dirty mouth." I laughed.

"The reason I swear so much is fuck you. Just listen to me. I give great advice. I just never follow it. Hence the late-morning fuck buddy."

"Who was it, Mel?"

She looked around before she leaned in and whispered, "My boss."

"What?" I yelled.

"Simmer down. It's no big deal. His wife was out of town and he texted me early this morning. It's not going anywhere. Just a stupid lapse in judgment."

"I'll say." I shook my head. Only Melody would get herself into that kind of situation.

"Don't tell Sarah. She'll get all judgy and I don't need that. Besides, I'm meeting Danny at the bar tonight. You going?"

"Yeah, I'll be there. Wait. Danny called? When did this happen?"

"Last night. He apologized for not getting in touch with me. Not sure how he got my number but anyway, we're meeting up tonight. No big deal."

"You always did have a thing for tall, dark, and handsome."

"And blond and ginger and, and, and. Besides, I bought a fabulous pair of fuck-me heels and I intend on putting them to good use."

"You're right." I blew on my nails. I was suddenly antsy to get home and have the heart to heart with Sarah.

We chatted for the next hour about nothing and everything. She was right. I had been off the grid. I silently vowed not to make that mistake again.

"Okay, I'm off. Gotta buy a new pair of panties."

The word still made me cringe a week later.

"Have fun. I'm off to chat with Sarah. Wish me luck."

"Good luck." She grabbed my boob. "What? Everyone knows good luck is imminent when someone grabs your boob."

"Who knows that?"

"Um, everyone? See you tonight, bitch face. Love you!"

"Yeah, yeah. Don't trip on your heels."

She blew me a kiss as she sashayed out the door. There was no other word to describe it. She didn't walk.

I took my time walking home, mentally going over what I wanted to say to Sarah. It wouldn't be fun but I knew Melody was right. I knew Sarah better than I knew myself and nothing she said or did was malicious. I should have known better than to think so.

When I entered the apartment, Sarah was nowhere in sight. I beelined for the kitchen to make a pot of coffee. I was pulling down the sweetener when I heard a thump. My skin tingled. There was no one in the apartment but me.

Like a maniac, I twirled around the kitchen looking for a weapon. I thought about a knife, but knives meant stabbing and stabbing meant blood and I just wasn't ready to stain my new kicks. Converse need to be broken in gently and blood would screw up the process. So I settled on a wooden spoon.

Tiptoeing with my back against the wall, I stealthily moved from the kitchen to the entrance to the hall. Another thump echoed louder. Ice slid through my veins. I psyched myself up before I peeked around the corner. Counting to three, I flipped on the light.

Nothing. All the doors were closed to the rooms and the bathroom. I longed for my cell phone but it was over by the door inside my purse. It may as well have been in the middle of the ocean. No way was I going to cross the room and expose myself to whatever terror was residing in my apartment.

Another thump.

Carefully, I opened the closet door and threw the spoon in there while I grabbed the long golf umbrella Steven left at the apartment years ago. I promised myself if the umbrella saved my life, I would be nicer to Steven the next time I saw him. My brain looped the word "if" over and over.

I was scared shitless as I heard a louder noise come from Sarah's room. Blessing myself with the sign of the cross, I placed my hand on the doorknob. Mentally counting backward from ten, I prepared to attack.

I turned the knob slowly until I heard a click, then I shoved it open, umbrella stretched out in front of me.

"Aha!" I hit the man in the head and he dropped to the floor.

"Caroline! What the hell?"

Sarah was handcuffed to her bed, stretched out in all her naked glory. She kept twitching.

I covered my eyes and turned away. "Oh my God! I am so sorry!"

"What did you do?"

"I thought there was an intruder! I didn't know!"

The naked man on the floor began to stir and I jumped back.

"Who is that?"

"It's Drew, you ass!"

"Hey, Care," Drew said.

"Hey, Drew. Sorry about that. Do you need an ice pack?"

"Um, a little help over here!" I peeked between my fingers. Sarah was still twitching.

"What's wrong with you? Why are you twitching?" I dropped the umbrella and stepped toward her.

"Don't come closer." She moaned.

"Are you sick?" I was becoming concerned. Her mouth kept opening and closing, her body looked like it was spasming, and something was wrong with her voice. "Are you having a stroke?"

"She's not having a stroke." Drew stood up, reached for his shirt, and held it in front of himself.

"Then what's wrong with her, I really should—"

I stopped midsentence and reexamined the scene. Drew was naked. Sarah was handcuffed to the bed. She was vibrating. She was moaning.

"Motherfucker! You're using a vibrator!" I collapsed to the floor, laughing so hard I thought my sides would split.

"And I was enjoying it until you barged in here!" I watched her eyelids flutter and her toes point.

"Um, Care?" Drew looked at me and then motioned to Sarah.

"Oh, right. You don't want me here. I shouldn't be here. I'm just um, going to go and, you know, find a noose to hang myself with." I closed the door behind me and leaned against it, laughing really hard.

"I can hear you!" Sarah yelled out before she yelled Drew's name in her big finish. I hopped back to the kitchen to get my coffee.

Twenty minutes later, Drew hightailed it out of the apartment as I sat on the couch reading a manuscript. Sarah strolled into the space moments later covered in her fluffy pink robe.

I snickered.

"I can hear you, you know."

"I'm sorry. It was just, so *not* you. I mean, I expect to walk in on Melody in that situation, not you."

"Well, then, you don't know me very well." She huffed as she poured herself a cup of coffee.

I put the papers down on the coffee table and turned toward her. "You're right. I don't know you as well as I should and that's on me." I patted the cushion next to me. "Come sit."

For the next hour we talked about everything. From Steven to the breakup to the one night stand. She told me her fears, her hopes, and what she wanted most in life. We reconnected in a way we hadn't since college.

We'd graduated from coffee to wine when Sarah said, "I was just sad when you disappeared. I felt like I lost my best friend. And when you came back, you were all weepy and shit. I mean, when you were with Steven you weren't the Caroline I knew but that sobbing six-week mess was not even in the vicinity of who I knew you were."

"I didn't know. I am so sorry. I deserve an oblivious asshole award or something."

"Nah. Sometimes I wish I was that wrapped up in someone. The kind of love that's the reason to look down at my phone and smile when he calls. Then promptly walk into a pole."

"Stupid love."

"Yes!"

"Steven wasn't my stupid love. I think Brian is." I ducked my head, waiting to hear the lecture that never came.

"I think he is, too. Come on, let's get ready. We're meeting at the bar in an hour and a half and I really, really need to shower."

"Bring that vibrator in there with you. That thing needs a good cleaning."

"Ha! Glad I have someone to use it with."

"You should have seen your face when I clocked Drew with the umbrella. Priceless!"

"Yeah, well."

"He has a nice ass, though."

"You saw?" She smiled.

"I saw more than I care to ever see again, seriously. I'm still trying to gather up enough brain bleach to get the visual of you handcuffed to the bed, spread out like jelly on toast, out of my mind."

"You loved it."

I laughed and stopped at my door. "So, we're good?"

"We're forever good."

I watched her strut into the bathroom and close the door. I went into my room to pick out my outfit for the night and pack my overnight bag.

Smiling, I ran and pulled my phone from my purse. Back in my room, I stripped off my shirt, snapped a pic, and sent it to Brian. Giggling at his open-mouthed, surprised selfie, I went back to getting ready.

Chapter Twenty-Eight

We didn't hit the bar until close to nine. Sarah and I stopped at the sushi place to stuff our faces. Apparently reminiscing and apologizing works up a massive appetite.

Everything was falling into place. I couldn't have been happier.

I bounced into the bar, walked right up to Brian, and planted a long slow kiss on his lips. When we pulled away from each other, the bar erupted in cheers. The old me would have been embarrassed but the new me took a bow.

"What was that for?" Brian wrapped his arms around me.

"No reason."

"Well, I like no reason. And thanks."

"For kissing you? That's hardly a chore." I gave him a quick peck on the nose.

"No. For talking to Ryan. He came over earlier and we had a little chat. Seems like you're a little Miss Fix-It."

"Yeah, well, I had to fix it with Sarah today, too."

"How'd that go?" He stepped away to pull a beer.

"The conversation went well. I'll tell you all about it later. The preconversation was a little spicy."

"Spicy?"

"Yeah. Let's just say I know how many freckles are on Drew's ass."

I heard him yell, "What?" as I walked toward the back. I was giggling when I reached the table.

"Caroline!" Berk and Danny exclaimed in unison. "Thank God you're here."

"Thank God, huh? Nice to see you, too." I flopped down on the chair Berk kicked out for me, grabbed an empty glass from the table, and filled it with what was left of the beer in the pitcher. I popped a French fry in my mouth and leaned back.

"Yeah. Apparently you know how Drew got the lump on his head," Berk offered.

"I already told you—" Drew began.

"Hush now. Caroline will clear the matter up."

Both Drew and Sarah stiffened and turned bright red. I looked between the two of them and smiled. "I think he fell down. Is that right Drew?"

"Yeah, that's what I said."

"Then how on earth"—Berk made an elaborate gesture with his hands—"did Sarah get those red marks on her wrist?"

I looked over as Sarah dropped her hands to her lap. "Rubber bands."

She looked at me.

"Rubber bands?" Danny asked.

"Yeah. You know, she's a teacher and she puts rubber bands on her wrists and they were too tight. Rubber bands that are too tight leave red marks. Everyone knows that."

Both Berk and Danny looked at me skeptically. Melody stifled a laugh. She didn't know the story but her imagination was probably on target.

"That doesn't sound right. We're missing something here." Berk stood.

"Well, that's my story."

"Right. I'm going to get more beer. Anyone want anything?"

"Yeah! Tell Brian to send over some shots." Melody leaned against Danny with a smile on her face. "So"—she looked between Sarah and me—"did you two square things away?"

"We did, actually. We had a good talk. Learned new stuff about each other."

"We did. I saw a whole new side of Sarah today. One that I won't forget for a long time."

"Will you be requiring the brain bleach?" Melody's eyes twinkled.

"I will, as a matter of fact."

"Oh shut up, Lots O'Lube." Sarah laughed.

"Lots O'Lube? That's that nasty shit Ryan buys." Danny's eyes widened. "You didn't!"

It was my turn to freeze.

"Who's talking about me?"

Ryan arrived at the table, beer in hand. He looked perplexed when the entire table erupted in laughter.

"What's so funny?"

"Nothin' man. Welcome back." Danny grabbed Ryan's hand and pulled him in for a hug.

Berk walked over with a tray full of shots.

"What do we have here?" I asked. "And why are you always delivering the drinks? Aren't there waitresses who work here, for tips?"

"Do you see any waitresses? I come bearing a tray full of Tight Snatches. Please, drink at your own risk."

"Why does yours look different?" Melody asked.

"Considering, even though you ladies are quite lovely, I don't prefer the snatch, tight or not, I decided to drink something that reflects my own personality."

"Which is?"

"A Dr. Pecker. I thought it quaint considering my new flavor is a doctor anyway." Berk winked and downed the shot without waiting for the rest of us.

"I'll never get used to the fact that you like dick, man." Ryan said.

"You'll never get used to the fact that I like dick or that I *don't* like *your* dick?" Berk leaned down and planted a juicy kiss on Ryan's lips.

"Get off me!" Ryan laughed as he wiped his mouth with the sleeve of his shirt. He spazzed out enough that Berk had to catch the chair from tipping over. "What the hell man? I have a reputation to uphold."

"As do I. I hope no one saw me kissing *you*. I wouldn't want anyone thinking I switched teams."

"What's wrong with kissing me? I'm a great kisser."

I secretly agreed but kept my mouth shut.

"A little sloppy." Berk made a show of wiping his entire face with a napkin.

"Sloppy? You don't know what you're talking about."

"The lady doth protest too much, methinks," I offered.

"Watch who you're calling a lady, lady." Ryan snorted into his beer glass.

Everyone grabbed a shot.

"Here's to none of us getting friend-zoned tonight!" Drew lifted the shot glass.

"Friend-zoned?" I asked.

"Yeah, when she doesn't change her mind when she's drunk," Drew explained.

"To not getting friend-zoned!" Brian appeared behind me and joined in the toast.

"No chance of that," I countered.

"I would hope not. Hey Drew, what's this I hear about freckles on your ass and why does Caroline know how many there are?"

"I knew there was more to the story!" Danny yelled, jumping out of his seat as his face broke into a huge grin.

Sarah spit out her shot and Drew found something on the floor suddenly very interesting.

"You and I"—Brian pointed from his eyes to Drew—"will chat about this later." He leaned down and whispered in my ear. "You need anything?"

"You?"

He looked around the bar. "Give me five minutes and meet me upstairs." He twirled his towel and snapped it at me.

"No fair!" Melody called out. "You can't sneak off when none of us can do it here!"

"Should I rent out my bedroom? A few hundred bucks an hour? I bet I could clean up."

"Why use a bed when you have a perfectly good bathroom to get freaky in? That's your thing, right, Caroline?" Danny shot back.

"*My* thing?" I shook my head in confusion.

"Yeah. Melody told us about your bathroom escapade from last weekend."

Danny flinched when Melody smacked him on the arm.

I whipped my head around. "You told him?"

"I didn't know it was a secret. It was pretty funny!"

"Do you know how long it took us to get her in that thing?" Sarah asked.

"About as long as it took me to get it off her?" Brian quipped.

"It's not funny! That thing was squeezing my insides out my ears."

"It's a little funny."

"It's a lot funny," Drew said.

"Hey." I pointed at him. "You want me to tell everyone what's so funny?"

He held up his hands. "Shutting up now."

"That's what I thought. I can't believe you told them."

I couldn't decide whether to laugh or crawl under the table.

"How about the next time I do something terrifyingly funny, you can tell everyone all about it?"

I made a face. "Deal."

"Shake on it?" Brian offered his hand.

"Nope. Kiss on it."

He kissed me quickly. "Like I said, five minutes. Be there."

"With bells on."

"How about that smile I left you with?" Brian winked and went back to the bar.

"Aww. That's cute." Melody pouted her lips. "I want to be cute with someone."

"You can be cute with me," Danny said.

"Is that right?" Melody's eyes shined.

"Sure. Why not?"

"We'll see. Anyway, I have to go to the little girls' room. Be back."

Melody made eye contact with Danny and tilted her head toward the bathroom.

"Um, I have to go, too." Danny jumped up and raced after her.

"So, Ryan. Did that waitress give you her number?"

"There was a waitress?" Drew took a moment from making out with Sarah to ask.

"Yeah. Well, I don't know. We're going out Wednesday night."

"Huh, maybe she can teach you not to be such an asshole." Drew laughed like he'd told the funniest joke he'd ever heard.

Ryan playfully shot back. "Hey, I'm not an asshole. I just don't give a fuck a lot."

It was my turn to shoot beer out of my nose. Sarah handed me a napkin.

Ryan and Drew continued the conversation about the waitress; Sarah got up to go talk to one of the other teachers she worked with. I watched Brian make drinks and check his phone. He looked up, whispered to another bartender, threw down his towel, and stepped out from behind the bar. I watched him walk to the apartment door and disappear.

I smiled, slid my chair back, and did my best not to sprint after him.

The upstairs entrance to the apartment was open and as I stepped through, Brian appeared out of nowhere, pulled me aside, and slammed the door closed. Smiling, I maneuvered him back so he was up against the door.

"What are you doing?"

"What?" I tilted my head as I worked his belt buckle open.

"You don't have to." He breathed as I shoved his pants and boxer briefs over the round of his ass.

"You don't want me to?"

"I didn't say that."

"Good." I gripped him in my fist as he continued to swell.

I kissed him hard on the mouth, allowing our tongues to tangle for only a moment before I dropped to my knees and ran my lips over his length.

He threaded his fingers in my hair and whispered my name when I spit on the tip and ran my hand up and down the shaft. I fit him in my mouth and his knees buckled. I wrapped my hands around him and gripped his ass, pulling myself in closer to him. He palmed the back of my head and kept rhythm with me as I worked to bring him to climax.

He yelled out my name as he came, his fingers knotted in my hair. I continued to hold on to him until he stopped shaking.

I leaned back and sat on the floor as he slid down the door until he was sitting in front of me. With his pants around his knees he brought his hands to his head and shook it hard like he was trying to focus.

"You okay?" I giggled. His reaction was priceless.

"No. Don't touch me. Not yet. I need a minute."

"You don't want me to touch you?" I ran my hand along his thigh.

"Caroline." He growled.

"What?" I put his earlobe between my teeth and pulled gently. He closed his eyes.

He didn't move, so I stood up and took off my shirt. He finally opened his eyes when it hit him in the face. "Well, if you aren't interested"—I slipped out of my flats and walked toward his bedroom—"I guess I'll just have to take care of it myself."

He shot up, pulled his pants back on, and chased me down the hallway as I screamed and ran toward the bedroom. He grabbed me right before I entered the room, lifted me up, threw me on the bed, and pressed himself on top of me.

"You're killing me." He moaned.

"I told you I would take care of it myself." Laughing, I tried to wiggle out from under him.

"Oh no you don't!"

"Oh yes I can!"

"I know you *can*. A real woman can do it all by herself, I know that. But a real man won't let her."

His lips met mine and we lost ourselves in each other.

An hour later we lay in the bed, quiet but for the sounds of our breathing.

"We should get back." I broke the silence.

"No." Brian nuzzled his unshaven face into my neck.

"Everyone is probably waiting for us, wondering where we are."

"Let them. The longer we're up here, the more studly I look."

"More studly?" I raised my eyebrows.

"You know what I mean. More studly. Studlier. Whatever." He reached down and smacked my ass.

"Ouch! Come on." I rolled over and looked for my pants.

"Fine. You're sleeping here tonight?"

"I was planning on it."

"Good. You know, Christmas is coming up."

I turned to him. His hair was disheveled and his eyes were sleepy and relaxed.

"Christmas?" I had totally forgotten.

"Yeah. It's in like, ten days."

"Wow."

He laughed and pulled on his pants while lying down. "Anyway, I was thinking we could go get a tree tomorrow."

"I haven't even started shopping yet. I can't believe it slipped my mind. I mean everything is already decorated. How did that slip past me?"

"I don't know. What do you say? We can go shopping in the morning, then get a tree before we come back here."

"I think"—I crawled across the bed and kissed him—"that sounds like a great idea."

"I was hoping you'd say that."

"Maybe I'll call out sick on Monday. We can sleep in and decorate it."

"Sounds like an even better plan."

He grabbed my ass and squeezed. I waited until he put on his shirt before we walked out to the living room. I pulled my sweater over my head and we went back downstairs hand in hand.

Chapter Twenty-Nine

I approached the table to see Melody with her hair spread out on the table and Sarah texting someone while she sipped a beer.

"Hey."

"Hey," Sarah replied.

"She returns!" Melody lifted her head and slurred before dropping it back to the table.

I cocked my head to the side and squinted before I leaned down and whispered to Sarah, "Does she know her shirt is inside out?"

"That's nothing, there was a used condom stuck to her shoe."

I crinkled my nose. "Ew."

"Yeah."

I looked around. "Where'd everyone else go?"

"Danny, Drew, and Ryan are playing darts, and Berk is in the back corner making out with his doctor friend. It's a shame. Two perfectly hot guys completely unavailable to me." She shook her head in disbelief.

I dug around in my purse and found my compact and lip gloss. "Looks like Melody's cut off."

I slicked on the gloss and puckered in the mirror before handing it to Sarah.

"Oh yeah. We're only staying a little longer, then I'm bringing her back home with me. I'd rather be able to walk her home than call her a taxi and hope she gets home."

"Blot?" I handed her a napkin.

"Thanks."

"Mel!" I yelled and kicked the table.

She lifted her head and looked at me. "What? Huh? Yeah?"

"You okay?"

She gave me a loopy smile and a thumbs-up, then dropped her head back down.

"She's down." Sarah laughed.

I nodded back at her and whispered to Sarah, "I'm not supposed to tell you, but she slept with her boss this morning."

"Which one?" Sarah's voice was serious.

"The married one."

"Shit."

"Yeah."

"She can't be doing that."

"You tell her that!" I pointed to Melody's sleeping head.

Sarah shook her head. "Always something with her. Smart as a whip but no common sense. You're staying here, right?"

"Yeah. Get this. We're picking out a Christmas tree tomorrow."

"That's a big step. Sure you're ready?"

"For real."

Sarah scrunched up her face. "Wait. It's Christmas already?"

"Right? I thought I was the only one who wasn't paying attention. Feels like yesterday we were taking in the sun in Jamaica."

"God. I know. Let's go back."

"Can't. It's Christmas and we are required to celebrate in New Jersey."

"I can't believe I didn't realize how close it was. There is no excuse. I'm a teacher. I look forward to this shit."

I shrugged and said, "Maybe we're too old for Christmas."

"Bullshit. We're never too old for Christmas. What do you want anyway?"

"A new pair of nude pumps? Mine are all scuffed."

"Consider it done."

"You?" I poured a glass of beer for myself and topped hers off.

"A man." She took a drink, keeping her eye on Drew.

I nodded toward him. "What about Drew?"

"Eh, I don't know. It's not serious."

"It sure as hell looked serious. I mean you don't just let anyone handcuff you to the bed. Maybe you do, I don't know. But I draw the line."

"Yeah. Not serious. Fun, yes. Serious, no."

"Why not?"

"I don't know. Maybe he's not into me."

"Doubt that."

"I'm happy for you, you know."

I smiled at her. "I know."

"Brian is a good guy."

"I think so." I looked over and caught his eye. The best feeling in the world is when a girl looks over and her guy is already staring. He winked and went back to pulling beers.

"I think," Sarah began, "we should play darts. I think these guys need to get their asses handed to them."

I got up and followed her. "But I don't know how to play."

"How hard can it be? You throw the arrow thingy at the target and try to get a bull's-eye."

"I don't know about you but the last time I tried to go after a target it didn't work out so well."

"Oh, it worked out. Just not the way you thought it would."

I looked over at Brian again and said, "Yeah, I guess you're right."

The rest of the night was spent with Melody asleep on the back table and the rest of us laughing, dancing, singing, and shooting darts. Brian's breaks were spent in the back with us. Even Berk pulled away from his man candy long enough to join us. We were a bunch of people, some who barely knew one another, starting relationships that would last longer than any of us could have anticipated.

Cocktail Recipes

Sex up Against the Wall

- 1 oz. vodka
- 1 oz. pineapple juice
- 1 oz. cranberry juice
- 1 oz. sour mix

Pour all the ingredients into a cocktail shaker filled with ice, shake, and strain into a cocktail glass. Serve.

Sex on the Beach

- 1½ oz. vodka
- ½ oz. peach schnapps
- 2 oz. cranberry juice
- 2 oz. orange juice

Pour the vodka and peach schnapps into a rocks glass filled with ice. Add the juices. Stir and serve.

Harvey Wallbanger

- 1¼ oz. vodka
- 3 oz. orange juice
- ½ oz. Galliano L'Autentico
- Orange slice

Pour the vodka and orange juice into a tall glass filled with ice. Stir. Carefully pour the Galliano over the back of a spoon to layer it on top of the drink. Garnish with the orange slice and serve.

Screaming Orgasm

- 1 oz. vodka
- 1½ oz. Irish cream
- ½ oz. coffee liqueur

Pour all the ingredients into a rocks glass filled with crushed ice. Stir and serve.

Slippery Nipple

- ½ oz. butterscotch schnapps
- ½ oz. Irish cream

Add the schnapps to a shot glass and layer the Irish cream on top. Enjoy.

Body Shot

- 1½ oz. tequila
- Willing partner
- Salt
- Lime wedge

Pour the tequila into a shot glass. Find a willing partner and lick a sensitive part of his or her body (neck, breasts, wrist, shoulder—you get the idea). Shake some salt on the moist skin and place the lime wedge in the mouth of your partner, with the pulp side facing out. Lick the salt from his or her body and down your shot. Eat the lime out of your partner's mouth. You'll never do a tequila shot any other way again.

Pink Panty Dropper

- 6 oz. light beer
- 1½ oz. vodka
- 1 to 2 spoonfuls frozen pink lemonade concentrate

Mix all the ingredients in a pint glass and enjoy.

Pop My Cherry

- ½ oz. cherry vodka
- ¼ oz. triple sec
- ¼ oz. orange juice

Add all the ingredients to a cocktail shaker filled with ice. Shake and strain into a shot glass. Enjoy.

Amaretto and Ginger

- 2 oz. amaretto
- 5 oz. ginger ale
- 2 maraschino cherries (optional)

Pour the amaretto and ginger ale over ice in a rocks glass. Garnish with cherries if you are so inclined.

Blow Job Shot

- ¼ oz. Irish cream
- ½ oz. amaretto
- Whipped cream

Pour the liqueurs into a shot glass and top with whipped cream. Place your hands behind your back, then pick up the shot glass with your mouth, tilt your head back, and drink.

Wet Pussy

- ½ oz. whiskey
- ½ oz. Irish cream
- 2 oz. energy drink

Combine all the ingredients in a large shot glass and slam back.

Perfect Erection

- 6 oz. raspberry vodka
- 6 oz. watermelon schnapps
- 4 oz. lemon-lime soda

Combine all the ingredients in a large frosted glass. Add ice and serve.

Stumble Fuck

- ⅓ oz. Jägermeister
- ⅓ oz. Rumple Minze
- ⅓ oz. Fireball Cinnamon Whisky

Pour all the ingredients into a shot glass and drink.

Dirty Whore's Bathwater

- ¾ oz. vodka
- ¼ oz. sour apple liqueur
- 1 tsp. powdered lemonade mix

Pour the vodka and apple liqueur into a cocktail shaker filled with ice. Shake and strain into a large shot glass. Add the lemonade mix, stir until dissolved, and serve.

Rum Punch

- 1 cup light rum
- ½ cup dark rum
- ¼ cup coconut rum
- 2½ cups pineapple juice
- 2½ cups orange juice
- Juice of one lime
- Splash of grenadine

Mix all the ingredients together in a pitcher or large punch bowl. Serve in glasses over ice. Makes about 12 drinks.

Piña Colada

- 1½ oz. light or gold rum
- 2 oz. coconut milk
- 2 oz. fresh pineapple juice
- 2 maraschino cherries
- Pineapple wedge

Pour the rum, coconut milk, and pineapple juice into a shaker filled with ice. Shake and strain into a large glass filled with crushed ice. Garnish with cherries and pineapple wedge and serve.

Dirty Banana

- 2 scoops vanilla ice cream
- 1 oz. crème de banana

- 1 oz. crème de cacao
- 1 oz. coffee liqueur
- 1 to 2 slices fresh banana
- Chocolate syrup

Combine the ice cream and a cup of ice in a blender and blend until smooth. Add the liqueurs and blend until combined. Pour into a tall glass and garnish with slices of a fresh banana and a drizzle of chocolate syrup.

Bull's-Eye Bomb

- ¼ oz. amaretto
- ¼ oz. peach schnapps
- 3 oz. energy drink

Mix the ingredients together in a rocks glass with ice and enjoy.

Tight Snatch

- 1 oz. vodka
- 1 oz. peach schnapps
- 3 oz. pineapple juice
- 3 oz. cranberry juice

Pour all the ingredients into a shaker filled with ice, shake, and strain into a large glass. Serve. Note that the juice amounts can vary depending on how you like your drinks.

Dr. Pecker

- 2 oz. whiskey
- 2 oz. cola
- 2 oz. cranberry juice

Pour all the ingredients into a tall glass filled with ice and serve.

Please turn the page for a preview of
Christine Hughes's next sexy romantic comedy

Operation Foreplay

Available Fall 2015

Chapter One

With nothing but a towel wrapped tightly around my head, I padded barefoot to the kitchen to open a bottle of wine. Turning up the music, I shimmied around the room as I searched the drawer for the bottle opener. I was giddy after checking the time; Zac would be at my apartment in an hour. For the first time since, well, the first time, he'd be on my turf. There would be no sneaking around the office, no stolen kisses when no one was looking. No rushing out of bed at three in the morning to take a cab to the train that would bring me home by four only to head back into the city by nine. He was coming to my place. My place. Sleeping over. Spending the night. Spending the weekend. And if I had a say in it, the weekend would be spent in bed.

I'd put on the slinkiest, sluttiest underwear I could find—purchased specifically for the occasion—perfected my barely there makeup, and dabbed on the expensive perfume he'd purchased for me during his last visit to France.

With thirty minutes to go, I pulled the towel off my head, and used the diffuser to ensure the honey-blond curls he loved so much were intact and full. I lit candles and slipped on my barely legal black dress in time to pay the Chinese delivery guy, whose eyes bugged out of his head when he saw the surgically enhanced cleavage I presented him with when I answered the door, and set the table. Looking around my ridiculously spacious apartment, I smiled because everything was perfect. Early dinner meant more time in bed. Or on the floor. Or in the shower.

After I polished off my second glass of wine, I shot him a text and picked at the dumplings. Within thirty minutes, there were none left and I was still starving. I checked out the market recap and flipped through the channels until I landed on a sitcom that highlighted one of the characters turning thirty. I opened the second bottle and lamented the fact that I'd be thirty in less than a month. I wasn't *not* looking forward to it, but I didn't see the big deal. Unfortunately my mother didn't agree. Especially since she'd learned my friends were moving in a direction I clearly was not. I mean, who cared if Caroline moved in with Brian? Why did it matter if Sarah was dating Drew regularly? Who said I needed any of that? I was an attractive young professional woman. I was successful. And I liked to have sex. Lots of it. And I liked to sample all the different varieties of dick being single introduced me to. At the moment, I was having lots of sex with my boss, Zachary Waterman. The things that man could do with his hands. The thought gave me goose bumps.

I reached across my chocolate leather sofa and grabbed a four-hundred-dollar pillow to rest my laptop on. Maybe he'd e-mailed. I'd eaten both eggrolls and started the second bottle by the time I finished perusing through the spam and department store sales advertisements. It wasn't a total loss. I'd ordered a sexy new pair of peep toes to go with the entirely too expensive suit I'd purchased the week before.

I clicked off the television and walked to my bedroom as wine sloshed from my glass due partly to my overpour and partly to my impaired balance. I call it my two-bottle strut. Everyone has one.

Relighting a vanilla candle that had snuffed out, I picked up my never-used landline and dialed my cell phone to make sure it was still working. He was an hour and twenty minutes late. I took a deep breath and reminded myself not to panic. Of course, he was a busy man. He ran a multimillion-dollar company. There was no need to worry.

Refreshing my makeup, I told myself over and over again not to worry. The voice in my head, unfortunately, was growing more frantic by the minute. I was never one to get all swoony and girly over a man. I had no time for relationships, no time for anything other than casual and mutually mind-blowing sex. I had a black book. I had notches on my bedpost and a belt with more holes than I cared to admit. It's not that I didn't care about the guys I slept with, it's just that I cared more about myself and my orgasm. Not a bad thing. I certainly wasn't selfish, any bedmate could tell you. I just wasn't relationship material. And it pissed off my mother.

So why were my panties in a bunch over Zac? What the hell made him so special that I'd sit home and wait for him? It was because he was unavailable to me in the relationship department. His wife would agree with me. I'd been involved with my still-married-but-going-through-a-divorce boss for the past five months. Not exactly going through, per se. More like promising-to-end-it-but-hasn't-yet. My friends thought I needed a new hobby.

I dialed his number and was slightly surprised when it went straight to voice mail. I didn't bother leaving a message. Instead I threw the phone on my couch and slinked back to the kitchen to grab a third bottle. I sat on the floor between the hallway and the kitchen cracking fortune cookies that gave shitty advice and refilling my glass until my vision clouded. It wasn't until that third bottle of Pinot sat unopened in my lap, mascara stained my cheeks, and he was officially two and a half hours late that I realized he wasn't coming.

That isn't true.

I realized it when he didn't return my text.

Calmly I walked to my bedroom and stripped off the slinky black dress I'd picked out for the evening, now noticeably stained with drops of wine, and let it fall to the floor. I yanked on the rattiest pair of sweatpants I could find from my drawer and pulled my old college T-shirt over my head. Even that had holes in it. Perfect metaphor for my life at that moment. Full of holes. I was crying by the time I called Sarah.

"Hey."

She was out somewhere. I could hear other people talking in the background.

"He didn't come." Unsteadily I made my way back to my living room.

"Oh, sweetie. I'm sorry."

"I've eaten five dumplings and two eggrolls. I have a pile of fortune cookie crumbs in my hallway. I am going to open my third bottle of wine and eat the lo mein I ordered without a fork. I will gain ten pounds and I don't care."

"We'll be right there."

"I will stick my face in the lo mein and eat it like a caveman."

"Do not eat the lo mein like a caveman. We will be there in less than twenty minutes."

The best part about having two best friends was there were no questions when one of us was down. I didn't have to ask. They'd be there. They'd answer the phone. They'd respond to a text and, barring a life-threatening accident, they wouldn't be two and a half hours late.

I barely heard them come in my apartment. It wasn't until Sarah plopped down on the floor next to me that I opened my eyes. Thankfully, I never opened that third bottle.

"You okay?"

I rolled my head and rested it on her shoulder. "Yeah. I'm okay."

"Can I be blunt?"

"I don't think it's a good time to be blunt. Caring and understanding. Not blunt," Caroline said as she settled on my other side and handed me a cup of coffee from my favorite place.

"It's okay," I reassured her, "I can take it." I sipped the strong black coffee and knew sooner rather than later, I'd be perked back up. I didn't want to be perked back up. I wanted to wallow and woe is me in the dark depths that only sleeping with a married man could bring you.

"How long are you going to keep doing this to yourself?"

"Oh, at least another dozen or so times."

Caroline was right. I didn't want to hear what Sarah, the constant voice of reason, had to say.

"He's married."

"I am more than aware." I rolled my eyes and tipped my empty wineglass, hoping to tease out one last drop.

"He's done this to you more than once. He's a no-show. Doesn't call. Doesn't text."

"That isn't fair." With a bit of latent enthusiasm, I shot forward and pointed a perfectly manicured finger at her. "The last time his mother was in the hospital."

"And the time before that he was stuck in traffic and the time before that—"

"I think she gets it, Sarah. Just like I think it's time for you, my dear, to get dressed."

Caroline stood, scooped her hands under my arms, and pulled me to my feet.

"I am in no shape to go out. I'm drunk." My point needed a drunk-girl arm flail but I was too tired to attempt it.

"It's nine o'clock. Since when do two bottles stop you? You're fine. Besides, if you stay here, you'll be in a food coma. Jesus"—she walked over to the dining room table—"how much did you order?"

"A lot."

"Drunk is fine. Drunk and holed up in your apartment crying about a married man who didn't show up is not. Don't be silly. We're just going to Murphy's. It's time for target practice." Sarah winked at Caroline. I had the feeling they'd been planning this for a while.

Target practice. Almost a year ago Caroline's boyfriend-turned-fiancé of five years broke up with her in the douchiest way imaginable—she walked in on him banging the intern. Needless to say she retreated, hid, gained ten pounds, and became a disheveled mess. Until Sarah and I stepped in and forced her to see herself without Steve. Target Practice: Operation One Night Stand was born. After a few bumps in the road, Caroline ended up with Brian, the bartender who owned Murphy's Bar. He was supposed to be a rebound, someone to pull her out of her funk. Two weeks ago, they moved in together and bought a dog.

Go figure.

"I don't need target practice." I moaned as the girls walked me back to my room.

"You need a distraction," Sarah piped in.

"Operation Distraction?" Caroline said with too much enthusiasm.

I shook my head and laughed. "Whatever."

Sarah and Caroline convinced me that night to shower, dress, and head to Murphy's. They reminded me that they'd warned me numerous times that getting involved with Zac wasn't the brightest of my ideas and eventually, I had to agree. After much discussion, it was decided that I would choose my target the following week, after, of course, dodging calls and advances from Zac and solidifying the platonic work-only relationship that was probably best but certainly not as fun.

With reluctance, I allowed Sarah to delete Zac's number from my phone, which would have been the perfect solution did I not work so closely with him. And if he were not the definition of tall, dark, handsome, and fucking sexy as hell.

I just needed to get through the week.

About the Author

Christine Hughes is a former middle school English teacher from New Jersey. After nine years teaching others to appreciate literature, Christine decided to take the plunge and write her first novel, *Torn*—a YA paranormal released by Crushing Hearts and Black Butterfly Publishing in August 2013. The sequel, *Darkness Betrayed*, and a third novel, a stand-alone NA Contemporary titled *Three Days of Rain*, were released by CHBB as well. Though she loved writing for the YA set, she really found her love with *Three Days of Rain*—writing for more mature audiences. And though she loves it, it was heart-wrenching to write, and she found herself drawn back into romance with a fun voice.

Christine has attended numerous book festivals such as the Baltimore Book Festival, YA Fest, the Collingswood Book Festival, BooksNJ, and, most recently, the Princeton Public Library's Local Author Day. Additionally, she's attended a SCBWI conference and a Writer's Digest Annual Conference. In 2012, she traveled to Hollywood, California, to receive an award for *Torn*.

Christine currently stays home to write while her husband works and her two boys attend elementary school. Don't bother her too much during football season—she's either cheering on her boys or crying in her pint glass over yet another Jets loss.

Learn more at:
Christine-Hughes.com
Twitter @HughesWriter
Facebook.com/ChristineHughesAuthor

www.ingramcontent.com/pod-product-compliance
Ingram Content Group UK Ltd.
Pitfield, Milton Keynes, MK11 3LW, UK
UKHW022258280225
455674UK00001B/84